In Our Image
A Novel

Susan Alan

ACKNOWLEDGEMENTS

This story is a tale of fiction. However the literary, art and electronic references are real. Following is a partial listing of books and websites which I used in my research. You are urged to investigate. Think. Draw your own conclusions.

Bibles: The King James Version was used for the quotes herein, with limited reference to the Catholic and Hebrew bibles.

The Lost Books of the Bible and the Forgotten Books of Eden published by Penguin Group

Slave Species of God by Michael Tellinger

Rulers of the Earth, Secrets of the Sons of God by Joe Lewels

The Lost Book of Enki – Memoirs and Prophecies of an Extraterrestrial God by Zecharia Sitchen

The Genesis Race by Will Hart

Disclosure by Steven Greer

The Alien Chronicles by Matthew Hurley

Alien Encounters by Chuck Missler and Mark Eastman

A Soul's Journey by Peter Richelieu

The Greatest Deception: The Bible UFO Connection by Patrick Cooke

Masks of God by Joseph Campbell

The Yahweh Encounters: Bible Astronauts, Ark Radiations and Temple Electronics by Ann Madden Jones

ACKNOWLEDGEMENTS, CONTINUED...

The Gospel of Judas published by National Geographic Society

crystalinks.com

greatdreams.com

slavespecies.com

DEDICATION

    Much of the research for this novel was performed by my dear friend Alan who spent much of his free time pouring through books and searching the internet in an attempt to help me connect the dots; and there were a lot of dots to connect. Thank you, Alan.

CONTENTS

Prologue

1 In the Beginning 1
2 We Are Not Alone 9
3 Genesis Revisited 16
4 Tale of Two Kitties 24
5 Slime of the Earth 31
6 Stone Age 38
7 Double Dipping 42
8 Adam, Son of God 49
9 The Glory of the Lord 55
10 Transfiguration/Ascension 60
11 An Unmoving Experience 67
12 Blood Relative 71
13 A Needed Break 74
14 First Night 83
15 For the Birds 91
16 Stormy Weather 96
17 Snow Scenes 108
18 Of Heaven and Earth 121
19 Bad Bat Karma 132
20 Food for Thought 146
21 In Black and White 154
22 So Much More to Learn 161
23 Kindred Spirits 170
24 Chatterbox 181
25 Truth is Stranger than Fiction 186
26 Six Fingered Giants 199
27 Be Careful What You Ask For 209
28 Blood Count 216
29 A Very Real Possibility 221
30 No Moon at All 224

Epilogue 226

PROLOGUE

The house was situated on the side of a mountain overlooking Lake Champlain and the Adirondacks. In all seasons, at all times of day and night, the view was spectacular.

It was the last house at the end of a winding, dirt road and sat on 20 acres. The crushed gravel driveway led through a wooded area, curved to the left and brought you to a courtyard. The barn formed the left side of the courtyard and the house and garage formed the rest. The house was a Cape built in the 1930's mostly of stone. Several acres immediately around the house had been cleared and the lawn to the west of the house had a gentle downward slope and spectacular views of the lake and mountains in the distance. There was a stone patio to the right of the house that wrapped around to the rear. Further toward the back of the property were the remnants of a stone foundation, presumably that of a barn.

This is where Constance and Alex lived. They called it "Meghalaya".

Chapter 1 – In the Beginning

I was running up the path from the sunken garden toward the house, waiting for something to grab me from behind at any second. I reached the porch and sprung to the back door. Was it behind me? I didn't dare turn around. Once inside, I quickly locked the door. I heard the snap of a twig and realized the screen window was open. I scrambled to close the window and then I saw it. This wasn't my imagination. There were two huge black almond shaped eyes staring in at me.

"Connie, wake up," Alex said and gently shook my arm.

"Oh, what an awful dream I was having," I murmured.

"I didn't even realize you had fallen asleep. We were sitting here staring at the stars in silence and the next thing I know you're screaming. You scared the hell out of me."

"I was dreaming that an extraterrestrial was chasing me though the backyard. I made it to the house and locked the door. Then I saw these enormous black eyes staring at me through the window," I said. "I guess that's when I screamed."

"Maybe the UFO you and your mother saw back when you were a teenager triggered the dream?"

"Actually I was thinking about that just before I fell asleep. On nights like this I can't help but think about it, it was a beautiful, clear summer night then as well. Little did we know that a short while later we'd be running into the house thinking a spaceship was coming for us!"

"Tell me that story again," Alex said.

Alex and I were sitting out on the patio on a late August night, looking out at the lake and mountains. Weather permitting, we sat on this patio most nights, gazing at the stars.

"I must have been around 14. My mother and I sat outside on summer nights in our backyard in Connecticut to enjoy the cool night air and watch the sky. We knew the flight paths of the airplanes from the New York airports to Boston and Europe. We knew the path of Telstar's orbit and we would watch for it as it passed overhead. We sat in the sunken garden for hours on a nice night and observed the stars, planets, shooting stars and everything else that occupied the night sky.

"One night I noticed a relatively dim light low in the southeastern horizon. It appeared to be stationary, but it was a light or star that I did not recall seeing before. I kept my eyes on it while taking in all that was going on in the sky above me. It seemed to me that it was moving ever so slightly. If you looked at it, you couldn't see movement, but if you looked away and then looked back several minutes later, it appeared to have moved northward along the horizon in relation to where it had been before.

"After watching this for probably a half an hour or so, I brought it to my mother's attention. She didn't remember seeing it before either and she kept her eyes on it as did I. Over the next half hour we both agreed that, yes, it was still moving north. Now we were really intent on watching it. It had progressed a little more than half way across the eastern horizon. We watched and watched and it appeared to have stopped. We continued to watch. Minutes passed and no movement. We were now up on our feet watching it. We were alarmed by the lack of movement. What could possibly stop dead in the sky? There were no sounds and it seemed to be very distant.

"Then, from that dead stop, it made a 90 degree turn and was zooming directly toward us. I felt that it was reading our minds…it knew we were watching it and it was coming to us. As it zoomed in our direction, the light was getting brighter and bigger with still no sound emanating from it. It was almost directly overhead. Scared, I took off and ran toward the house. I could hear my mother's footsteps following me. We reached the back door and ran into the kitchen and locked the door behind us. We were afraid to look out the windows for fear something would be looking in. We discussed this episode quite often in later years and often wondered if we had lost any time that night....were we abducted? We couldn't recall losing time and we had no evidence that we were abducted. But now, more than 45 years later, that memory is still alive and I still wonder."

Alex and I sat there for a while longer, looking at the night sky and speculating on the nature of those celestial beings.

"It's getting chilly and I can almost feel the dew falling on me', I said, 'I'm going in."

Alex got up, too, and we both walked inside. There were two sets of French doors in the living room leading out to the patio, one set on either side of the fireplace. The living room ran from front to back on the right side of the house.

On the other side of the central staircase and through hall, was the dining room. The two exterior walls were stone, as were all of the exterior walls of the house, but the two interior walls were covered in mahogany paneling with a notched small shelf toward the top on which I displayed some of my brown and white transferware plates. Alex had also built a niche into the wall so that I could display small pieces of transferware such as creamers, sugar bowls, pitchers and other assorted shapes. There was also a two-sided fireplace in the rear wall which backed up to the den, so we had fireplaces in both rooms.

The den at the back of the house was more a library and TV room and it opened up to the kitchen that occupied the L which attached to the garage.

All of the floors in the house were the original 1930's fir floors. Every room had Persian rugs, some of them antique.

Alex had a friend, Bashir, who was originally from Kashmir and he was a rug merchant. Alex had designed and helped with the carpentry work on several of Bashir's shops in various cities throughout the country. Alex learned to appreciate the beauty of these rugs, and many times Alex's services were traded for some of the rugs which now were in this house. I, too, became a fan of these works of art that graced our floors, and I purchased some to add to this collection.

The entire layout of the house was perfect for us; it wasn't too large, yet it gave us enough space to get out of each other's way when necessary.

So I went upstairs to bed and Alex stretched out on the sofa in the den and watched TV. He usually fell asleep watching TV.

The next morning was misty and foggy and the lake and mountains were not visible. It was a good morning to laze around, drink coffee and read. We had a large oak table in the living room that was piled high with books. It was an ideal spot for reading and doing research. Alex had a fire going in the fireplace as there was a cold damp chill in the air and the stone construction of the house seemed to capture that cold.

I brought a carafe of coffee into the living room and sat down at the oak table.

Over the years Alex and I had separately acquired many books, his mostly landscape design, building design, horticulture, history and fiction; mine were mostly health, religion and UFO's. Alex did have a few books by Erich Von Daniken including 'Chariots of the Gods" as he, too, had an interest in extraterrestrials and UFO's.

We had a variety of books stacked on the table, each stack containing different subject matters. On top of the stack of religious books was the bible. I picked it up and opened to Genesis and began to read. Upon reaching Genesis 1:26 I read the following:

"And God said, Let us make man in our image, after our likeness: and let them have dominion over the fish of the sea, and over the fowl of the air, and over the cattle, and over all the earth, and over every creeping thing that creepeth upon the earth."

Alex had just sat down and was pouring himself a cup

of coffee. I said, "Listen to this…" and I read him the verse, emphasizing : 'Let *us* make man in *our* image, after *our* likeness…'

"Who is 'us' and 'our'?" I asked him. "I have read this many times before and I never picked up on that."

"Keep reading," Alex said, "are there more references to plural gods?"

I continued to read further in Genesis, but my mind strayed to Alex and his disbelief in any god. We had many heated discussions in the past over the existence of God. He felt that the concept of God had been fabricated by man and exploited by organized religion; the result was greed and hatred and war. I couldn't help but agree on his observation regarding organized religions, but I still believed there was a God.

I was brought up a Roman Catholic. I went to a parochial grammar school and parochial high school. I was taught that if you weren't a baptized Roman Catholic, you were going to hell. Simple as that. We had a family friend who was a priest and I can remember my mother saying to him "Say there's this little Jewish woman who was a good daughter, and is now a good wife and mother and never did a bad thing in her life, and you're telling me she's going to hell?" And he'd kind of talk his way around it, but still basically say "yes, she's going to hell." That would drive my mother crazy.

And you never questioned your faith. I can remember my best friend's father back then, and the word was that poor Mr. Wallace had lost his faith; he was researching other religions. And I felt sorry for him and his family. We were taught to never question; we were taught to "accept it on faith".

Over the decades that had passed since then I did start to question my faith. What I specifically questioned was the role of the Roman Catholic Church. How can the Roman Catholic Church be the one true church and yet orchestrate the Inquisition? What about the Crusades? What about all those corrupt popes that had existed over the centuries? Pope Alexander VI was a Borgia and had seven children during the time he was cardinal and then pope (Lucrezia Borgia was one of his daughters). So I had my own issues with organized religion, but I believed in God and I believed in the teachings of Jesus.

So now here I was reading "And God said, Let *us* make man in *our* image, after *our* likeness...." What did it mean? I continued reading until I came upon the following, in Genesis 3:22-24:

"And the Lord God said, Behold, the man is become as one of us, to know good and evil: and now, lest he put forth his hand, and take also of the tree of life, and eat, and live for ever: Therefore the Lord God sent him forth from the garden of Eden, to till the ground from whence he was taken. So he drove out the man; and he placed at the east of the garden of Eden Cherubims, and a flaming sword which turned every way, to keep the way of the tree of life."

"I've found something else," I said to Alex, and I read him the passage. "'...man is become as one of *us*...' another reference to plural gods."

"It sounds like those gods wanted to keep man dumb and short-lived, doesn't it? Makes me think of a lab experiment. They weren't too sure how this new creature was going to work out and they certainly didn't want it to gain too much knowledge or live forever, if the experiment went bad." Alex said. "They didn't succeed with keeping man from partaking of the tree of knowledge, but they weren't going to let him get to the tree of life."

"Something just came to me," Alex continued, "Do you think the reference to 'cherubim' and 'flaming sword which turned every way' could be extraterrestrials and a space ship?"

"And the plural gods that created us were extraterrestrials as well?" I asked.

"It's an interesting theory, isn't it?" Alex asked. "Otherwise, how can you explain 'man has become like one of *us*?' If it wasn't extraterrestrials, then it was multiple divine beings of some sort."

The implication of what we had read and the conclusions to which it was leading us was overwhelming to me. I got up and looked out across the patio toward the lake. The fog was still thick and I could barely make out the mountains on the other side of the lake. Could it be that we were created by extraterrestrials?

Alex got up and stood next to me and we both stared out into the fog in silence. Could it be that we had been living in a fog our entire lives and now that fog was lifting?

"We have a lot of research to do," Alex said. "You continue reading through Genesis and see if you come across any other interesting text. What version of the bible is it?"

"King James Version...I do think I have another version, which I believe is the preferred Roman Catholic version, and I also think I have a Hebrew bible."

"Okay, I'm going to get online and start doing some research and you continue reading Genesis."

I picked up the bible again and continued to read. The next questionable text I found was in Genesis 6:1-4:

"And it came to pass, when men began to multiply on the face of the earth, and daughters were born unto them, that the sons of God saw the daughters of men that they were fair; and they took them to wives of all which they chose. And the Lord said, My spirit shall not always strive with man, for that he also is flesh: yet his days shall be an hundred and twenty years. There were giants in the earth in those days; and also after that, when the sons of God came in to the daughters of men, and they bare children to them, the same became mighty men which were of old, men of renown."

I said to Alex "Okay, are you ready for this?" and I read him this latest passage.

The response exploded out of him. "Sons of God and giants? Doesn't it sound like the extraterrestrials were mating with humans? And from the prior passages it appears that humans were created by extraterrestrials. Can you believe this is in the bible? I'm going to do a search on the web for giants in Genesis."

A few minutes later Alex said excitedly, "I did a search on giants in the bible and found a reference to 'Nephilim' which are described as the off-spring of fallen angels and daughters of men and they reference that same Genesis verse. They also say that the Nephilim were giant in stature. The most famous Nephilim was the biblical Goliath who was over 13 feet tall."

I kept reading further in Genesis and I noted out loud to Alex that there were listings of genealogy, like who begat whom and the age of each individual was stated. And it appeared the longevity of the individuals listed was generally declining after each generation. Adam lived 930 years, Seth 912, Enos 905, Cainan 910, Mahalalel 895, Jared 962, Enoch 365 (but there was a notation that Enoch didn't die, he "walked with God"), Methuselah lived 969 years (older than all those before him) and Lamech lived 777 (and begat Noah when Lamech was 595 years old).

We debated what this could mean and we came to the possible conclusion that perhaps the earlier individuals had some genetic make-up/DNA of the "gods" and this was being diluted as the generations passed, with Methuselah being an obvious exception.

Alex said "I think it's time for a trip to that really good bookstore in Burlington. Want to take a ride?"

Chapter 2 – We Are Not Alone

A short while later we were driving north up Route 7 heading toward Burlington. The fog was gone and it was a beautiful sunny day. We took my 1964 Dodge Dart GT convertible and had the top down. My brother had bought the car when it was new and sold it to me 5 years later when he was ready to trade up to a new car. The car was a dark blue metallic with light blue leather interior. It drove like a little tank and didn't have a scratch on it. I kept it in very good condition for the past almost forty years. Forty years! Where did all that time go and how did I get so old? At least I don't feel old, definitely a good thing.

We drove past antique shops that we've gone to many times before. Even if I didn't buy anything, or need anything, I still liked looking at antiques. We were passing a shop that we call "Uncle Jim's". I don't know why we call it that, because that's not the name. This shop was huge. When you walked in the front door, there was so much stuff crammed into the place that it was hard to focus on anything. I remember Alex pointing out to me a stuffed monkey that was enclosed in a glass box in the corner. It was scary looking at first, but then you wondered about who would stuff a monkey, how old was it, and how did it get to this antique shop. I swear I saw that same monkey recently behind a man being interviewed about Sasquatch on the History Channel. I really should stop in at Uncle Jim's some time to see if that monkey is gone. But even though Uncle Jim's was crammed full of stuff, it was all organized. It certainly was an entertaining way to spend a few hours.

But, we didn't stop; we just kept on going as we were on a mission to do some research at the bookstore!

We passed by the Pacific View Motel on the right. I don't care how many times I see that sign, I still laugh. Why would someone name their motel the Pacific View if they are on Route 7 in Vermont not far from Lake Champlain? Because it's right next to the Pacific Gas Station of course…Pacific View. I love it!

We were getting close to Burlington now. I took the left at the fork and headed straight into town. If I had taken the right, I'd be up in the Hill section of town. The Hill section was lovely; there were beautiful older houses and marvelous neighborhoods and you could walk downtown as well as to the waterfront. The city of Burlington itself was alive. Church Street was not open to traffic and the resulting pedestrian mall was always teaming with activity. There were many interesting shops and restaurants and on a beautiful day like this people would be sitting on the benches and around the fountain just observing the passersby.

There were several bookstores on Church Street, including a large national chain, but our favorite was up at the end of the street in the basement of a building. It had new books and used books and some hard to find books. We headed straight there.

The space was large. We stood half way down the stairs and peered over the railing; from there you could take in the vastness of the store and also see the signs for the various sections.

"Okay, where do we start? Religion, paranormal, new age, occult or what?" Alex asks.

"Beats me," I said, "let's just start walking and looking."

"We could just go to the Information Desk and ask."

"Sure, we could say 'Pardon me, could you point us in the direction of books on the creation of the human race by extraterrestrials?' Anyway, that would take all of the adventure out of it," and having said that, I wandered off down the first aisle on the right and kept walking until I found the religion section. Alex was not far behind me.

There were various versions of bibles and other sacred

texts as well as books on Buddhism, Christianity, Hinduism, Islam, Judaism, and other Eastern religions among others. At this point I didn't want to start comparing the religious beliefs of each. I needed to get through Genesis first! I just wanted to know if anyone had questioned the verses we had questioned in Genesis and if anyone had done research on it.

So we kept on walking. When we got to the new age section we found what we were looking for. Alex was the first to pull out a book, 'Slave Species of God' by Michael Tellinger. The back cover mentioned our DNA being manipulated by our creator resulting in a less intelligent species. Sounded promising.

I found 'Rulers of the Earth, Secrets of the Sons of God' by Joe Lewels. "Sons of God," I said, "now we're really cooking. And look at the picture on the front, it's the Blessed Virgin and baby Jesus with a UFO over their shoulder!" I found a disclaimer inside the book that the UFO was inserted by the author and wasn't original to the painting, but even though, this book really sounded good.

We quickly located 'The Lost Book of Enki – Memoirs and Prophecies of an Extraterrestrial God' by Zecharia Sitchen, 'Alien Encounters' by Chuck Missler and Mark Eastman and 'The Genesis Race' by Will Hart.

We thought that we had enough to do some preliminary research and were about to head to the check-out desk when Alex spotted 'The Alien Chronicles' by Matthew Hurley. "Look at this,' he said, "the cover has a picture of the baptism of Christ with a big UFO above shining its light rays down on Jesus." I said "That can't be a real painting". Alex found the credit inside the cover and he said, "Yes it is, get this, it was painted by Aert De Gelder in 1710, it's entitled 'The Baptism of Christ' and it's housed in the Fitzwilliam Museum Cambridge. The cover also states 'Compelling Evidence for UFOs and Extraterrestrial Encounters In Art and Text Since Ancient Times'. We have to get this."

We checked out with our six books and headed up the

stairs toward the street. I wanted to grab a cup of coffee and sit down on one of those benches around the fountain and start pouring through the books right away. But instead we headed to the car and started our drive back down Route 7 toward home.

Alex said "Don't you have some grocery shopping you need to do? We're passing by the Hannaford."

I didn't want to stop for anything, but he was right, we did need some items and it was a distance from the house to any grocery store, and since we were almost right in front of Hannaford, I pulled in.

He said "I'll wait here in the car."

"Oh, so you can thumb through those books first? No, you lock them in the trunk and come with me. We're going to look through them for the first time together." He was not in an argumentative mood that day, and surprisingly he did as I requested.

Normally, my trip to Hannaford was a laid-back, pleasant experience. It had wonderful produce and an excellent fresh fish section, and I usually took my time, sipped a cup of coffee and looked at everything, but not today. I just wanted to get what I could remember I absolutely needed and get out of there. But Alex was heading over to the fish section and I followed.

"They have sea bass!" he said, "let's get some and I'll grill it for dinner. You still have some of that pineapple salsa you made, right?" Before I could respond, he was asking for a pound of the fish. When the clerk handed the package to him, I took control of the shopping cart and wove my way through the store at a brisk pace to pick up what we needed. We were out and on our way in no time.

There were no other side excursions, and it was mid afternoon when we pulled into the driveway. I drove the car into the garage, popped open the trunk, grabbed the books and headed inside. Alex was right behind me with the groceries. We quickly put our grocery purchases away and headed toward the living room to look at the books.

"Okay, which one do you want to start with?" Alex asked.

"I'll take the one with the portrait of 'The Baptism of Christ' on the cover."

"Sure, leave it to you to take the book full of pictures. Then I guess I'll take 'Slave Species of God' ".

I looked again at the front cover of this book, and said to Alex, "This picture takes us from the Old Testament to the New Testament. There is a possibility that celestial beings created us, and now there is also a possibility that there was a connection to Jesus. Like the Star of Bethlehem...maybe it wasn't a star, maybe it was a UFO? Maybe every time you read 'angel' in the bible, it's really an ET and every time you read 'star' or 'cloud' or some such thing it's a UFO."

Alex said "I'll try to do a 'find and replace' function of the bible on the internet and see what I come up with. I agree, this probably involves the entire bible, not just the Old Testament." He got up and walked towards the computer and I started to thumb through the book.

I turned to the table of contents and found a chapter entitled 'Creation Stories'. The chapter was broken down into sections: 1) Asia, Mesopotamian Civilizations, Bible Stories, Islam, 2) Africa and Egyptians, 3) North America, 4) South America, 5) Australasia. It referred to a common thread appearing in creation myths and legends of cultures around the world. The common thread was that beings from elsewhere with "Godlike" powers tried to assist in the development in the culture of civilizations around the world. The Indian 'Vedas' actually contained descriptions of flying machines, which were called 'Vimanas'.

I quickly browsed the rest of this chapter and realized that I needed to sit down and read every word, not just browse. The existence of the types of books that we purchased today was evidence that our preliminary suspicion that the 'god' reference in Genesis might be extraterrestrial was supported by others.   But the newly acquired books were too much of a distraction. I needed to focus on one thing at a time, and I felt that one thing was to finish reading Genesis.

I started to put down 'The Alien Chronicles' and then curiosity got the better of me. I turned to the table of contents again and saw there was a chapter 'UFOs in Western Religious Art'. I had to take a peek at this. The picture on the cover was too enticing.

The first work of art shown in this chapter was 'The Annunciation, with Saint Emidius' by Carlo Crivelli, 1430 to 1495. The painting shows the Virgin Mary kneeling inside a building with what appears to be a dove (the holy spirit) above her. But outside in the sky is a UFO which is emitting a beam of light down, through the wall of the house, through the dove, and into the head of the Blessed Virgin. The Angel Gabriel was outside the building speaking with Saint Emidius.

Another painting was that of 'The Virgin Mary with Saint Giovannino'.   The artist is unknown, but has been credited to the School of Lippi, 1406-1469. This picture was amazing. It showed the Blessed Virgin with the baby Jesus. Off to Mary's left shoulder is a UFO hovering in the sky. There is a man and his dog in the background. The man has his hand up to shield the sun from his eyes and both the man and the dog are looking up at the object. If you missed the UFO at first glance, then looking at the man and dog looking up would draw your attention to it.

Then there was the 'Glorification of the Eucharist' by Bonaventura Salimbeni, 1595. This was the most bizarre of all! Toward the upper right side is God the Father, to the left is Jesus, and above is the dove which symbolizes the Holy Spirit. In between Jesus and God the Father is a round object that has two antennae, kind of like rabbit ears, sticking out of the top. And toward the bottom is a round protrusion that looks like a camera or telescope.   To me this object resembled a Russian sputnik or one of the earlier satellites. What did this mean?

There were other paintings and tapestries included in

this chapter ranging from the 1300's to the 1800's. Why did these works contain portrayals of UFO's? What did these artists know?

I needed to put this book down and get back to Genesis. Resisting any further temptation, I closed the book, put it on the table, got up and went into the kitchen to make myself a cup of tea.

I was just about to call Alex to see if he wanted some tea when he walked into the kitchen with a beer in his hand. Guess he didn't want any tea. He said he just did a search of the bible on the internet and he found 271 references to the word 'angel', 90 references to 'angels', 16 'star' and 98 'cloud' in the New and Old Testament combined. Each reference was identified by chapter and verse. So much research to do.

I told him I was going to complete my reading of Genesis. Actually, I was going to go back to Chapter 1 and reread what I had already read to see if there was anything that I had missed.

Chapter 3 – Genesis Revisited

"Aren't we going to eat soon?" Alex asked?

"I know it's getting late. I'll read just the first two chapters over. You get the grill going and make a salad. The fish will only take a few minutes to cook."

"I'll shuck some of that corn, too. Want some of that extra-extra-extra sharp cheddar and some crackers?"

"You must be hungry! No, I'll pass on the cheese and crackers, thanks."

I went back to the living room and picked up the bible and opened to Genesis. I slowly began to reread Chapter 1. I got to Chapter 1:26 and read:

"And God said, Let us make man in our image, after our likeness: and let them have dominion over the fish of the sea, and over the fowl of the air, and over the cattle, and over all the earth, and over every creeping thing that creepeth upon the earth."

This is the sentence that got things started this morning. My world had changed over the past few hours and now I felt consumed to read everything I could to find the truth. I continued to read:

"So God created man in his own image, in the image of God he created him; male and female he created them. And God blessed them, and God said unto them, Be fruitful, and multiply, and replenish the earth, and subdue it: and have dominion over the fish of the sea, and over the fowl of the air, and over every living thing that moveth upon the earth... And the evening and the morning were the sixth day."

This section said "God created man in his own image". This made me think that one being, of the multiple beings who had agreed to this creation experiment, actually performed the experiment.

And that was the end of Chapter 1 of Genesis. God had created male and female "in his image". So if God had created man in "his image" then "God" must have had a physical form and was not just a spiritual being. And if humans were created in the image of "God", then our creator didn't look like a stereotypical extraterrestrial with a big head and big dark eyes and grey skin. But who's to say how many different kinds of celestial beings there are out there; each group could look different.

Chapter 2 began with reference to God ending his work and resting on the seventh day. I read on but became confused as I read in verse 5 "…there was not a man to till the ground." What had happened to the man he had created in Chapter 1 whom he told to be fruitful and multiply? Reading further, verse 7 said:

"…the Lord God formed man of the dust of the ground, and breathed into his nostrils the breath of life; and man became a living soul."

Was this a second creation or a restatement of what was described in Chapter 1? How did I miss this when I read it earlier this morning? And I saw that "God" was "God" in Chapter 1, but now a quick scan of Chapter 2 shows that this has been changed to "the Lord God". What did this mean? Was this a different entity and a second creation story?

As I read further it described that the "Lord God planted a garden eastward in Eden; and there he put the man whom he had formed. And out of the ground made the Lord God to grow every tree that is pleasant to the sight and good for food, the tree of life also in the midst of the garden, and the tree of knowledge of good and evil."

The creation story in Chapter 1 did not have reference to Eden and it did not contain reference to the tree of knowledge of good and evil nor the tree of life. In verses 16 and 17 the Lord God told man:

"And the Lord God commanded the man, saying, Of every tree of the garden thou mayest freely eat: but of the tree of the knowledge of good and evil, thou shalt not eat of it: for in the day that thou eatest thereof thou shalt surely die."

Chapter 2 continued with the Lord God saying "it is not good that the man should be alone." And then, for the second time, God continued to form every beast of the field and every fowl of the air. But for the man there was not found a "help meet" for him. The creation of woman, again for the second time, follows beginning with verse 21:

"And the Lord God caused a deep sleep to fall upon Adam, and he slept: and he took one of his ribs and closed up the flesh instead thereof; and the rib, which the Lord God had taken from man, made he a woman, and brought her unto the man."

Verse 25 said "...they were both naked, the man and his wife, and were not ashamed."

Then the serpent shows up in Chapter 3 and we all know how that goes. I especially noted the verses that read "And the serpent said unto the woman, 'Ye shall not surely die: For God doth know that in the day you eat thereof, then your eyes shall be opened, and ye shall be as gods, knowing good and evil." And once they had eaten of the tree, they did not die as God had said, but they did know they were naked.

I wondered who the serpent was. Was he 'Satan', or was he an emissary of an extraterrestrial community interfering with this little creation experiment for some reason? And if so, exactly what was their agenda?

I also noted that the serpent uses the word "God"; yet throughout Chapter 3 the words "Lord God" are used. "God" was the creator back in Chapter 1. Were 'God' and 'Lord God' two separate entities? Was the serpent connected with the 'God' of Chapter 1 and out to sabotage the 'Lord God' of Chapter 2?

Then in Chapter 3, Verse 8 "...they heard the voice of the Lord God walking in the garden..." which again refers to the physicality of the Lord God.

Reading further in Chapter 3, I came across that reference to "plural gods" that I had read this morning when the Lord God says "Behold, the man is become as one of us, to know good and evil…"

I noted that once I got into Chapter 4, the Lord God became just "Lord" and again wondered if that had any significance. I kept reading past Noah and the flood story and came to Chapter 11 which began "And the whole earth was of one language, of one speech." And described the building of a city and "a tower, whose top may reach unto heaven; and let us make us a name, lest we be scattered abroad upon the face of the whole earth." And this was followed with:

"And the Lord came down to see the city and the tower, which the children of men builded. And the Lord said Behold, the people is one, and they have all one language; and this they begin to do; and now nothing will be restrained from them, which they have imagined to do. Go to, let *us* go down, and there confound their language, that they may not understand one another's speech. So the Lord scattered them abroad from thence upon the face of all the earth: and they left off to build the city. Therefore is the name of it called Babel: because the Lord did there confound their language, that they may not understand one another's speech. So the Lord scattered them abroad over the face of all the earth."

Okay, I had to stop here. This was enough to take in for one day. I got up and walked into the kitchen with the bible in hand. Alex looked up as I walked in and said, "Find something good?"

I told him about the two separate creation stories in Chapters 1 and 2. And that God could not just be a spiritual entity as man was created in his image, or should I say "their image".

And then I got to the tower of Babel story and read out loud to him the verses from the bible where he says "let *us* go down" and confuse their speech. I mentioned that up through Chapter 11 there were three separate references to plural gods, and in each of them it is a direct quote of "god" speaking to others who appear to be of similar standing. And in the Babel story he is saying "let *us* go down"…like fire up the spaceship we've got to go down there and confuse the hell out of those people because they're getting too smart for their own good.

"Chapter 11, I thought you were going to read just the first two chapters over," Alex said.

"I guess I got carried away. Sorry! But isn't it amazing that here it is in black in white in the bible that there are plural references to God, and not just references, these are direct quotes. God is speaking, and he is clearly talking to others who are with him about what they are about to do to man. How could people be reading the bible for centuries and not question this?" I asked.

"Maybe they're not really reading the bible, or at least not questioning the meaning of what they are reading," Alex said.

"You're right. I've had twelve years of religious education, and I've read the bible before and I never picked up on any of this. I wonder what made me open the bible this morning and read it; I mean really read it?"

"Isn't there some saying about 'when you are ready to receive, it will come to you' or something like that?"

"Something like that. Maybe I haven't been ready to receive this information before." I replied.

"Do you have any idea when the Tower of Babel was being built, just to get some kind of reference to a time line?" Alex asked.

"I have no idea. You put the fish on the grill and I'll look it up."

I walked over to the computer and did a search on Tower of Babel. It appeared that the tower had been built, at least in part, during the reign of Nebuchadnezzar so that put in at approximately 500 B.C. I wondered how that time frame fit in with the Mayan civilization and all other major ancient civilizations who had built similar structures.

It was time to trade in my cold cup of tea for a nice cold Tanqueray martini and join Alex out on the patio.

I plopped myself down into a nearby Adirondack chair

and sipped my martini.

"I found that the Tower of Babel is believed to have been constructed around 500 B.C. Of course, it took many, many years to build, but it is believed that at least part of the construction occurred around 500 B.C. That amazes me because I would have thought it was built long before that."

"Me, too. I was thinking more like 2,500 B.C. We'll have to check out a time line to see how that relates to other civilizations. And tomorrow morning I think we should check out the other two bibles you have, the Catholic version and the Hebrew version, to see if they say the same thing as the King James Version," Alex said.

"Good idea," I said, "I can't believe what we have uncovered today. It's amazing, isn't it?"

"You mean that the human race was created and manipulated by extraterrestrials? You think that's amazing?" Alex chuckled.

"And if we've been manipulated by them in the past, then it's possible that they're still manipulating us," I said.

"Hmmm, a definite possibility there."

"Do you think you might be going down this path if you hadn't seen a UFO when you were younger?" Alex asked.

"I'd like to think I had an open enough mind to consider the option, but I'm not sure. You haven't seen a UFO, but you're seriously pursuing this train of thought," I said.

"It's more logical than some white bearded "god" floating around in the clouds, all knowing, all seeing, all powerful, who always was and always will be. And this "god", who supposedly loves us, lets all the suffering and cruelty continue on this earth."

"Remember, he even got fed up with us a few times. He wiped out Sodom and Gomorrah, and then there's the flood," I said.

The fish was ready and we decided to eat outside as it was a beautiful evening. After dinner, we continued to sit on the patio for a long while, mostly in silence, looking at the sky and thinking.

Just before I was ready to go in, I said "Did I ever tell you about my reoccurring dreams about the vortex?"

"I don't recall you mentioning anything about that."

"This must have been 20 plus years ago. At that time I was reading spiritual and new age type books and each night after I put my book down on the nightstand and turned out the light, I would lay in bed and silently ask for guidance and knowledge. I wasn't directing this request to any specific entity, I was just putting that request out there to whomever was out there listening to me. This was a ritual of mine every night for months. Then one night I had a very vivid dream, at least I think it was a dream, of seeing a vortex created of clouds. I was floating on the clouds and I was being pulled closer and closer to the edge of the vortex. I was terrified. I tried to resist. But then an awareness came over me that if I let myself go into the vortex, all that I had been asking for would be given to me. I would be given knowledge of eternal truth; all that is yet unseen would be revealed. This was the answer to my prayers. Yet I couldn't let myself go into the vortex. I was at the edge, I could feel one leg being pulled in. With all my might I resisted. It seemed this struggle went on forever and at times I thought I would never get free. And then with one mighty effort on my part, I pulled my leg out of the vortex, and I immediately woke up. My heart was pounding and I was sweaty. I got up and got a drink of water. I was afraid to go back to sleep for fear of going back to that same dream. Or was it a dream?"

"That is an amazing story. You never told me that before." Alex said.

"And you know, I thought of myself as having failed. I was given an opportunity that few have been given. And I turned it down. And what is even worse, I had the same dream twice more within the next few weeks, and both times I was petrified and pulled myself out of the vortex. I was disgusted with myself. I vowed to myself that if this opportunity were given to me again, I would allow myself to go into the vortex. But the opportunity was never given to me again."

"What made you think of that now?" Alex asked.

"It must be because I feel that I am on the edge of that vortex again, and that all truth is about to be revealed to me. And this time I am not afraid."

We sat there again in silence for several more minutes, and then went in for the night.

Chapter 4 – Tale of Two Kitties

I felt Itzy jump up on my bed and I could hear the birds chirping outside. I had slept very soundly all night, which surprised me. There were so many thoughts racing around in my head when I went to bed, I expected to toss and turn all night.

Itzy came over to me, touched my cheek with her paw and meowed softly. I petted her and told her what a pretty girl she was, and she curled up next to me.

Itzy was a white cat with celery green eyes. She was "given" to me a few years ago by an elderly couple who lived down the road. Itzy was just a tiny kitten then who showed up in their backyard. Her throat had an ugly gash across it and she was very weak. The couple watched her for several days as she lay in the sun under one of their bird feeders. It seemed she was getting weaker by the day. They knew I had recently lost my cat, Black, and they decided to catch Itzy and bring her to me. They didn't know if she was a he or a she at that time, so they referred to her as "it" and then started calling her Itzy.

I was shocked when they arrived at my front door with the tiny white kitten in a 'have-a-heart' trap. To me the cat didn't look like it would live through the night. It could barely pick its head up to look at me, but when I looked in those eyes, I knew I had to do something fast. I called the vet who had taken care of Black and explained the situation with this new kitten. He said to bring her over right away.

When I arrived he immediately started to examine Itzy. He said the wound on the throat did not look infected. He guessed that perhaps some animal grabbed her by the throat but she managed to escape. Her weight was only two and a half pounds. He said she was too small and too weak for him to draw blood. He suggested that I buy orphan kittens milk at the local Agway and feed her that along with wet and dry kitten food. He said to do that for three weeks and then to bring her back.

I did just that. I kept her in my bedroom and she sucked down that orphan kittens milk and gobbled up all the food I gave her. She got bigger and stronger each day. I brought her back to the vet three weeks later, he took blood and all the tests came back negative and she was given a clean bill of health. That was a little over four years ago and now my little Itzy was a big beautiful muscular fourteen pound cat. And I was glad to have her as I had missed having a cat after Black died. Black had a story to be told, too, as he came with the house when I bought it.

The first time I saw the house, I noticed that there was a huge bag of cat food in the basement and two dishes outside by the garage door. I thought that was peculiar as the house had been cleared out and was completely empty except for that bag of cat food.

The house was a sad looking Cape. It, and the surrounding grounds, appeared to have been neglected for a while. But, oh what possibilities, especially the yard with that beautiful view of the lake and mountains. I could also see there were iris and peonies, roses, daisies, clematis, rhododendrons, dogwoods, two huge holly trees and a beautiful crab apple. However, raspberries, bittersweet and poison ivy had encroached into the flowerbeds and other open areas. The undergrowth in some areas was so thick that you couldn't really see what was in there. As Alex, the real estate agent and I tramped through bittersweet vines we noticed the side of what appeared to be a stone bench that was under a huge old Beech tree. We made our way slowly over to the spot and Alex pulled the bittersweet away from the structure and, sure enough, it was a beautiful stone bench. It was positioned for a perfect view of the lake and mountains. What a spot to sit and take in the scenery.

"Look," Alex had said, "there is a word cut in the stone on the front of the seat ….M..E..G..H..A..L..A..Y..A.. Meghalaya. I wonder what that means."

We knew that this is where we wanted to be, and an asking price offer was put in that very day.

When we got home that night we looked up the word 'Meghalaya' and found it was Sanskrit for "Abode of the Clouds". This must have been what the prior owners had called it, and we loved the name as well. How appropriate for the little stone house on the side of the mountain.

The second time I was inside the house was during the walk through the day of my closing. I noticed the bag of cat food was still in the basement, and this time I noticed that there was some food and water in the dishes outside the garage door. Someone obviously was entering the house (which I was about to close on in an hour or so) and feeding something (a cat would be my guess) outside. The "who" was kind of unsettling.

During the closing, the seller's attorney acknowledged that he believed there was a cat that lived on the grounds around the house and he thought a neighbor might be feeding the cat. Hmmm.

A few days later I was outside whacking away at the weeds and raspberries and Denise stopped by and introduced herself. She lived up the street and had known Gene and Hilda very well. Gene and Hilda were the couple that had built the house almost 60 years earlier when they were newlyweds and had lived the rest of their lives, very long lives, in the house. Gene was the last to go, about 18 months earlier. I mentioned the mystery cat to Denise, and she said, yes, her husband, Mark, had promised Gene he would continue to feed "Black" and he had done so every day since Gene had died.

Mark stopped by later that day with his copy of my house key in hand. He explained that he believed Black was around 20 years old. As he understood it, someone had dropped off a litter of kittens on the property all those many years ago. Gene and Hilda were able to catch all but one, the little black cat. They found homes for all of the other kittens, but the little black one remained elusive. They put food out daily for him, which he did eat. But he never wanted to come into the house, even during the harshest winters. They decided to call him Black. So for all those many years, Black managed to survive outdoors, supplemented by that one daily meal left for him by Gene and/or Hilda.

Mark said if I did not want to accept the responsibility for Black, he would take Black and bring him to the Humane Society. I didn't want that to happen (I love cats) and said I would be happy to continue to feed Black. Mark said most likely, I would never even see Black, as Black was basically a wild cat. Mark saw Black infrequently. Over the 18 month period Black accepted Mark and would walk up to him on occasion, but that was it. Mark just wanted to warn me that I might never see him, but the food would be gone the next day.

So, sure enough, for about a month I continued to put the dry food and water out every day and it would be gone the next day. I would sometimes get the feeling that I was being watched as I put the food and water out there, and sometimes I thought I could hear a faint rustle of leaves, but I never saw Black. He was my phantom cat.

Then one late afternoon, as I put the food dish on the ground I heard a distinctive snap of a twig and rustle of leaves. It was a very bright summer day. I strained to see into the shadows under the large yew trees that were up on a slight slope a few feet away. I could see a movement. And then I saw two yellow eyes looking back at me. I was looking into Black's eyes! I said hello to him. He just kept staring at me. I knew there was no chance that he would come down to the dishes while I was standing there. I told him I was going to leave so that he could eat, and that I was very happy to have finally seen him. As I walked up the steps toward the back door, I heard more rustling of leaves and knew he was descending down toward the dishes to eat.

Over the course of the next couple of weeks, I saw Black several times. He would sit there in the shadows and stare at me. Whenever I saw him, I would sit down for a few minutes on a wooden pallet near to his dishes and just talk to him. I'd tell him how handsome he was, and how happy I was to be able to feed him and care for him. He'd just sit there and listen, but wouldn't come down until I left. He started making a daily appearance in the shadows, accompanied by a deep, gravelly Louie Armstrong kind of sounding "meow".

Then one day, as I sat on the pallet talking and he sat there in the shadows listening, he got up and walked down toward me. I kept talking with a soft, soothing voice like nothing was happening, but my heart was racing. He sat down several feet away from me and just kept looking at me. I could see his ears were a little torn, his coat looked dull and his eyes were runny. He was a big cat. Kind of thin, yet muscular. I kept talking for a few minutes, and then got up and slowly left. He sat there watching me go. As I got to the bottom of the steps to go up toward the back door, he got up, walked to his food and started eating.

After several more days of Black coming down and sitting near me, he finally went over to his food and ate while I continued to sit there and talk to him. And this continued for a couple more weeks; I'd talk and Black ate.

Then one day, I had just finished putting down his food and Black approached. He slowly came up to me and rubbed against my leg! I couldn't believe it. He stood there looking up at me. I reached down and patted his head and he just continued to stand there and let me pet him for a few seconds. Not wanting to wear out my welcome, I turned and walked away. He turned and started to eat. This was a momentous event, at least to me. Black actually let me touch him! I went in the house and called Mark. He was amazed as well.

Every day thereafter, Black let me pet him. I would sit down on the pallet and he would come over to me and eventually we worked our way up to multi-minute sessions of him rubbing up against me and me petting him. He would purr, a deep rattley kind of purr.

I didn't know where Black slept. However, early that fall I found out. There was an old dog house out by the barn.

Alex and I were going to move it closer to the barn. It was a good-sized structure and made out of solid wood, so it was heavy. Alex and I grabbed it by the eaves of the roof and the roof came off! And, to our shock, there was Black groggily looking back at us. He jumped out and ran off. The roof of the doghouse was structured so that it sat on top of the bottom structure, but was not nailed on. The floor of the roof only extended ¾ of the way across, so that it was kind of like a loft. That gave Black enough room to jump up to the loft area and sleep. So this is where he was sleeping. And here we went and disturbed him!

The floor of the roof was not in good condition and there was some old crumbly foam rubber on it. Alex decided to cut a new wood floor for the roof and cut a semi-circular opening in one corner so Black could jump up there. I thought it might be nice if Alex could put a step in there to help Black get up to the loft (as he wasn't getting any younger) and he did this. I bought a dark green fleece blanket and put it on the floor of the loft so he would be nice and cozy.

But Black was no longer going to the doghouse (or cathouse). All of our good intentions had backfired. I made several attempts of trying to lure Black into the cathouse by walking out there in the dark, using a flashlight to see, and carrying his dinner. He would follow me. I'd put his dinner inside the cathouse and position the flashlight so that he could see in there. This would drive Alex crazy because he kept saying that cats can see in the dark. I knew that, but I figured a little light on the subject, in this case, dinner, wouldn't hurt. Sometimes Black would step into the house and eat a little, but it was obvious that he didn't want to be there. So after several days of trying, I gave up.

After a while we discovered that Black was sleeping in the window well, hidden under the evergreens at the backside of the house. Alex kept telling me that a lot of heat was escaping from the basement through the window. That, coupled with the density of the evergreens above, assured

Black was warm and dry. I couldn't believe it.

We were into fall and the weather was getting cooler now. We had our first snow before Thanksgiving that year. And that was the beginning of the worst winter we've had in years. Snow, ice and bitter cold. I'd bring Black's breakfast out to the back porch every morning. He looked like he was shivering some mornings. I'd pick him up and hold him next to me and wrap my coat around him. He seemed to like that warmth very much.

Alex had been talking about building a room in the basement for Black. Now that the weather was really turning for the worse, he began construction. Every morning I'd tell Black that Alex was building a room in the basement for him. He'd look in my eyes and seemed to understand. Temperatures overnight at that point were down in the teens, and I remember looking at the thermometer one morning and it was 5 above. I really had my doubts that Black made it through the night, but I went out on the back steps and called his name, and out he came from his window well under the shrubs. I picked him up and put him under my coat. His ears were cold; his paws were cold. I massaged them and held him for an extra long time, then put him down so that he could eat.

Finally, just in the nick of time, Alex finished Black's room. The day it was completed, I picked Black up and carried him into his room in the basement. He seemed to take the whole room in, and Alex, who was standing behind me, thought that Black looked pleased.

Black lived with us for almost a year before he died of old age. I missed him terribly and Itzy did a wonderful job of filling that void.

The sun was coming up and Itzy was looking at me like "aren't you going to get up and feed me my breakfast?" I laid there for a few more seconds and wondered what today would bring. Yesterday had been truly amazing. I got up, put my robe on, and went downstairs. Itzy beat me down and was waiting.

Chapter 5 – Slime of the Earth

Itzy wasn't the only one who beat me downstairs. Alex had already made the coffee and was sitting in the den reading the Koran. I could see he had the Catholic and Hebrew bibles on the table as well

"Good morning, you're up early," I said.

"I really didn't sleep well last night; my mind was racing," he said. "Instead of continuing to toss and turn, I got up around 4 a.m. and made my first pot of coffee; this one is the second which just finished brewing so it's nice and fresh.

I placed Itzy's bowl of cat food on the floor as she seemed to be ravenous. Then I poured myself a cup of coffee and sat down opposite Alex.

"So you've been reading the Koran since around 4 o'clock?" I asked.

"Yep, just about. However, I did do a timeline search on the internet. Remember we were talking about the Tower of Babel and how that fit in with similar structures built by other civilizations? I found that the Pyramid of the Sun and the Pyramid of the Moon were built in Central America around 300 BC. And I found that the Mayan civilization was flourishing around 300 AD."

"I also learned that ziggurats were a form of temple common to ancient Mesopotamia, with the earliest dating from the end of the third millennium BCE and the latest dating from the 6th century BCE.'"

"They were built in receding tiers in a pyramidal shape, with a shrine or temple at the highest level. They were believed to be dwelling places for the gods, and each city had its own patron god."

"Only priests were allowed inside the ziggurat and it was their responsibility to take care of the god that lived there."

"I found a discussion on Joseph Campbell and his book, *Masks of God*. According to Campbell, ziggurats first appeared "during a sudden scientific and philosophical golden age". The first use of the written word occurred at this time, the wheel was invented, and astronomy and the calendar came into being. Again, all of this happened suddenly, this did not evolve over time. And this advanced culture spread from Mesopotamia around the world.

"Okay, I have a question. Weren't the ziggurats in Central and South America built after the 6th century BCE? Why did they say that the most recent were built in the 6th century BCE?"

"From what I have read, they refer to the Central and South American structures as 'ziggurat-like' structures. Which means to me that the only official ziggurats are the ones that were built by the Sumerians, Babylonians and Assyrians."

"What I really find interesting is the fact that they were built as dwelling places for the gods. And that ziggurats first appeared during a sudden scientific and philosophical golden age. Maybe there were extraterrestrials on this earth then, who were considered to be gods, who were teaching the beings on this planet."

"Could well be. Interesting, isn't it?"

"Oh, and I found those other two bibles for you so you could start checking them out to see if they match what you found yesterday in the other bible."

"Gee, thanks. Don't you feel drained from yesterday?" I asked.

"No, I'm energized. I'm ready to research every lead we get. Can't wait."

I sat there sipping my coffee and stared at him. Usually it was the other way around; I'd get up early and make the coffee, eager to start a new day, and he'd be watching the television in the den, constantly clicking the remote, and driving me crazy doing it. Today the TV wasn't even on.

I reached over and picked up the Catholic version and opened to Genesis Chapter 1:26 and read:

"And he said: "Let us make man to our image and

likeness; and let him have dominion over the fishes of the sea, and the fowls of the air, and the beasts, and the whole earth, and every creeping creature that moveth upon the earth."

"Well, Genesis 1:26 in the Catholic bible uses the same phrase "our image".   Some of the words in the sentence vary, like God is "he" and instead of "in our image" it's "to our image", things like that.   But get this, the Catholic bible has footnotes at the bottom, and the footnote related to this verse reads: "This image of God in man, is not in the body, but in the soul; which is a spiritual substance, endued with understanding and free will.""

"They felt compelled to include this footnote in the Catholic bible to explain that we are not talking about God as a physical being, but as a spiritual being.   Yet they don't say anything about the usage of the words 'our image'.""

I next went to Chapter 2, verse 7, and almost spit out my coffee as I read:

"And the Lord God formed man of the slime of the earth; and breathed into his face the breath of life, and man became a living soul."

Alex was looking at me like I was crazy.   "What does it say?" he asked.

I read the verse to him.   "Just like the Catholic Church to use the word "slime" instead of dirt.   Man is made out of slime…slimy creatures are we. I'm amazed I survived twelve years of Catholic education.   Here I always thought it was 'Dust thou art and to dust thou shalt return' and instead it's 'Slime thou art and to slime thou shalt return'.""

Alex was laughing and I started laughing and the tears were running down our faces. Ah, we needed a good laugh.

I composed myself, poured myself another cup of coffee and continued reading.   Chapter 3, verse 8 stated "And when they heard the voice of the Lord God walking in paradise at the afternoon air..." How could a voice be walking?   This was a strangely worded phrase, and perhaps they were trying to convey that this was not a physical being walking, just the voice of a spiritual being walking. It made absolutely no sense.

I then went to Chapter 6, and the part about the "sons of God" and the "giants". The Catholic bible read as follows:

"Now giants were upon the earth in those days. For after the sons of God went in to the daughters of men, and they brought forth children, these are the mighty men of old, men of renown."

I read this to Alex, and then said, "But wait, there's another footnote concerning the sons of God. It reads:

"The descendants of Seth and Enos are here called sons of God from their religion and piety; whereas the ungodly race of Cain, who by their carnal affections lay groveling upon the earth, are called the children of men. The unhappy consequence of the former marrying with the latter, ought to be a warning to Christians to be very circumspect in their marriages; and not to suffer themselves to be determined in their choice by their carnal passion, to the prejudice of virtue or religion."

"Wow, it must have taken a lot of thinking to come up with that explanation. It's going to be interesting to see how the Hebrew bible reads," Alex commented.

"And of course they had to add that bit about Christians being circumspect in their marriages. You couldn't marry within the Catholic Church if you married a non-Catholic."

Okay, I'm going to check out the Tower of Babel story now. I turned to Chapter 11 and read, and although some of the phraseology was a little different, it was basically the same as the King James Version and verse 7 did say: "…let us go down…"

I told Alex what I had found in this chapter and commented that overall the only major difference was that pesky little reference to "sons of God" in Chapter 6 which had to be explained away by the footnote.

"Wait a minute," he said, "don't forget dust was replaced with slime. That's a major difference!"

That had been very entertaining! I felt a little perkier now. I had consumed two cups of coffee and was pouring a third. This slimy little creature was ready to tackle the Hebrew bible. Bring it on!

In the Hebrew bible, Genesis was one of the Five Books of Moses contained within the Torah. I had absolutely no idea what I would find, but I was ready for it.

I opened to Genesis 1:26 and read:

"And God said, "Let us make man in our image, after our likeness. They shall rule the fish of the sea, the birds of the sky, the cattle, the whole earth, and all the creeping things that creep on the earth.""

Well, this was basically the same as contained in the King James Version. Okay, now on to Chapter 2 to see if dust or slime was the basis of man's creation. And it was dust! Yes! And man became a living being and not a soul. We're on a roll here.

I conveyed all of this to Alex. He was relieved that at least two of the bibles used the word "dust" instead of "slime". Said he might have gotten a complex otherwise. He got up to get the dictionary and sat back down.

Chapter 6 was interesting, because instead of using the phrase "sons of God", the phrase "divine beings" was used. This made it perfectly clear that we're not talking about the descendants of Seth and Enos here, we are talking about divine beings. Divine beings who could take human form and mate with human women. Not spirits, but physical beings. I like this bible! It read:

"When men began to increase on earth and daughters were born to them, the divine beings saw how beautiful the daughters of men were and took wives from among those that pleased them…It was then, and later too, that the Nephilim appeared on earth – when the divine beings cohabited with the daughters of men, who bore them offspring. They were the heroes of old, the men of renown."

I read this to Alex and he agreed this was the most

enlightening version of the three. The Nephilim were the resulting offspring of the divine beings cohabiting with the daughters of men. The Nephilim were the heroes of old, the men of renown.

I mentioned that we could use some Nephilim on earth today, as there were few if any heroes or men of renown.

Alex responded, "The information I found on the internet indicated the Nephilim were giants and that they were the offspring of fallen angels and daughters of men. Do you really think we need giants on this earth that are the offspring of fallen angels?"

"Oh, you're right. I was thinking 'divine beings' and daughters of men producing heroes and men of renown."

"Different translations can really alter the meaning. The other versions said they were 'mighty men of old, men of renown' and I don't think anyone could argue that giants were mighty men of renown. But the word 'hero' conveys something else. Let me get the trusty old dictionary and look up the word 'hero'."

He reached for the dictionary, found the word 'hero' and read: a: 'a mythological or legendary figure often of divine descent endowed with great strength or ability b: an illustrious warrior c: a man admired for his achievements and noble qualities d: one that shows great courage'.

"You see, most people today wouldn't think of the 'a' definition."

"I know I didn't," I said.

Alex said "Okay, now I'm going to look up Nephilim." A minute later he said "Listen to what I found. There was no reference to Nephilim in the dictionary. However, I did find 'nephology' and 'nephogram'." He stopped and gave me a look.

"And, what are the definitions?"

"Nephology is a branch of meteorology that studies clouds, and nephogram is a picture of a cloud. So perhaps Nephilim had some relationship with clouds, like perhaps they were the offspring of divine beings from the clouds. Maybe the Sons of God aren't fallen angels, maybe the Hebrew bible is correct in their interpretation and they are divine beings from the clouds," Alex said.

"But, right after that reference to Nephilim in the bible, it mentions the increasing wickedness of mankind, as if there is a connection between this increasing wickedness and the Nephilim. Noah and the flood story follow, as if all the abominations on earth had to be wiped out," I responded.

"I think we should look at all of references to clouds in the bible," I continued. "Remember in 'Close Encounters of the Third Kind' when they showed the UFO's coming out of the clouds? What a beautiful job they did with those special effects!"

"We've got the DVD of that movie, we should sit back, relax, and watch that again tonight. What do you think?" Alex asked.

"Sounds good to me. In the meantime, I'm going to take the bible and sit outside on the patio and read."

Chapter 6 - Stone Age

A light breeze was coming off the lake, and the intensely blue sky was dotted with fluffy cumulous clouds.

I sat down with bible in hand. I just wanted to take in the view for a few minutes. I looked at the patio and the stone sitting wall and thought how hard Alex had worked to build them. Stone is what brought Alex and me together.

I thought back to the house in Connecticut. I happened to see Alex's ad in the local paper and made an appointment for an estimate for a stone patio. I could remember the first time I saw him. He was medium height and slim build. His brown hair had a few streaks of gray, and was pulled back into a ponytail. I especially noticed his nice strong arms and hands. We walked around to the back of the house and I described what I had in mind for the patio. I wanted a flowerbed right next to the house for perennials and I wanted the patio large enough to place a table and chairs; that I was certain of. But other than that, I had no clue.

Alex said he'd draw up some plans and give me a call when he was ready to come back and review them with me.

A few weeks later he called, and came over that very night with plans in hand. He envisioned a patio area that was not rectangular, but more of a trapezoid shape, with a sitting wall on the side opposite the house, with another planting bed behind the wall. The bed curved from behind the wall to the far edge of the patio. He suggested that an ornamental tree of some type be planted in the bed. The back edge of the property was wooded, and there were tall pine trees up a slight hill on one side, but otherwise the backyard was devoid of trees.

He also suggested a waterfall toward the far edge of the patio on the house side. The land had a slope to it on that side, and he thought it would be a natural for a waterfall there. He had sketched in the waterfall in his drawings and I could see how perfectly that fit in and seemed to complete the entire area.

Work began a few weeks later. Most evenings, if the weather was good, I'd come home from work and Alex and his crew would still be there. He'd show me what they had done that day, and discuss what would be done the next. If there were any questions, that's when we'd discuss them. I looked forward to those brief talks with him.

The day came when the patio, wall and waterfall were completed. He had planted an Amur maple in the bed on the backside of the sitting wall. It had a very pleasing shape to it and he said it wouldn't get too big, but big enough to provide a little shade to the patio in a few years. That tree made such a difference!

The finished product of all the stone work was beyond words; it was so much more than I had ever expected. And the sight and sound of the waterfall was a delight. It did not look man-made, and it looked like it had always been there.

I didn't see Alex again until next spring, when I came home from work and found him out on the patio.

"What a surprise," I said, "nice to see you."

"I thought I'd stop by and see how everything wintered. I like to check on my work periodically to make sure there are no problems," he said.

"And, what do you think?"

"Everything looks great, stones are all in place, no heaving. The Amur maple is in bud and looks like it wintered well. You get the north wind whipping through here, and although this is a hardy tree, you never can tell what the wind will do. But it looks just fine. I see your perennials are starting to come up, too. Really nice."

"So how are things going with you," I asked.

"I'm going to be relocating to Burlington. It's a great little town and I've found a place in the Hill Section where I can walk into town and even to the waterfront."

"Burlington, Connecticut?"

"No, Vermont! Some of my crew are going to move up as well. The young single ones are looking for a change of scene, and it is a college town. Lot's of activity and nightlife."

"It was kind of hard to imagine you were talking about Burlington, Connecticut. I don't know what I was thinking. So when are you going?'

"Tomorrow."

I don't know why I felt so sorry that he was leaving, but I did. At one point last summer, I thought he fancied me a bit. One morning I looked out the upstairs window and I could see the garden hose lying on the grass and it looked like it was in a heart shape. Did someone place it like that on purpose? I told myself it was all my imagination, and I got through the winter barely thinking of him. But now I felt so sad. He was leaving.

He said, "Would you mind if I wrote or called you?"

My sadness changed to euphoria. I tried not to show any change of expression as I said "I'd like that."

"Good, then we'll be talking. Take care," and with that he turned and left.

A couple of weeks later, I received a letter from him. He sounded happy that he had made the move, but said it was difficult getting started in a new place. He was trying to come up with a new name for his business. He wrote a few down and asked me for my opinion: "Rock and a Hard Place", "Rock My World", "No Stone Unturned", "Rock Bottom", "Rock Hard", "Rocky Road" and the one that really cracked me up, "Flintstone".

Although he had built a patio, stone wall and waterfall for me, he specialized in stone structures that I thought resembled ancient stone ruins. One summer evening last year he had brought his portfolio and showed me pictures of jobs he had done pretty much all over New England.   They were unique, and no two were alike. They included cairns, sunken gardens with stone pillars, pergolas with stone support columns, stone bridges and arches, and one amazing creation that resembled Stonehenge, only in a smaller version.

One picture showed what looked to be two sides of a crumbling stone foundation built into the slope of a hill. Actually, it kind of looked like the stone foundation we had out back, but ours was an actual foundation and not a recreation. The one that Alex had built had a pea stone floor, with a wrought iron table and chairs in one corner, huge urns filled with flowers here and there and this amazing periwinkle blue passionflower vine crawling up the side of one of the stone walls. It was breathtaking.

I couldn't envision a man who created such marvelous unique structures naming his company "Rock Bottom" or "Flintstone", even though I did like "No Stone Unturned". I gave it some thought, and a couple days later I wrote back to him with my suggestions, "Stone Age" or "Set in Stone".

Alex called me and told me "Stone Age" was perfect. He said he already had the graphics for his business cards before he heard back from me. He chose a stone arch which looked like something out of Machu Pichu or Cuzco, and the name "Stone Age" was a perfect match for the graphic. It was so good to hear his voice.

We continued to communicate by letter, or an occasional phone call. His business was doing very well and he sounded happy. One day, about a year later, we were talking on the phone and he said "Why don't you drive up to Burlington for a visit?"

The long and short of it is, I did. That was a little more than ten years ago.

Chapter 7 – Double Dipping

"Find anything else, yet?" Alex asked and sat down beside me.

"I haven't even started to look," I said.

"What have you been doing out here?"

"Wondering."

"Wondering about what?"

"Wondering if you placed the garden hose in the shape of a heart when you were working at my house in Connecticut."

Alex gave me this incredulous look and said "You mean you saw that? You never said anything."

"So you did do it! I thought it was my imagination and I didn't want to embarrass myself, so I didn't say anything. But you did it, right?"

"Yes, I did. And now over ten years later you're sitting here thinking about that?"

"Weird, huh? I was looking at this patio, and remembering the patio you built back in Connecticut, and then the picture of that heart-shaped hose came to mind."

"And here we are sitting together on another patio all these years later. I guess my plan of attack worked."

"Plan of attack! You finished the job and I didn't see or hear from you for almost a year, then you tell me you're moving to Vermont the next day, and then I don't see you again for almost another year. That was your plan?"

"Absence makes the heart grow fonder."

"Right, and familiarity breeds contempt."

"I guess I had better leave you to your reading," he said, and he got up and walked around the back of the house.

I opened the bible to Genesis and resumed my reading. I noted that in Chapter 17:16-17, God told Abraham "...I will also give you a son by her (Sarah)...then Abraham fell upon his face, and laughed, and said in his heart, shall a child be born unto him that is a hundred years old? Shall Sarah, that is ninety years old, bear?"

Then in Chapter 21:1-3, I read "And the Lord visited Sarah as he had said, and the Lord did unto Sarah as he had spoken. For Sarah conceived, and bare Abraham a son in his old age, at the set time of which God had spoken to him. And Abraham called the name of his son that was born unto him, whom Sarah bare to him, Isaac."

Those words "…the Lord visited Sarah… and the Lord did unto Sarah as he had spoken…" were chilling to me. This sounded like a physical being visited Sarah and impregnated her. I thought to myself, "Wait, I've got to get the Catholic bible and see what they have to say about this!" I got the Catholic bible and it said "…the Lord visited Sarah and the Lord fulfilled what he had spoken." There was no footnote. 'Fulfilled', at least, didn't sound as bad as 'did to'. But still, 'god' did do something to Sarah.

To me, this was similar to the story of the Virgin birth. And it was similar to the story of Mary's mother, Anne, who also was past childbearing age. In fact, it was the same story as Elizabeth, Mary's cousin, who was the mother of St. John the Baptist. I made a mental note that I'd have to research the stories of Anne and Elizabeth. I was pretty sure I was correct in my recollection that an angel of the Lord appeared to each of them and told them they would have a child, even though they were beyond childbearing age.

So if the Lord "did to Sarah as he had spoken", and it appears the Lord also did to Mary and Anne and Elizabeth as he had promised, why was Mary's child more special than the others? I had to think that it was because Mary, too, was the offspring of extraterrestrial intervention, and, to the best of my knowledge, Sarah, Anne and Elizabeth were not. So Jesus, Mary's offspring, had more extraterrestrial DNA than did the others. Isaac, Mary and St. John the Baptist were very highly regarded entities in the bible, but Jesus had twice the amount of DNA of our creators than the others.

I had to tell this to Alex. I got up and walked into the house and called him, but no response. I walked out the front door and walked over to the barn, but he wasn't there. I looked in the garage, but no Alex. I walked around the back of the house and I spotted him up the hill at the edge of the woods, continuing with building the cairn he had started a few months ago. It looked like he was almost finished. It looked to be about 5 feet tall and 5 feet wide. He had cleared out the woods of stone and he thought he'd have enough to build a good size cairn, and he was right. Looking at it, I thought it would be great to put a solar spot light on it as it was completely dark on that side of the property. It would not only illuminate the cairn, but also provide under lighting to the tree branches overhead.

As I approached, Alex said "What's up?"

I said "The cairn looks great! You'll finish it today, right?"

"Yup, just a few stones more and I'll be through. And it's good and solid. How does it look from down below?"

"Wonderful. I think we should put a solar spot light on it."

He gave me this look, like 'oh, no', but didn't say anything. He was not fond of solar lights.

"How's your bible reading going?" he asked.

"Very interesting. I read the story about Sarah, Abraham's wife. She was 90 and childless. Abraham was 100. God told Abraham that he would give him a son by Sarah and Abraham thought that was very funny. But then it says "the Lord visited Sarah…and the Lord did unto Sarah as he had spoken."

"That sounds kind of creepy…he did to her as he had spoken."

"Doesn't it? But this made me think of the other women who had similar stories. Anne, mother of Mary; Elizabeth, mother of St. John the Baptist; and Mary, mother of Jesus all were impregnated by divine intervention. By divine intervention, I mean extraterrestrial intervention. And then I started to think why Jesus was more special than the other offspring. And my conclusion was that Mary had extraterrestrial DNA in her, and then she gave birth as a result of extraterrestrial intervention, so Jesus had twice as much ET DNA than the others."

"Like a double dip of DNA. That makes sense. I don't know how you ever thought of that," Alex said.

"It just came to me, but it does make perfect sense."

"Are you sure about Anne and Elizabeth?"

"Pretty sure. I'm going to research that next." As I turned to leave I said, "Don't work too hard."

I went into the house and poured myself a glass of water and went back outside to look for references to Anne and Elizabeth in the bible.

After a few minutes, I found the reference to Elizabeth (spelled Elisabeth in the King James Version of the bible) that I was looking for in the Gospel according to St. Luke. Chapter 1 of this gospel contained the story of Zechariah being visited by an angel of the Lord while Zechariah was in the temple praying. The angel told him that his wife, Elizabeth, will bear him a son, and that his name shall be called John. Verses 18-20 read:

"And Zechariah said unto the angel, whereby shall I know this? For I am an old man, and my wife well stricken in years. And the angel answering, said unto him, I am Gabriel, that stand in the presence of God; and I was sent to speak unto thee, and to shew thee these glad tidings. And, behold, thou shalt be dumb, and not able to speak, until the day that these things shall be performed, because thou believest not my words, which shall be fulfilled in their season."

Well, Gabriel was really full of himself, wasn't he? The story continued that Elizabeth did give birth, and when the neighbors asked what they would name him, she said "John". And the neighbors thought this was strange as none of their 'kindred' was called by that name. So then they turned to Zechariah and asked him, and he wrote down "His name is

John", and at that moment he could speak again.

Another interesting passage in Luke was the part about Mary, now pregnant, going to visit her cousin, Elizabeth, who was six months further along in her pregnancy than was Mary. In Chapter 1, verse 44, Elizabeth said to Mary "For lo, as soon as the voice of your salutation sounded in mine ears, the babe leaped in my womb for joy." Sure, I thought, one extraterrestrial baby would probably recognize another…in this case, both Mary as well as the baby in her womb. Those little extraterrestrial babies had probably already developed extra sensory perception.

Well, now that left the Anne, mother of Mary, story to verify. I looked all through the New Testament and couldn't find anything. I went into the house and picked up the book "The Lost Books of the Bible and the Forgotten Books of Eden" which was first published in the 1920's. I had bought this book several years ago at a tag sale and rediscovered it when Alex found it on the shelf next to the Catholic bible.

As luck would have it, "The Gospel of the Birth of Mary" was right at the very beginning. It said Mary's father's name was Joachim and her mother's Anna. And in Chapter 2 it states that an angel of the Lord appeared separately to both Joachim and Anna and told them that Anna would conceive and give birth to a daughter, whom they should call Mary.

This angel also stated that other barren women had also given birth through the intercession of God, which I now took to mean extraterrestrial intervention. Sarah brought forth Jacob, Rachel gave birth to Joseph and the angel noted that Samson and Samuel were both born to barren women.

So although it wasn't one of the books that had been accepted in the New Testament, I did find written corroboration to my recollection about Mary's birth.

I also found the angel's reference to not only Sarah, but Rachel and the mothers of Samuel and Samson very interesting. All of the offspring of these supposedly barren women were men of renown. The inference being that all of these women were impregnated by an extraterrestrial.

Just then Alex walked out onto the patio. "Still reading?" he asked.

"Very interesting indeed! I found the reference to Elizabeth's pregnancy in Luke. I couldn't find any mention of Anna's pregnancy in the bible, but I did find it in the 'Lost Books of the Bible'," and I read him the entire section.

"There is one difference between Sarah and all of the other women, though." I said. "There was no angel involved in the Sarah story. The Lord directly told Abraham that he would give Abraham a son by Sarah. And then the Lord visited Sarah and did to her as he had spoken. With the other women being visited by angels, you have to draw your own conclusions as to what had happened. With Sarah we are being told, without any doubt, that the Lord visited her and made her pregnant."

"So these barren women were giving birth to super humans who were fathered by extraterrestrials," Alex said. "Maybe these barren women weren't really humans, maybe they were barren because they were extraterrestrials and couldn't conceive with human sperm. Then, when the experiment with each failed, they were inseminated with extraterrestrial sperm, which of course worked, and then they gave birth to what appeared to be super human beings."

"Your mind really works in amazing ways. But I like it. Could be. Why not?"

"Sure, then Joseph could write a book 'I Married an Extraterrestrial'."

"Very funny. But seriously, this is just what we need on earth today. Seeding of extraterrestrial sperm to elevate the abysmally ignorant human race to a higher level."

"I wouldn't use the word ignorant; some humans are extremely intelligent and have accomplished great things. But as a whole, I believe the human race is generally complacent and a great many are consumed with greed and hate. There are those who live a hedonistic life style and worship materialism. Just for instance, look at the current financial crisis. Either there was complete ineptitude or downright fraud going on, or a combination of both. High level executives are getting paid obscene amounts of compensation even though their companies are going down the tubes. They take the money and run. As a result there are massive layoffs and worthless or non-existent pension plans. What happens to all those people who worked years, decades in some instances, who counted on the company pension plan? Or people who depended on their investments to help fund their retirement? Greed and incompetence destroyed it. I do agree that we could use some men of renown today."

"Men and women of renown."

"Absolutely, men and women of renown."

"I do think that we are being programmed to become dumb and dumber, though," I said.

"Right, masses of people are being sucked slowly into stupidity by the media," Alex interjected.

"How many people actually think today? They have I-pods stuck in their ears, or they're on their cell phones, or playing video games or watching drivel on TV. How many are reading anything meaningful? And then there are the others who spend most of the time working. Even when they're not physically at work, they're on their laptops or Blackberries and working from home, on weekends, on vacation. And for what, for an employer who just wants to suck all the life out of these people to fuel that corporate greed. Those same employers would layoff those workers in a heartbeat without a second thought if it would improve the bottom line. In both instances, these are empty, wasted lives. When these people breathe their last breath, are they going to be proud and satisfied with what they've done with their lives?"

"They're probably too ignorant to realize that they have wasted their lives; they just don't know any better," Alex said. "So I guess your use of the word 'ignorant' was correct."

"I think it's time for dinner and a movie, how's that sound to you?"

"Great. I'm starving."

CHAPTER 8 – ADAM, SON OF GOD

Over coffee the next morning, I said to Alex "I was pontificating yesterday about how ignorant people are, and how they don't think and pretty much waste their existence on this planet. Really, I'm no different than they are. I shouldn't have had that moment of feeling somehow superior."

"What are you talking about? Do you have an i-Pod or a cell phone? No. Do you own any video games? No. I'll admit you do watch a few movies every now and then. And you do have an affinity to 'Close Encounters of the Third Kind'."

"I do hate phones," I said. "If I didn't feel I needed to have one in the house to at least be sociable with my family, or in the case of emergency, I wouldn't have one. But I did work for more than a couple of decades for a huge publicly traded corporation, so I contributed to that corporate greed."

"But did you have a Blackberry, laptop, and work at nights, weekends and vacations?"

"No. I worked to make a living. But I knew the value of my own time and I always knew there was something better out there and I hoped I would find it. Colored stones were my avocation, and, thankfully, helped me escape the corporate jungle early. But, thinking of that, what value does jewelry have to society? At least you work with stone and create structures that are beautiful, functional, and could conceivably last for hundreds of years. That's a contribution to society. You know, like the creators of the pyramids and Stonehenge; they contributed to society as they are a link today to the civilization that existed then."

"Right, and the builders of those structures are still unknown." Alex, said.

"Hmmmm, so you're saying that hundreds of years from now someone will be looking at the cairn you built up on the hill and wonder what kind of primitive man built it and for what purpose. Was it for some pagan ritual?"

"Right. And I guess what I'm saying is that, in my opinion, we do read meaningful books, and we do have relatively serious conversations and thoughts. And the odyssey we are on right now is proof of that."

"Okay, I'm not going to dwell on my value to society right now."

"Good. So what are your plans for today?"

"The first thing I want to do is take another look at the Gospel of Luke. He seems to have a slightly different twist to things."

"So you're giving up the Old Testament for the New?"

"No, I'll go back to the Old Testament. But Luke is calling to me right now."

"Okay, you go back to Luke. See if I care."

I moved into the living room and picked up the bible and opened it to Luke. In Chapter 3 it described Jesus' baptism. It read "...it came to pass, that Jesus also being baptized, and praying, the heaven was opened, and the Holy Ghost descended in a bodily shape, like a dove, upon him and a voice came from heaven which said, Thou art my beloved son; in thee I am well pleased." Verse 23, gave a genealogy of Jesus. It read: "Jesus...being (as was supposed) the son of Joseph, which was the son of Heli, which was the son of Matthat..." and went on and on backward in time until it got to "...which was the son of Seth, which was the son of Adam, which was the son of God."

I had to stop and read that again "the son of Adam, which was the son of God." Luke was saying that Adam was the son of God. I didn't see any other way this could be interpreted. I knew that Adam was created "in our image". I didn't recall reading anywhere else that Adam was the son of God. Yes, Adam was created by the gods, but the son of God? Adam was created out of dust (or slime if you read the Catholic version of the bible). But to be a son, you would have to have the DNA of the father. No?

I continued reading Luke, but didn't find anything as startling as "Adam...the son of God."

I decided to go back to the Old Testament. I started reading Exodus and took note in Chapter 19 when I started reading Verses 16-21:

"And it came to pass on the third day in the morning, that there were thunders and lightnings, and a thick cloud upon the mount, and the voice of the trumpet exceeding loud, so that all the people that was in the camp trembled. And Moses brought the people out of the camp to meet with God; and they stood at the nether part of the mount. And mount Sinai was altogether on a smoke, because the Lord descended upon it in fire: and the smoke thereof ascended as the smoke of a furnace, and the whole mount quaked greatly. And the voice of the trumpet sounded long and waxed loud and louder, Moses spake, and God answered him by a voice. And the Lord came down upon mount Sinai, on the top of the mount: and the Lord called Moses up to the top of the mount, and Moses went up. And the Lord said unto Moses, Go down, charge the people, lest they break through to the Lord to gaze, and many of them perish."

I couldn't help but think of 'Close Encounters of the Third Kind' when they're at Devil's Tower and the spaceship sends out this blast, much like a very loud trumpet.

I continued to read as God gave Moses a verbal summary of the Ten Commandments. Then in Chapter 24, Verses 15-18, I read:

"And Moses went up into the mount, and a cloud covered the mount. And the glory of the Lord abode on mount Sinai, and the cloud covered it six days: and the seventh day he called unto Moses out of the midst of the cloud. And the sight of the glory of the Lord was like a devouring fire on the top of the mount in the eyes of the people of Israel. And Moses went into the midst of the cloud, and gat him up into the mount: and Moses was on the mount forty days and forty nights."

"The glory of the Lord" abode on Mountain Sinai.

And "the glory of the Lord" was like a devouring fire on the top of the mountain. It sure sounded to me that "the glory of the Lord" was a spaceship.

Okay, time for a break. Where was Alex? I walked around the back of the house and saw him coming down the hill. It looked like he had finished the cairn.

I went into the kitchen, put the bible on the table, and opened a can of tuna to make salad for sandwiches. Of course, as soon as she heard the can opener, Itzy was right there for her 'tuna juice'. I drained the water out of the can into a little bowl and put it down on the floor for her. She immediately began lapping it up.

Alex walked into the kitchen and said "That cairn really does look good from down here. Maybe we should try a solar spotlight on it and see how it looks. Don't we have one still in the box?"

Well, what a surprise! I said, "Yes, I think it's on the shelf to the left of work bench in the garage. You've got to charge the solar battery in the sun for several hours first."

"I was hoping you'd make tuna salad sandwiches. I'm going to put that solar battery out in the sun right now. I'll be back in a minute."

I made the sandwiches, poured some iced tea, took out the chips and sat down at the table in the den.

"Okay, I've got the solar battery out in the sun," Alex said as he walked in the back door.

He sat down at the table, and took a sip of iced tea. "So did you find anything interesting in Luke?"

"I guess you could say I did." I picked up the bible and read him the Luke verse that ended "...son of Adam, which was the son of God".

Alex finished swallowing a bite of sandwich and said "So Luke was saying that Adam was the son of God?"

"Right, not just that Adam was created by God, Luke's genealogy states that Adam was the son of God."

"Which means that he had his creator's DNA. How

can people be reading the bible for centuries and never have picked up on any of this? I know I've said this before, but didn't anyone ever stop and think about what they were reading? This is amazing! It was there all along in black and white."

I said, "It was amazing when we realized that man was created by extraterrestrials. But if Luke is saying what we think he is saying, then extraterrestrial DNA was not just in certain people; it was in mankind from the start. And Luke was a physician. I think that adds some credence to his statement. He knew exactly what he was saying, and it has been there for centuries waiting for us to discover it."

"And come to think of it, remember the genealogy in Genesis which started with Adam and listed each succeeding generation and the age of each and there was a general downward decline in age for each subsequent generation from Adam? Now it makes sense! Adam was not just created by extraterrestrials, he had extraterrestrial DNA in him that was being diluted with each passing generation."

"So those men of renown had a little more extraterrestrial DNA than the rest of us, and that is what made them better human beings."

"Must be," I said.

"And there is hardly any extraterrestrial DNA in the population today. That is why the majority of us are pathetic little sheep who can't use our brains and think for ourselves. We pay for and drink bottled water, some of which comes from London's public water supply and who knows where else, when the stuff that comes out of the tap is perfectly good and free. We walk around with cell phones and i-Pods attached to our heads, drive gas guzzling SUV's, buy McMansions and spend money like drunken sailors, and are now 'going green' because it's the thing to do although we've been polluting the environment for decades. And we let our elected officials get away with murder, literally and figuratively, with hardly a whimper out of us. It's pathetic," Alex almost shouted.

"Okay, calm down. I have to agree with you. Look at women's shoes!"

"What?"

"Women's shoes! Women torture themselves because they think they look better wearing high heels. When I was decades younger I wore pointy toe high heel shoes just about every day of the week. I had calluses and corns and now have bunions because of those stupid shoes. I haven't worn anything but Earth shoes for about 15 years now. No more corns and calluses. No more sciatica, shoulder pain, neck pain, back pain. But it took me the majority of my life to figure this out. Yes, I was one of the sheep, following the trend. Baa."

CHAPTER 9 – THE GLORY OF THE LORD

I then told him about Moses, Mount Sinai and the glory of the Lord. Compared to the Adam story, it seemed hardly important at all.

He responded, "I have a vision of this spaceship, fire shooting out from it, sitting in a cloud on the top of Mount Sinai with the word 'Glory' painted on the side. Get it? 'Glory' of the Lord? Like they used to give female names to aircraft during the first and second World War? Like the Betty Lu, or something?"

"You are quite the comedian." I said.

"I'm going to take a look in the dictionary to see what definitions they have for 'glory'." He got up, walked into the living room and returned with dictionary in hand.

"Okay, let's see what it says."

I sipped my tea and watched him turn to the word 'glory' and start to read. A few seconds later he looked at me and said "You're not going to believe this."

"What?"

"There are various definitions, but this is one of them: "…a nimbus; halo."

" 'Nimbus' like cloud?"

"Yep. Now I'm going to look up 'nimbus'."

A minute or so later he was reading "nimbus: luminous emanation or atmosphere believed to envelope a deity or holy person; glory; a low formless dark gray cloud."

"Well," Alex said, "that all ties it together, doesn't it? The 'glory of the Lord' is the cloud that envelopes him."

"Right, but this cloud has a devouring fire in it…like a spaceship."

"You know, someone could write a book just using the bible and a dictionary. Most people read the bible and interpret the words in the context they are commonly used today. Who would think 'glory' could mean 'low cloud'? We certainly didn't."

We finished our lunch and I decided to continue reading Exodus to see what would happen between Moses and God for the 40 days Moses was up on Mount Sinai with God.

Dark clouds had suddenly blown in across the lake and large droplets of rain started to fall. I sat down in one of the large comfortable chairs by the fireplace, turned on the lamp, and continued to read. Chapter 33,18-23 was interesting. It read:

"And he said, I beseech thee, show me thy glory. And he said, I will make all my goodness pass before thee, and I will proclaim the name of the Lord before thee; and will be gracious to whom I will be gracious, and will show mercy on whom I will show mercy. And he said, Thou canst not see my face: for there shall no man see me and live. And the Lord said, Behold, there is a place by me, and thou shalt stand upon a rock: and it shall come to pass, while my glory passeth by, that I will put thee in a cleft of the rock, and will cover thee with my hand while I pass by; and I will take away mine hand, and thou shalt see my back parts: but my face shall not be seen."

Chapter 34 continued, in verse 2-5, with the Lord saying:

"And be ready in the morning, and come up in the morning unto mount Sinai, and present yourself there to me in the top of the mount. And no man shall come up with thee, neither let any man be seen throughout all the mountain; let no flocks or herds feed before that mount...and the Lord descended in the cloud, and stood with him there, and proclaimed the name of the Lord."

And then, starting with Verse 29 it read:

"And it came to pass, when Moses came down from mount Sinai...Moses wist not that the skin of his face shone while he had talked with him. And when Aaron and all the children of Israel saw Moses, behold, the skin of his face shone: and they were afraid to come nigh him...but till Moses had done speaking with them, he put a veil on his face. But when Moses went in before the Lord to speak with him, he took the veil off, until he came out. And he came out, and spake unto the children of Israel what which he was commanded. And the children of Israel saw the face of Moses, that the skin of Moses' face shone: and Moses put the veil upon his face again, until he went in to speak with him."

I put the bible down on my lap and laid my head back on the chair and thought about what I had just read. I could envision Moses perched in a cleft in the stony face of a mountain, with the Lord in his UFO, partly enveloped in a cloud, flying by. And I could see Moses with his shining face coming down from the mountain and all the people backing away from him as they were afraid of his strange countenance. The Lord had told Moses not to bring anyone up on the mountain with him, and let no flocks or herds feed before the mountain. I'm assuming that there was radiation or some energy source emanating from the glory of the Lord. How could Moses withstand it? Obviously it must have affected him severely enough that he had to cover his face with a veil.

Earlier in Exodus, Chapter 25, verse 8, the Lord had said to Moses "And let them make me a sanctuary, that I may dwell among them." And the Lord provided Moses with exact details as to the pattern and size of the tabernacle, its furnishings, the alter, the ark, the courtyard. The information provided was so detailed, in fact, that the Lord even stated that he wanted blue, purple and scarlet curtains.

I picked the bible up again and continued reading. In Chapter 35, actual construction began. Verses 30-35 were noteworthy:

"And Moses said to the children of Israel, See, the Lord hath called by name, Bezaleel the son of Uri, the son of Hur, of the tribe of Judah; and he hath filled him with the spirit of God, in wisdom, in understanding, and in knowledge, and in all manner of workmanship; and to devise curious works, to work in gold, and in silver and in brass, and in cutting of stones

- 57 -

to set them, and in carving of wood, to make any manner of cunning work. And he hath put in his heart that he may teach, both he and Aholiab the son of Ahisamach of the tribe of Dan. Them hath he filled with wisdom of heart, to work all manner of work of the engraver, and of the cunning workman, and of the embroiderer, in blue, and in purple, in scarlet, and in fine linen, and of the weaver, even of them that do any work, and of those that devise cunning work."

In reading these words, I couldn't help but think of countless conversations Alex and I have had in the past about all of the great civilizations that created works of wonder: the Sumerians, Egyptians, Incas, Aztecs, Mayans and many more. Our belief is that they were taught, coached and helped to create all of the wonders that still remain on this Earth by those from another galaxy who were more advanced than we. How else could you explain the Egyptian and Mayan pyramids, the stone work at Machu Picchu, Stonehenge, the Moai (stone statues on Easter Island, some over 60 feet high and weighing over 200 tons) and other "wonders" of the world?

And the ziggurats that had been constructed from the end of the third millennium BCE to 600 BCE had also been constructed as dwellings for the gods. This was very similar to this bible story where God is instructing the people on how to build the tabernacle.

It seemed to me in readings Verses 30-35 that the Lord was very particular and wanted only the finest surroundings, exactly as he had designed, in which to spend time with the Israelites, and that meant that the Israelites would have to be "filled...in understanding, and in knowledge, and in all manner of workmanship" to create as the Lord instructed. And the Lord, obviously, was a physical creature who demanded all of these creature comforts exactly to his liking. So he filled Bezaleel with the knowledge and ability for work in every skilled craft and also inspired him to teach others. There it was, right there in the bible. I always thought this was pretty much what had happened, but I never thought I'd be reading the details in the bible. Early "advanced" civilizations had been filled with the knowledge and ability to create all of these amazing structures and artifacts.

I continued reading on to the conclusion of Exodus. The last few verses of Chapter 40 were also very noteworthy:

"Then a cloud covered the tent of congregation, and the glory of the Lord filled the tabernacle. And Moses was not able to enter into the tent of congregation, because the cloud abode thereon, and the glory of the Lord filled the tabernacle. And when the cloud was taken up from over the tabernacle, the children of Israel went onward in all their journeys: But if the cloud were not taken up, then they journeyed not till the day that it was taken up. For the cloud of the Lord was upon the tabernacle by day, and fire was on it by night, in the sight of all the house of Israel, throughout all their journeys."

Hmmm. In contemplating this last section of Exodus, the thought came to me that the same energy source that made Moses' face shine, was illuminating the tabernacle so that it looked like fire was in it at night.

In describing all of this to Alex later, he laughed and said maybe they needed to do repairs on the spaceship, and that's why they needed a temporary place to live on this planet.

Could be.

Before I fell asleep that night, I thought about Moses' face shining after being with the Glory of God. I recalled (from my many years of Catholic education) that during the Transfiguration, when Jesus was on a mountain top with some of his disciples, his face shone like the sun. I thought there was a cloud involved in the Transfiguration episode as well. Kind of a coincidence, both events taking place on the top of a mountain, with clouds and shining faces. I made a mental note to look this up tomorrow.

Chapter 10 - Transfiguration/Ascension

The next morning Alex said to me. "You know what I was thinking?"

"No, my mental powers are not too keen today; what were you thinking?"

"I was thinking it is quite a coincidence that we are living in a place called 'Meghalaya...abode of the clouds', considering all the research we've been doing on clouds in the bible."

"I never thought about that; you are absolutely correct. It is amazing, isn't it?" I responded.

"And it seemed like it was destiny that brought us here." Alex said. "Remember how we found this place? We were out for a ride one Sunday afternoon and we got lost. We turned onto this dirt road; it didn't say it was a dead end. We kept driving higher up on the mountain until we came to this driveway at the end of the road, and there was a "For Sale" sign hanging by the entrance to the driveway. We were very bold and drove down the driveway and found a vacant stone house with amazing views of the lake and mountains. We got even bolder and got out of the car and walked around the property and looked in the windows of the house. We both knew that this was it. This was where we were meant to be."

"We found our way home and called our agent, and the next day she was showing us the house." I said. "We offered the asking price, and it was ours."

"And we've lived here happily ever after."

"We certainly have."

"So what's on your agenda for today?" Alex asked, and sipped his coffee.

"I was thinking about Moses' shining face. I think Jesus' face shone when he was transfigured. I'm going to do some research on the transfiguration."

"It's a good thing you've had all that Catholic

education."

"Oh, I'm sure the nuns would be very pleased to know that I'm using all that knowledge to convince myself that we were created by extraterrestrials and that Jesus had a double dose of extraterrestrial DNA in him."

"Hey, at least you are putting all that education to good use. Right?"

"Right."

"And what's on your agenda for today?"

"I've got an appointment to look at a property in Charlotte. They're interested in building a sunken garden with stone retaining walls. Ron and I are going over to check it out."

"Will you be home for dinner?"

"Sure. The appointment is at 1 p.m."

"Good. Do you think you could pick up something for dinner?"

"I had a feeling this line of questioning was leading somewhere. What do you want?"

"Use your imagination."

"You might be sorry. Remember that time I made the black olive soup?"

"Yes and it was truly revolting. Please try to do better."

After finishing some chores, I grabbed the bible and started to research the transfiguration.

I found several references to the transfiguration, one of which was in Matthew, Chapter 17:1-9:

"After six days Jesus taketh Peter, James and John his brother, and bringeth them up into a high mount apart, and was transfigured before them: and his face did shine as the sun, and his raiment was white as the light. And behold, there appeared unto them Moses and Elias, talking with him. Then answered Peter, and said unto Jesus, Lord, it is good for us to be here: If thou wilt, let us make here three tabernacles: one for thee, and one for Moses and one for Elias. While he yet spake, behold, a bright cloud overshadowed them, and a voice out of the cloud, which said, This is my beloved Son, in whom I am well pleased; hear ye him. And when the disciples heard it, they fell on their face and were sore afraid. And Jesus came and touched them and said, Arise, and be not afraid. And when they had lifted up their eyes, they saw no man, save Jesus only."

I was struck by the fact that the voice from the cloud said "This is my beloved Son, in whom I am well pleased; hear ye him." Isn't this the same thing the voice from the clouds said during the baptism of Christ?

I quickly turned to the Gospel of Luke, Chapter 3, where he describes the baptism of Christ, and sure enough, the voice from the cloud spoke directly to Jesus saying, "Thou art my beloved son; in thee I am well pleased."

I then searched for a reference to the Ascension, and found it in the Acts of the Apostles, Chapter 1:9-12:

"And when he had spoken these things, while they beheld, he was taken up; and a cloud received him out of their sight. And while they looked steadfastly toward heaven as he went up, behold, two men stood by them in white apparel; which also said, ye men of Galilee, why stand ye gazing into heaven? This same Jesus, which is taken up from you into heaven, shall so come in like manner as ye have seen him go into heaven. "

This clearly stated that Jesus was taken up into a cloud. And it also said that Jesus will return from heaven in like manner, meaning that he will return in a cloud.

I turned on some music and walked through the open French doors out onto the patio. "Crystal Blue Persuasion" by Tommy James and the Shondells started to play. I could almost feel the hint of fall in the air. The light was different; the sun was a little lower in the sky. The air smelled fresher; it had almost a sweetness to it. The atmosphere was crystal clear and the greens of the grass and leaves and blues of the lake and sky were vivid. It was a spectacular day. And Tommy's song fit perfectly with the day and how I was feeling.

I heard a vehicle coming up the driveway and into the

courtyard. I heard a door open and close and I heard Alex talking, presumably to Ron.

I walked around the corner of the house and went over to Ron's truck.

"Hi, Ron. How's it going?"

"Great. How 'bout you?"

"No complaints. Did you guys go to the store for me?"

"Certainly did. I made sure he got something good," Ron said.

"How does grilled lobster tails, baked potato and asparagus sound?" Alex said.

"You're kidding, right?"

"No, I'm not. When's the last time we had lobster? Anyhow, we really hit it off with the homeowners. They loved everything we suggested for the sunken garden, and we've got the job. So we're going to celebrate." Alex said.

"Ron, will you join us for dinner?" I asked.

"Thanks, Con, but Cheryl has other plans for me tonight. I'll take a rain check, though."

"Okay, how about you and Cheryl coming over for dinner some night. Any night. Just let me know what works for you guys."

"Will do. Thanks. Better be off now."

We turned to go inside as Ron drove away. Alex seemed very pleased with the day's turn of events. What he enjoyed most is being creative, and today was one of those successfully creative days.

"I'll go fire up the grill. Could you grab me a beer? And could you put the potatoes in the microwave for a few minutes?" Alex said.

"Sure, I'll be right out."

I made myself a martini, got the beer for Alex, put the potatoes in the microwave and went out to the patio.

"So how was your day? Did you find anything new?" Alex asked.

I told him all about the transfiguration, with Jesus' face

and clothes shining, and the voice coming out of the clouds saying basically the same thing as the voice that came out of the clouds during the baptism of Christ.

Then I told him about the ascension and how Jesus was taken up into the cloud and the angels telling the apostles that Jesus would return in the same way.

"Well, it sounds like you had quite a productive day. What you read today builds on what you've discovered before. It's quite a compilation of information you've amassed."

"Sure is, but what am I going to do with it?"

"It should be shared with others."

"But how?"

"I don't know, but I'm sure we'll figure something out."

"You know, it's all there for us to read and discover the truth. Back when the Old Testament was written, they were not technologically advanced. When they saw a spaceship, of course they figured it had to be supernatural. It had to be of the gods. They could not comprehend anything else. Today we look up in the sky and see an airplane and it's no big deal because we know the technology exists. But back then that technology didn't exist, at least not here on earth," I said.

"More and more people today accept the fact that there must be intelligent life in other galaxies, and that we are being visited by those intelligent beings, and have been visited by them in the past. Yet there are those who cannot accept this. They think anyone who has seen a UFO is a nutcase and they laugh. The U.S. government conceals the truth. The media pokes fun at it, and even buries legitimate stories about sightings. At some point there has to be a shift of consciousness where the majority believes in extraterrestrial life." Alex said.

"There are those who believe, or who want to believe. Remember 'The Day the Earth Stood Still' which was first made back in the early 1950's? And look how well 'Close Encounters' did three decades ago. And today there are more shows on TV about UFO's and ancient astronauts, so the entire media is not poking fun at it."

"Right, and then there's movies like 'Mars Attacks!', 'Independence Day' and 'Men in Black' that make extraterrestrials out to annihilate the human race." Alex said.

"There might be extraterrestrials out there who do want to annihilate the human race. We don't know. But I'm convinced some group of them did create us. I believe that some group of them did send Jesus as an emissary to teach us to love each other. They were trying to help us."

"And we all know how that went. We've had religious war after religious war. Millions of people have been killed in the name of religion. Maybe that was their plan all along." Alex almost shouted.

"We just don't know, do we? I can't help but think about being taught in Catholic school to 'accept it on faith'. 'Don't question; accept it on faith.' And yet, Jesus said 'Ask, and it shall be given you; seek, and ye shall find; knock, and it shall be opened unto you.' He also said 'He who has ears to hear; let him hear!' To me, that doesn't sound like he was preaching that we should accept something on faith," I responded.

"So that brings me back to my earlier statement; you have to share your research with others and let them decide if you're a nutcase or if you're on to something here."

I took a sip of my martini and watched Alex cook.

"Hey, not to change the subject, but how about you make a Caesar salad? I think that would go really well with everything else." Alex said.

"Excellent idea!" I got up and went to make the salad.

The potatoes were still slightly hard, so I wrapped them in foil and brought them out to Alex to throw on the grill to finish cooking.

That night we did have a spectacular dinner. The lobster tails were tender and sweet. The grilled asparagus was cooked perfectly.

"You outdid yourself with this meal.   This even surpasses your famed black olive soup." I said.
"Why thank you very much."

Chapter 11 – An Unmoving Experience

I had no trouble falling asleep that night. A cool breeze was coming in the bedroom window and I pulled the quilt way up to my chin. It seemed I fell asleep within seconds of my head touching the pillow.

I woke with a start during the night. I went to turn to look at the clock, and realized I couldn't move. I couldn't move any part of me. I was fully awake. I remembered having these sleep paralysis episodes when I was younger, but this hadn't happened to me for decades.

I thought that the best thing I could do would be to try to relax and just go back to sleep. Concentrate on something else. Count backwards from 100…maybe that would work. Concentrate!

Don't panic!

I started counting 100, 99, 98…and then I stopped. I could hear something behind me. It sounded like breathing. Heavy, labored breathing.

Now I was in a panic. My heart was pounding. I was trying with all my might to move some part of me. To fling myself around and face whomever or whatever was behind me. But I couldn't.

Even though the room was cool, sweat was pouring off me. I was telling myself this was all in my mind. I was imagining this entire thing.

But it seemed like the breathing was closer to me. I was waiting for whatever it was to grab me or kill me or do something to me.

I tried to will myself to move. I strained to move just one finger. Finally, in one tremendous effort to move, I became free and swung around to face whatever was behind me. And there was nothing there.

I looked at the clock. It was 3:33 a.m. I sat up in bed. Itzy wasn't with me. That was very unusual.

I knew I hadn't dreamt this. I didn't want to go back to sleep because I was afraid it would happen again.

I got up, put on my robe and slippers and walked downstairs.

Alex was asleep on the couch with the television on. Itzy was lying on top of him, which was highly unusual. As I tried to be very quiet not to wake him, I heard him say "What's the matter?"

"I just had a strange experience."

"What kind of strange experience?"

"I had a sleep paralysis episode."

"A what?"

I sat down on the chair opposite the sofa and explained what sleep paralysis was. I was surprised he had never heard of it. I told him I had these episodes several times when I was a teenager and young woman. Then I told him that this episode had a slightly different twist to it; there was something breathing behind me!

This got his attention. He sat up and looked at me, and then said "Are you sure you weren't dreaming?"

"No, I wasn't dreaming. I was wide awake. Even though it seemed like an eternity to me, I'm sure it didn't last more than a minute or two. When I was finally able to move and turn around, there was nothing behind me."

Alex was up now, putting on all the outside lights and looking out all the doors and windows. But there was nothing unusual.

It was now around 4 a.m. I knew I wasn't going back to sleep. I asked "Want me to make some coffee?"

"Good idea."

I watched him go over to the computer and turn it on.

"What are you doing?"

"I'm going to do a search on sleep paralysis. It might be serious, you know."

A couple of minutes later he said, okay, listen to this: "The isolated sleep paralysis event occurs most often at sleep onset. An individual, even though aware and awake, is actually atonic, similar to the atonia experienced during REM sleep, and has great difficulty moving. This experience also may produce great anxiety and fear, while the individual struggles to 'wake up'. Individuals who experience sleep paralysis often report concurrent hallucinations. Commonly reported is the feeling of a presence or entity in the room in which the individual sleeps. At times this presence may seem threatening and evil giving rise to the folklore belief of the 'night-mare,' the 'old hag,' and the 'incubi'."

I poured the coffee and brought him a cup. He said "Do you know what an 'incubi' is?"

"I think it is a male devil of some sort."

"I'd better look that one up, too."

As I took a sip of coffee, Alex said "Okay I found it. 'The incubus ...... was an angel who fell because of lust for women according to many of the church fathers. This being appears to women often in the form of a sexual dream/
nightmare, and in fact the Latin word for nightmare is "incubo", meaning to lie upon'. "

"Believe me, there was nothing sexual about this. This was pure terror!"

"You know what is weird?" Alex asked. "This description is of a fallen angel. You know what we've been thinking lately, that angels are really extraterrestrials. Maybe there was an extraterrestrial behind you."

"You are not helping me to relax; I just want you to know that." I took another sip of coffee.

"Sure, drink some more coffee; that will help to settle your nerves. Did you have these episodes before or after you saw the UFO when you were a teenager?"

"After, I think. It started during my middle to late teen years and continued into my twenties."

He came over and sat down and looked at me.

"Do you think maybe you were abducted?"

"I have no physical evidence that I was. I have no

memory that I was. And if I was, then my mother was as well. We always wondered about it. We'd talk about it as a possibility, but we never really believed that we were."

"Okay, you've seen a UFO that picked up on your thoughts and zoomed in your direction. You've had sleep paralysis episodes thereafter, with the latest one having some entity behind you. Have you ever experienced anything else a little strange, anything unusual?"

"The only other strange thing that happened to me was when I was very young. I'd say I was four years old. I was standing in my backyard. Next to me were my cousins Andrew and Tom. We were standing back by the edge of the vegetable garden. I can't remember what we were talking about. But all of a sudden I had an out of body experience. I can remember floating slightly above the three of us, and looking down and thinking 'Something is wrong. I should be in my body, and I'm not.' Meanwhile my body seemed to be fine. I was standing there with my cousins, looking perfectly normal. Yet 'I' wasn't in that body. I was above it looking down. I was wondering if I'd be able to get back into it. And then all of a sudden, I was back in. I remembered what had happened. I remembered then, and I've never forgotten. It was a little unsettling to say the least."

"I'm speechless," Alex gasped.

"Come on, you've never had an out of body experience?" I said. For some reason now I was finding all of this kind of amusing.

"No, I've never seen a UFO, I've never had a sleep paralysis episode and I've never had an out of body experience."

"Well, they do say opposites attract."

Chapter 12 – Blood Relative

Later that morning, I was out back by the stone foundation pulling weeds when Alex came over and sat down on the grass next to me.

"I was on the internet doing a search on Jesus' DNA which took me to the bloodline of Jesus, and I came across some interesting sites talking about Rh negative blood."

That got my attention. I asked, "And what were they saying?"

"They were saying that only 15% of the world's population has Rh negative blood. The other 85% has Rh positive and the Rh stands for Rhesus like in monkey. So those with Rh positive blood have a factor in their blood that can be traced back to the Rhesus monkey. But the earthly origin for Rh negative blood is unknown. Scientists have no explanation for it."

"An Rh negative pregnant woman's body rejects the positive blooded baby in her womb. Her blood builds up antibodies to destroy the alien substance. Conversely, an Rh positive woman's body does not reject an Rh negative fetus. Isn't this interesting? And there's more."

"Very interesting," I said. "Go on."

"Scientists can clone the Rh positive factor, but they are not able to clone the Rh negative factor."

"There are some sites that suggest that perhaps these Rh negative people are related to the ancient astronauts. And it's believed that there is a high percentage of alien abduction of people with Rh negative blood."

"I have Rh negative blood," I said.

Alex gave me a long look and said "Are you kidding?"

"No, I'm not kidding. I have A negative blood. I've got a card in my wallet to prove it if you'd like to see it."

"So we can add that to your out of body experience, UFO sighting and sleep paralysis list. I always thought you were one in a million, and now, statistically speaking, you probably are. I'm going to do more research on Rh negative blood. Is there anything I can get you? Want some water or iced tea?"

"Actually, I'm about finished with this weeding. I'll get an iced tea when I get inside in a few minutes. Thanks."

Alex got up and I watched him as he slowly walked back toward the house. Added to everything else, this Rh negative thing was unsettling to say the least. What was going on? Was it all just a coincidence?

A short while later, I was sipping my iced tea and watching Alex search on the internet.

"The Basque people of Spain have the highest incidence of Rh negative blood and their origin is unknown," he said.

A couple of minutes later he said, "This is interesting. This site discusses the Hyperboreans. Ever hear of them?"

"No, I don't think so."

"There was a legendary polar country named Hyperborea, and the capital was named Thule. It was believed that Thule was the gateway to another world, the entrance to the "Hollow Earth', a place where humans could leave this planet. It continues by saying that it is believed by some that the Hyperboreans were in contact with extraterrestrials and were interbreeding with them."

"It is speculated that the descendants of this race were the Celts who spread out across the earth and spawned the Scots, Irish, Basques, Spanish, Scandinavians, Icelanders and the Portuguese. These nationalities all have one common genetic trait, a large percentage of Rh negative blood types."

"It is reported that the majority of alien abductees are from Rh negative blood groups, is this a possible indication that UFO cultures are tracking their cross-bred progeny?

"I never even heard of a Hyperborean before," I said and continued to watch Alex as he searched further.

"Here's a site that is linking Rh negative blood to the

fallen angels who mated with human women."

"And here's another linking them with shape shifting Reptilians."

I couldn't help it, I just started to laugh. I mean laugh hysterically. It was really ridiculous. No one had a clue. The only truth in the whole matter was that no one knew where the Rh negative blood factor originated.

"It says here that Queen Elizabeth is a shape shifting Reptilian!"

I howled with laughter. Tears were rolling down my cheeks. Alex started to laugh. Whoever said that laughter is the best medicine was right. I felt much better.

"And you know what? I'm glad I can't be cloned like Dolly the sheep. It makes me feel special, protected somehow."

Chapter 13 – A Needed Break

We had immersed ourselves in reading and researching all we could find on the subject of creation, religion and UFOs for over two months now. The table in the living room was piled high with books. Alex had written over 400 index cards with different subjects and reference material related to those subjects as a cross reference; they were filed alphabetically by subject in a wooden box, also on the table. Most of our conversations centered on this subject, and at night when I went to bed I would lay there and think about extraterrestrials and their relationship to this earth. Sometimes I would even dream about it. But, thankfully, I had no more sleep paralysis episodes.

I had tracked down a print of 'The Baptism of Christ" on the internet from somewhere in England, and bought a copy. It was now matted and framed and hanging in the living room. It really was an amazing picture. There was no doubt about what the artist had painted, there was a round object hovering over Jesus and John the Baptist in the River Jordan, and it was sending down beams of light on them. I would stand in front of this picture several times a day and just stare at it.

One of Alex's searches had brought him somehow to the "Venus of Willendorf", which was a tiny statue of a very round, voluptuous woman. It was only 4 and 3/8 inches long and was estimated to have been made somewhere between 30,000 to 25,000 BC. It was found near Willendorf, Austria. It was made out of limestone that was not indigenous to the area. This "woman" had no visible feet or hands and there were no features to the face, instead there were what appeared to be woven horizontal strands covering the entire head. It was one of the oldest pieces of sculpture on earth.

Alex and I speculated that maybe this little statue was a prototype of what the human female was to look like. Maybe our creators were discussing the physical attributes of the first woman and one of them said "I think she should have enormous breasts, and round belly and chubby little legs, and look something like this..." No need to waste any time on hands, feet and facial features at this point. We both thought this concept was as good as any other, because no one had a clue as to the origins of this little Venus. I located a copy of this statuette on the web. The little footless form was attached to a marble base. I ordered one and we now had it proudly displayed on the mantel in the living room.

In any case, I felt that I really needed a break from this obsession, because that is what it now was. And then one morning early in November, the phone rang. It was my sister, Mary. She wanted to know if we were up for a visit as she and my other sister, Anne, were thinking of coming up to Vermont later in the month. Anne and Mary lived on Hilton Head Island in South Carolina and our visits were few and far between. And they never came up to Vermont when the weather was colder. This is the break I needed. I told her this is wonderful news and to come on up!

So they firmed up their plans, and I started planning on where we would go and what we would do while they were up. Then it dawned on me that I could decorate the house for Christmas. They would be here for Thanksgiving, but since they never visited at Christmas, I thought it would be fun to decorate the house for Christmas and kind of celebrate two holidays at once. They would be shocked when they entered the house and saw all of the Christmas decorations.

I hated it when the days got shorter. I always looked forward to December 21st and the winter solstice because then I knew, minute by minute the days were getting longer again. I always put up my Christmas decorations early because the trees with their little white lights provided enough illumination to compensate for the darkness outside. The earliest I had ever started to put up Christmas decorations was many years ago back in Connecticut. It was Halloween. I was dressed as a witch and in between waiting for the trick or treaters, I started putting up one of my Christmas trees in the family room. The corner in which I put that tree was opposite a large bay window facing the road, so the tree was very visible to those passing by. I got a chuckle out of the cars that would slam on the breaks, sometimes even back up, to look in at that tree in late October. They must have thought I was nuts.

Now, here in Vermont in mid November I started pulling out the decorations and artificial trees and began to put them up. I put up the tree in the corner between the kitchen and den first. This tree had some old ornaments which my mother and I had made ourselves around 45 years or so ago. They were sequin and bead covered and we made them in an assortment of colors. Then there were miscellaneous ornaments, some birds, some cats, some martini glasses, some hot peppers and even one pickle ornament. Let's just say it was eclectic.

That tree was followed by the tree in the dining room which was a slim tree which fit nicely next to the corner cupboard. This tree had all of the really nice elegant type ornaments. These included many clear glass, as well as varieties of silver and gold.

And the last tree that went up was my favorite. Alex had made it several years ago out of PVC pipe and papier mache. He complained about my Christmas trees and said they took so much floor space. He suggested that he make a tree which would stand in a corner. Just the trunk of the tree would be fitted into the corner and then branch out along the ceiling. So standing underneath it you would feel like you were standing under the lower branches of a very tall pine tree. I said that sounded like a wonderful idea. He gave me a look, like the reality of the situation was sinking in; he would have to construct what he described. He was his own worst enemy. He would come up with ideas for this or that, be it a stone wall, bathroom renovation concept, or a Christmas tree, and I invariably said "that sounds great" and then he'd have to make it or do it.

It took him a long time to construct the tree. He made the frame out of the PVC pipe and then covered it with the papier mache to make it look more like a tree trunk and branches. Then once that was all shaped and dried, he painted it brown. He then attached pieces of some artificial green branches from an old Christmas tree no longer in use. I put tiny white lights on this tree and strands of red berry vines, and some vines that looked like ice crystals, and then hung glass ornaments that looked like icicles, and threw on a few birds and pine cones for good measure. This tree was certainly unique and I loved the way the trunk stood in the corner and the branches crept out along the ceiling, all sparking with lights and crystal. It was magical.

The weather outside had not yet been bad thus far into the month of November. The ground was not frozen and the temperature had been relatively mild. I had been intrigued with solar string lights and wanted to try using them this year. They were expensive, but at least I wouldn't have extension cords running all over the place. I strung lights up the trunk and part way up the branches of the crabapple out in the front courtyard area. I wrapped the columns by the front entry area. And off to the rear of the house, where it was so dark because there was nothing out there but woods, I put lights on the blue spruce which could be seen from the kitchen, den and living room. I cut a variety of greens and bittersweet and filled the urns on either side of the front door and that was that! Oh, and I also cut more greens to use to fill baskets placed here and there inside the house, just because I needed some of the evergreen smell!

It was my sisters' day of arrival a few days later. On the way out the door to pick them up, I looked in the front hall mirror and realized that I needed a little color, as I was dressed in various shades of gray. I ran upstairs, went over to the jewelry chest, and reached for my necklace with the chakra pendant and put it around my neck. I quickly looked in the mirror and thought that looked much better.

As I drove to Burlington International Airport, I thought about my chakra pendant and how it had dramatically changed my life. For as long as I could remember, I had always been fond of colored gemstones. White diamonds did nothing for me, but colored stones were my passion. I had many books on gemstones and went to gem and mineral shows whenever they were in the area. When I was in my mid 40's I decided that I wanted to enroll in a class on colored stones offered by the Gemological Institute of America (GIA). I obtained my certificate in colored stones upon passing the final exam. I decided I wanted to continue with the next class offered after that, colored stone grading. I had to go down to the GIA offices in New York City to take that final exam, which I also passed.

After leaving the GIA building late that morning after the exam, I wandered around the Diamond District on West 47th Street. The sheer number of jewelers was amazing as was the variety of jewelry offered. One large store that I went into was set up with many booths, some vendors selling their own creations, some selling antique or estate jewelry, some selling just jewelry findings, some selling loose stones, etc. Those that sold loose stones were the most interesting to me, and some of the prices seemed to be quite reasonable.

Riding home on the train that afternoon, I kept thinking of those loose stones. I had recently been reading about chakras, which were energy centers in the body located at major branchings of the human nervous system, beginning at the base of the spinal column and moving upward to the top of the skull. There were seven of them, and each one had a corresponding color: red/lower body, orange/reproductive, yellow/stomach, green/heart, blue/throat, violet/forehead, purple/top of head. I was thinking it would be wonderful to create a pendant with corresponding colored stones.

I kept thinking of those colored stones, and started to do some pricing of stones locally to familiarize myself with what I could expect to pay. And then I started doing research on goldsmiths in the area and I identified a handful to approach. I sketched a picture of what I wanted the pendant to look like. It would have 7 mm trilliant shaped stones at either end, and 7 x 5 mm ovals set horizontally in between.

I decided that the next time I was in New York City, I would revisit some of the vendors in the Diamond District and see what stones were available and at what price.

My real job was in insurance. At that point in the late 1990's, I had worked in insurance over 20 years. Early on I had tremendously enjoyed working in this field, as I worked for a wonderful man, and a small company. We were like family and the business was very profitable. But the company was acquired by a larger company, then again by a larger company still. It was no longer enjoyable to me; there were too many layers of bureaucracy and too much inefficiency.

I went to New York City on business quite often back then. After a morning meeting and early lunch with a client, I had time to go back to the Diamond District before I caught a train back to Connecticut. I went into that large store with many vendors and identified those who specialized in loose gems. I went from one to another, explaining that I was looking for seven stones the colors of the rainbow: purple, violet, blue, green, yellow, orange and red. I found one vendor who was extremely easy to talk to and I felt he wanted to work with me on this. I said I wanted vivid colored stones, nothing washed out. He suggested amethyst for the purple, iolite for the violet, blue topaz for the blue, Siberian green quartz for the green, citrine for the yellow, Mexican opal for the orange, and garnet for the red. I explained that I needed the garnet and the amethyst in 7 x 7 millimeter trilliants and the others in 7 x 5 ovals. He went through his inventory and pulled out samples of each. The color of each was intense, and laid out in order next to each other they looked marvelous. His prices were better than I had anticipated. He asked how many I wanted, and I told him I'd take 50 of each, which brought the unit price down even more. I was sure I could sell these pendants, so I might as well have a few of them made up.

I can remember riding home on the train and looking at the packets of colored stones. I was so pleased with myself. I could not have asked for more vivid colors or better pricing. And the vendor said that if I wanted more, to just let him know.

A few days later I had reached agreement with a goldsmith who would cast the setting and he had a stone setter to set the stones. Approximately a month later I had my finished pendants. They were spectacular, if I do say so myself. The first day I went out wearing one, I had a couple women stop me and comment on it. One of them gave me her phone number when I told her I manufactured and sold them, and she was my first sale!

Ah, but it wasn't that easy. Marketing was expensive. I put ads in several new age type magazines, and they resulted in only a couple of sales. I approached local jewelry stores and department stores to see if they would take some on consignment, and they weren't interested. I sent in a vendor application to one of the TV shopping channels, and they turned me down. I couldn't understand it; my product was nicer and better priced than anything out there. And it was unique! But I couldn't sell it. It was extremely frustrating.

I almost gave up. And then I sent a vendor's application and sample of the pendant to another TV shopping channel and waited. Several weeks later they contacted me and told me they loved it. We worked out details as to number and pricing. And I contacted my stone guy at the Diamond District as well as the goldsmith and made appropriate arrangements with them. The finished pendants were delivered to the shopping network, they went on the air, and sold out during their first showing. I received another order for a larger shipment this time, and again they sold out. I knew they would be well received, but I didn't anticipate this kind of overwhelming response.

Then I came up with another idea. I had been stopped several times by women who asked if the chakra pendant were a "mother's" pendant, similar to a "mother's" ring where you would put the corresponding birthstones of your children in the ring. Each time I was asked, I would say no and then explain the significance of the stones. But the concept of creating a "mother's" pendant was implanted in my head and I continued to think about it.

I finally came up with an idea of creating a pendant where you could add or remove stones as needed. So if you have one child and she was born in September, you have a sapphire pendant as sapphire is the September birthstone. The pendant is hinged, so it opens up like an enhancer would. The stone is emerald cut and set east to west, and at the bottom is a bar of gold that is attractive in its own right, yet would accept another hinged pendant should you wish to add one, and another and another. I thought a fun selling technique for this pendant would be to say that should you disown a child, you can just remove his/her stone from your pendant, simple as that!

And another good thing about this pendant is that there would be 12 birthstones, and you could just create a pendant with the colors you like, depending on what you're wearing, so this could be marketed to all women and not just mothers and grandmothers.

I was really excited about this idea. I knew I could get the appropriate stones from my stone guy, but I needed to make sure the goldsmith could actually create what I envisioned. I went to visit him with my sketches and we sat down and talked it over and he came up with a design that would work and be beautiful as well. He got to work on fabricating it and I contacted my man in New York for the stones. The only stone that presented a little bit of a problem was the June birthstone. The primary birthstone for June is pearl, which really didn't lend itself to the emerald cut shape we had going in the pendant. The alternate birthstone for June is Alexandrite. Genuine Alexandrite is one of the most expensive gemstones on earth, so we decided Russian lab created Alexandrite was the way to go.

I only purchased two of each of the twelve stones and had the goldsmith make 24 hinged pendants. I kept one set of twelve and sent the other twelve to the shopping channel with a written description of how they could be used, either as a mother's pendant or as a mix and match/create your own type pendant. You didn't have to buy all twelve stones, you could buy one pendant at a time if you wanted and then add to them as you desired. Well, they loved them too! I wasn't surprised by this, as I really had a lot of fun with my own twelve stones and received many compliments on them.

This line of pendants outsold the initial offering of the chakra pendants. Now, several years later, both types of pendants are still in production and being sold on that shopping channel. We are also offering earrings similarly constructed.

This wonderful turn of fortune allowed me to retire early from my insurance job and move to Vermont. And I couldn't have been happier.

Chapter 14 – First Night

In my reverie I almost missed the turn for Burlington International Airport. It was a beautiful little airport. There was a parking garage attached to it, and it was wonderfully easy to get in and out of. It was a crystal clear day and I got there a little early so I could get a cup of coffee and sit down by one of the big windows and watch the planes come and go for a while. It brought back memories of my teenage years when my girlfriend Meredith and I would drive every Sunday afternoon from Connecticut to LaGuardia Airport in New York to have lunch at one of the airport restaurants. Thinking back I wondered where we got the money to do this. We'd ask for a table by the window and Meredith would take out a cigarette and no sooner had she taken out the cigarette when a waiter would immediately appear to light it for her. I don't think she even inhaled, she just liked to have a waiter light the cigarette for her. She never smoked anywhere except at that airport restaurant. Ah, those were the days. Gas was cheap and smoking was allowed just about everywhere.

The girls' plane had landed, so I swallowed the last bit of coffee and walked over to position myself by the gate. They appeared a few minutes later and there were hugs and kisses all around. It was so good to see them! We collected their luggage and in no time we were on Route 7 heading south. They commented on how beautiful the lake and mountains looked as they flew over them. I had never flown into Burlington myself, but I could imagine the views must be breathtaking from above. I thought they were amazing from the ground!

We arrived at the house and I could see smoke coming up from the chimneys, so I knew Alex had lit fires. He was right on hand as soon as we got out of the car and there were more hugs and kisses. When we walked through the front door, the fires in both the dining room and living room fireplaces were visible as was the tree in the dining room and the tree in the corner of the living room that branched out across the ceiling. I must say everything looked perfect. The girls "ooo'd" and "ahh'd" about the fires and the Christmas trees. They sat down on either side of the living room fireplace and I poured some wine for them.

It was now late afternoon and the sun was starting to set behind the Adirondacks. Mary got up to look out at the sunset and Anne joined her. The sky was an incredible blend of gold, apricot and pink along with blue and the mountains in the foreground were a deep purple. Many years earlier when I had seen my first such sunset and I noticed the purplish color of the mountains, I recalled the phrase "purple mountain majesty" from 'America the Beautiful'. I had never seen purple mountains before and these truly were majestic.

I went into the kitchen to get some cheese and crackers and make myself a martini, and Alex grabbed a beer. My sisters followed us into the kitchen and stopped to admire the Christmas tree there. They recalled that time all those years ago back home in our parents' house when the dining room table was covered with sequins and beads and little Styrofoam balls during the period when my mother and I had made those ornaments. It was quite a little production we had going for a while.

The girls sat down by the fire in the den and started nibbling the cheese and crackers and assorted olives and I poured them another glass of wine. It was starting to get dark outside and the lights on the blue spruce magically came on; those solar lights are great! I put the already assembled JFK Seafood Casserole in the oven. The recipe came from an old dog-eared paperback cookbook entitled 'White House Cookbook' that had been my grandmother's. This recipe was incredibly easy, could be made ahead of time, and was delicious. I started preparing the saffron rice with peas as well.

I sat down next to my sisters for a while to relax and Alex started making the salad. I have to admit he did make a great salad. His favorite combination was spinach, celery, red grapes, apples and walnuts, kind of like a Waldorf salad type mix and then he'd make his own poppy seed dressing. He didn't have the dressing recipe written down, he'd just whip it together and, voila, an incredible combination.

Anne said she noticed that there were quite a few books piled up on the table in the living room and asked if there were some research project going on. Alex and I gave each other a look, and I said "Yes, I guess you could say that." Both sisters gave me a quizzical look.

Alex said "Go get the bible and read them some Genesis."

I got up to get the bible and the girls followed me into the living room. I opened to Genesis 1:26 and read the sentence about "in our image". Mary said maybe that was like the royal "we". I said, okay, then listen to Genesis 6:1-4 and I read the section about the "sons of god" and the "daughters of men" and the "giants". There was just silence.

I said "come over here and take a look at this picture" and brought them over to 'The Baptism of Christ' hanging on the back wall. Alex had installed a brass picture light above it, so it was nicely illuminated. I told them it had been painted in 1710 and the original is housed at the Fitzwilliam Museum Cambridge.

Mary said "That's a UFO overhead with beams of light shining down on Jesus."

I brought them back to the table with all of the books piled on it and picked up "The Alien Chronicles" by Matthew Hurley. I showed them that same 'Baptism of Christ' picture on the front cover. Then I turned to the chapter on UFOs in western religious art and showed them the remainder of the art work in that section. They were pretty much speechless.

Alex called us back into the kitchen as he could see their wine glasses were empty and my martini was ready to be refreshed. Our drinks were refilled and the three of us sat around the prep sink and work area where Alex was finishing whipping together his salad dressing.

"Did you ever consider that the star of Bethlehem was a UFO?" Alex asked. Mary and Anne stared at him.

"And that the Virgin birth was really the result of artificial insemination performed by extraterrestrials?" he continued.

"Are you saying that Jesus is part ET?" Anne asked.

I said "Yes, and more than just half ET, because the Virgin Mary was also conceived this way. Her mother, St. Anne, was long past child bearing age. An angel appeared to both St. Anne and her husband, Joachim, and told them a child would be born unto them. Sure enough, a child was born and that was Mary. The Immaculate Conception means that Mary was born without 'original sin' and although I don't agree with the concept of original sin, I think this reference is probably linked to Mary's ET lineage."

Just then the oven beeper went off. I got up and took the casserole out of the oven.

"Let's eat in the dining room," Alex said. "That way you'll get to see the other side of this two sided fireplace!" He quickly grabbed four place settings and in no time we were seated in the cozy dark room eating by firelight and candlelight.

We rarely used this dining room. It was basically a repository for all of my transferware and my mother's mahogany dining room furniture. The flickering light danced across the brown and white transferware. And out the front window you could see the crabapple tree with its little white lights. Everything looked lovely.

Alex said "Can you imagine a movie being made today that opened with shepherds and their flocks looking up at the sky and there is this glowing 'star', which is really a spacecraft, slowly moving toward Bethlehem, and they start to follow. And then the scene switches to another location with the Magi following that same 'star'. After days of following this glowing light in the sky, the shepherds and the Magi meet and proceed together. The 'star' is lower now and is clearly not a 'star' but a glowing, metallic spacecraft. It comes to a stop over a cave and casts this amazing golden glow on the ground and objects below. The Magi and shepherds approach the cave, and there is the newly born baby Jesus with Mary and Joseph. Jesus also has a glow about him. The Magi and shepherds fall down on their knees in adoration."

"Wouldn't this be too controversial? You'd have Christians the world over boycotting this movie." Mary said.

"Free advertising." Alex said. "And the vast majority of people worldwide do believe that we are being visited by extraterrestrials."

"Being visited is one thing, having these beings somehow involved in the birth of Christ is another thing," Mary said.

"If the evidence we have compiled is somehow introduced in this movie, concrete evidence that each person can then verify for themselves and from which they can draw their own conclusions, I think this movie will change the world as we know it."

"I know I'd love to see it," Anne said.

"And," I said "the story would continue with the baptism of Christ, for example, showing the UFO hovering over Jesus and John the Baptist in the River Jordan, with the rays of light shining down and this voice saying 'This is my beloved son, in whom I am well pleased.' And of course the transfiguration story would be included where Jesus brought James, Peter and John to the top of a high mountain and a bright cloud overshadowed them and a voice from the cloud said 'This is my beloved son, in whom I am well pleased: hear ye him',".

"You mean that 'this is my beloved son, in whom I am well pleased' was said on two separate occasions and it came from an object in the sky above?" Mary asked.

I answered "Yes, and can you picture a swirling glowing cloud like the ones they created for 'Close Encounters of the Third Kind' hovering over that mountain top with the voice booming out?"

"Actually, you could start with a little vignette of the Genesis story to introduce the concept that we were created by beings not from this earth, and then turn to their artificial insemination of Mary (not graphically, of course). The screen would go dark, and then the words 'almost nine months later …' would appear on the screen and then we could begin with the Magi and shepherds following the 'star'.

"There's so much material here that actually you could do two separate movies. The first would be the Genesis story, then the giants finding the daughters of men attractive story, the destruction of Sodom and Gomorrah by the extraterrestrials, Noah and the flood, and the Tower of Babel and the dispersal of humans around the world. We could also tie in the civilizations who acknowledge in their creation stories that they were created by gods who had human forms, and these gods were instrumental in the development of those civilizations. The sequel would then center on Jesus."

"I was thinking about the religious art with the spaceships; the Catholic Church must be aware of these paintings. I wonder what their explanation of it would be," Anne asked.

"I think they know we are being visited by extraterrestrials, why else would they have the Pope Scope. Maybe they are also awaiting the second coming, and they are focusing on watching the sky," I said.

"Pope Scope, what's that?" Mary asked.

"They have a large modern observatory in Arizona and their telescope is called by some the 'Pope Scope'," I said. "Actually they have two observatories, the one in Arizona and another one at the Pope's summer residence at Castel Gandolfo just outside of Rome."

"Is this common knowledge?" Mary asked. "I've never heard of it."

"I don't think it's very well publicized," Alex said,

"but it certainly isn't a secret. The information is out there for those with inquiring minds."

"I believe the Catholic Church has a considerable amount of information that they are keeping secret, though. I'm sure that Vatican Library is just full of interesting stuff," I said.

"And so much information has been destroyed by representatives of the Catholic Church. For example, many of the Codices of the Mayans and Aztecs were destroyed by Jesuit missionaries," Alex said.

We sat and talked a while more, before clearing off the table. It had been a long day for Mary and Anne and they were tired, I could tell. I suggested they go upstairs and put on their nightgowns and robes and get more comfortable. Alex brought the girls' luggage upstairs and showed them to their rooms.

By the time they came back down, the kitchen was clean, and I had made a pot of chamomile tea. We sat down in the living room in front of the slowly dying fire and sipped our tea. I said that tomorrow's plans were to go to Uncle Jim's antiques in the morning and then head to Middlebury. There were wonderful eclectic shops there, some shops that featured local artists and contained everything from jewelry to furniture. We could have a late lunch at the café overlooking the falls.

Anne said that there were very few antique shops in Hilton Head, there were consignment shops, but antique shops were few and far between.

Tomorrow's agenda sounded great to the girls. And Alex and I were looking forward to it as well; we really needed a break from all the research we had been doing.

Anne took a sip of the tea and looked up at the Venus of Willendorf on the mantel and said "What is that?" I have to admit, it was a bizarre looking creature.

Alex explained how our investigation had somehow brought us to the Venus, and he explained that it was created between 30,000 and 25,000 B.C. He shared our thoughts on what it was…our prototype.

Mary and Anne sat there by the flickering fire light, sipped tea and stared at the little statuette.

It had been a nice day. It was good to have the girls with us and it was good that they were interested in our research and conclusions. They were not reticent women; if they thought we were crazy, they would have told us so. At least I think they would have said so. Not that it would make any difference.

As we got up to go to bed, Anne asked if she could take one of the books upstairs to read. Mary said she'd like that as well. I chose two that I thought they would find very readable and extremely interesting. They took their books in hand and climbed the stairs.

Chapter 15 – For the Birds

I got up early the next morning, but was extremely quiet as my sister Mary was not an early riser. Anne, however, was. I wanted to have a pot of coffee going for Anne when she got down. And of course I had to feed my little Itzy first.

And where did you sleep last night, you little bum?" I whispered to Itzy. "You weren't with me." I suspected she sneaked in to one of the girl's bedrooms.

Alex had been asleep on the sofa in the den, but he heard me and gave me a waive. He lay there a few minutes more, then got up, folded his blanket and put it away.

"Howdee," he said, as he approached me. "Sleep well?"

"Great, how about you?"

"Pretty good."

"Could you please get the cream cheese out of the refrigerator? There are two containers, plain cream cheese and bacon horseradish," I said. I had the coffee brewing, and I got the bag of bagels out of the breadbox and sliced them.

I lined a wicker serving tray with a clean towel and arranged the bagels. They came from the Burlington Bagel Bakery. In my opinion, they were the best bagels anywhere. Better than New York bagels. They were crisp on the outside, and had a dense chewy texture inside. My favorite was the sunflower seed, but I had an assortment on hand. Even the cream cheese that I got at the Bagel Bakery seemed better than any other cream cheese.

"Oh, and could you please get the peanut butter out and sweet butter and blueberry jam as well, just in case someone wants it? And there's a bowl of fresh fruit in the fridge too; could you grab that as well?"

I could hear footsteps coming down the stairs, and Anne appearing around the corner.

"Good morning!" she said. "I slept like a log. I don't

think I moved all night."

"Nothing like a good night's sleep," Alex said.

The coffee was ready, and I filled cups for the three of us. Alex put on one of the local television stations to check on the weather.

Anne helped herself to some fruit salad, and went over and sat down on the couch with Alex.

"Can you believe it's going to get up in the 70's today? A cold front is coming through late in the day and there should be heavy rain, maybe even lightening and thunder. This is not typical November weather for us," he said to Anne.

"Hopefully we'll be home by the time the bad weather hits," I said.

I filled the thermal carafe with the remainder of the coffee, and started another pot. I joined Alex and Anne on the sofa. The three of us were sitting there sipping our coffee and watching the news when we heard the pitter patter of little footsteps approaching.

Mary appeared around the corner with her soft pink robe and matching slippers. She looked so cute.

"Helloooo!" She called. "Helloooo!" we called back.

"Do you know Itzy slept with me last night?" Mary said.

"I knew she wasn't with me, and guessed she might be with either you or Anne," I said. "Did she bother you?"

"No, she just snuggled up next to me, and barely moved all night."

I poured Mary a cup of coffee and took orders for bagels. Mary helped herself to some fruit salad and sat at the table. Anne and Alex got up and joined her.

When the last bagel was toasted, I joined them at the table. Mary started right in about the book she had brought upstairs last night. She said ancient civilizations of Peru, Mexico, China, Indus River Valley, Egypt and Mesopotamia all built similar pyramid type structures. And creation myths for each were similar; human-like "gods" descended from the sky, created human beings and taught them mathematics, agriculture, astronomy, metallurgy, science and assisted in helping them to construct cities. Mary said she had no idea there were ancient pyramids in China, but there were many of them located southwest of Beijing.

"And," she continued, "the thing of it is, these civilizations sprung up relatively suddenly. It's fascinating reading."

"Alex and I believe they truly were instructed in all forms of craftsmanship by the 'gods', meaning extraterrestrials. There is even a reference to this in Exodus when the Lord God infused Bezaleel with knowledge and ability to create beautiful works of art and also the ability to instruct others in this craftsmanship."

Anne said she wished she could remember what she read last night, but she was so tired, she couldn't remember any of it.

Just then a bulletin came on the local weather that strong storms were predicted for late afternoon.

"Gee, and it looks so beautiful out," Mary said.

"It's in the high 40's right now and it's supposed to get up into the 70's this afternoon," Alex said.

"So that means that we better get an early start. Finish up those bagels ladies and gentleman, and let's get this show on the road!"

"Hey, could I at least have a second cup of coffee first?" Anne asked.

"Sure, actually take your time, the antique shop doesn't open until 10 a.m. anyway," I said and refilled everyone's coffee cups.

"This blueberry bagel with sweet butter and blueberry jam is incredible," Anne said. "You can't get bagels like this down in Hilton Head."

"And they freeze really well. You slice them first and put them in those freezer bags, toast them up and they're wonderful," I stated.

"Hmmm, I wouldn't mind a few dozen for a Christmas present," Anne said.

"Okay, you got it," I responded.

"I can't believe what I just saw," Alex said. "I just looked up at the TV and they were interviewing a guy from one of the southern states that got hit by severe storms last night, and underneath his picture it said his name was Larry Crow, Mayor of Birdtown."

"Get out. You're kidding." I said, and quickly looked at the television, but a commercial was on now.

"No, I swear that's what it said. Larry Crow, Mayor of Birdtown."

We were still laughing when Alex said, "Gee, I wonder if that's Larry Bird and Charlie Byrd's hometown."

The volume of our laughter increased.

"And Peter Finch," Anne said.

We roared.

"Walter Pidgeon," Mary uttered.

And we continued to roar. I think our brains were all working overtime to come up with another 'bird' name.

"Jack Sparrow," I said.

"Ethan Hawk," Mary exclaimed.

"Debra Winger," shouted Anne.

"Sheryl Crow," Alex said. "Wonder if she's related to Mayor Larry Crow."

"Lady Bird Johnson," Alex bellowed.

"Robin Williams," I said.

"Christopher Wren," Anne yelled.

"Gregory Peck," Mary said.

"Gregory Peck?" I asked.

"Yes, peck, like a bird pecks. Gregory Peck."

"Okay, we'll let that one in," I responded.

"Chick Corea," Alex said.

We were all straining to come up with one more, but a couple of minutes passed and no one said a word. We just continued to laugh.

Alex said "Do you know what breaking an egg is in Birdtown?"

"What?" Mary asked.

"A cardinal sin."

We laughed and laughed, and after a minute or two we were finally composing ourselves, and wiping the tears from our eyes.

I picked up my coffee cup and took a sip, and then Alex said in a hushed voice "Mother Goose".

The coffee spurted out of my mouth and we all got hysterical again. But "Mother Goose" was the last, no one came up with another name, and the laughter finally subsided.

We finished our coffee, got dressed and soon thereafter headed out the door for the day's adventures.

"Should I take the convertible? It's going to be warm enough for it."

"No, you better take the wagon; we might have some large purchases today," Alex said.

"Right, we might have some large purchases today!" Mary chimed in.

We all got into the Outback, and off we went.

Chapter 16 – Stormy Weather

We got to Uncle Jim's just after 10 a.m. and were his first customers. Alex and I said hello to him, and I introduced Mary and Anne. I told him they came all the way from South Carolina to visit his shop.

I then looked at the corner by the front door where that stuffed monkey had been, and it wasn't there.

"You sold that monkey?" I asked.

"Yes, several months ago this guy came in and bought it. Didn't haggle the price, just said he wanted it. He didn't look at anything else. It was like he knew it was here. He walked in the front door, took one look, said he wanted it, and that was that."

"I swear I saw that same monkey recently behind an anthropologist on TV who was being interviewed about Sasquatch."

"Hmmm, could be. Never saw the guy before and most likely will never see him again."

I noticed my sisters were a little further in looking at the jewelry cases. Mary had already asked Jim's wife to unlock one of the cases as there were some earrings she wanted to try on.

I don't know how they zeroed in on the jewelry so quickly. Even though I had been in that shop many times before, I was always overwhelmed by the amount of things to look at. The first room alone had Christmas ornaments hanging from the ceiling. I mean the entire ceiling was completely covered by Christmas ornaments. There were old glass bottles on shelves that had been built in front of a row of windows. There were antique dolls and antique toys, and there were cases and cases of jewelry.

Alex was looking at pressed steel toy trucks over on the right side of the room. I went over to where Mary and Anne stood. Mary had the earrings on, and they suited her perfectly. She didn't have pierced ears, and these were clip-ons with a screw back so you could adjust the tightness. Sometimes clip-ons were so uncomfortable, but this combination with the screw back eliminated that. Mary said she'd take them.

Then Anne asked the woman to take out a gold bangle bracelet that had stones that looked like turquoise and blue sapphire embedded. This was costume jewelry, but the detail work was incredible. The gold looked like it could have been 18kt Italian gold; it was a beautiful buttery color. It was an exquisite piece of jewelry. Anne put it on her tanned wrist and it did look lovely. She said she'd take it.

Mary asked to see a gold necklace with a pendant that looked like a 4ct diamond. When the woman took it out, she looked at the price tag and said "This can't be right, but it does say $3.50!" We all scrambled to see this. What must have been a cubic zirconium sparkled as much as, or more than, a real diamond. It was amazing. Mary tried it on and we all commented on how real it looked and it even included the chain for $3.50! She said, "Okay, I'll take it. Actually, if you could please just cut the tag off, I'll wear it."

We continued to look at jewelry. I felt left out; I hadn't found anything that appealed to me. If I had seen that bangle that Anne bought first, I would have bought it. If I had seen that $3.50 pendant (included chain) that Mary bought, I would have bought it. So now I was intently searching the cases, looking for something special that would call out to me.

Instead, I heard Anne say "Could you show me that gold ring with the blue stone?" The woman took it out and said it was labeled "blue topaz and 14kt gold". Anne tried it on and it fit her perfectly. And it looked wonderful with the bangle she was buying with the blue stones. She asked me to take a look at it. It was only $55 and she couldn't believe it was really 14kt gold with a genuine blue topaz. The stone was bezel set. Inside the band it was stamped "14K". The stone certainly looked genuine to me. Actually, I was wearing my chakra pendant, which had a blue topaz of the same color and I held it up to my pendant and said to Anne, "It looks like a genuine blue topaz to me, see how it compares with the stone in my pendant? And it is stamped 14k gold and it looks to me like it was handmade. Anne put it back on again, and said "Okay, I'll take it."

No sooner had Anne said she would take it than Mary asked if she could see a bracelet. It was a gold link bracelet, kind of an art nouveau design, with emerald cut yellow stones that looked like citrine. Before she tried it on, Mary asked me to look at it. It was gold-filled, not solid gold, but the workmanship was wonderful, the design was a classic, and the stones appeared to me to be genuine citrine. Mary tried it on, and at the same time spotted a ring in the case which she asked to see. This was a Mystic topaz band ring set in 10kt gold. She tried that on as well, then she said she'd take both of them.

We had pretty much worked our way through the jewelry cases. We approached the next room which was off to our left. Alex was already in there, looking through the pottery. This room was completely filled with china and pottery. It was in this room that I had found many pieces of Burgess and Leigh, Hill Pottery, Rustic pattern. This was the pattern that I went on to collect and which now filled my entire corner cupboard. But that was many years ago, when there was a considerable amount of brown and white transferware out there. Today, it was rare to find any piece that was not damaged. We had fun going through that room, looking for a hidden treasure, but we didn't find any.

The next room was filled with books. I have to give Uncle Jim credit; he had everything in that shop well organized. Even the books were arranged by general subject. Alex went to the gardening section, and I gravitated to architecture and religion. I found a book entitled 'Houses of Stone' that had a 1933 copyright. It contained text as well as drawings and floor plans of stone houses. I showed it to Alex, and he looked at me and said "You already own that book." I knew I liked it! Oh well, I put it back on the shelf. We left that room empty handed.

The huge room in the back had oriental rugs, furniture and art. This room really was overwhelming. So much furniture, and so many rugs. Anne and Mary followed Alex around and he explained the different types of rugs they saw. He identified Heriz, Tabriz, and Sarouk. He explained about knots per square inch and turned the corner of the rugs over so the girls could see for themselves. He talked about warp and weft, wool and silk. My sisters were wall-to-wall carpeting types; they really didn't know much about Persian rugs. But they seemed to be enjoying what he was telling them. The prices of some of those rugs ran into several thousands of dollars.

After spending quite a bit of time looking at the rugs and furniture, we headed upstairs where there was a section for textiles, another for old small appliances, like toasters, and another huge area with everything else. After a while, Mary said "I'm getting hungry."

Anne looked at her watch and said "It's after 1 p.m.; we've been here for over 3 hours!"

"I guess we'd better head out to lunch," Alex said. "We don't want anyone fainting from hunger."

We went back downstairs and retraced our footsteps through the different rooms, and the girls checked out with their jewelry purchases. I was feeling depressed. I didn't find one thing that I couldn't live without.

We walked out into the sunshine and it was as warm as a summer day. We took our coats off, and got into the car. I even had to put the air-conditioner on for a brief while to cool down the interior of the car.

I drove south toward Middlebury and I could hear my sisters talking about their jewelry purchases. I was pleased that they seemed to be so happy with their new acquisitions. I looked in the rearview mirror and I could see Anne holding up her arm admiring her new bracelet and ring.

A short while later we were in Middlebury. There were many shops to see, but since everyone was starving at this point, we headed toward a little café with a view of the falls. Luckily, as it was rather late, the lunch crowd had come and pretty much gone, and we were seated at a table by a window overlooking the falls. A quick perusal of the menu, and my sisters knew exactly what they wanted, tuna melts. We ordered and the food was served very quickly; maybe the fact that we told the waitress that we were famished helped.

After taking one bite of her sandwich, Anne said to Mary, "Isn't this the best tuna melt you've ever had?"

I thought she was kidding, but Mary replied "Yes, there's something different about it, but I don't know what it is. It's marvelous."

I said "You're both so hungry anything would taste good to you."

"In Hilton Head you can't find a real grilled tuna melt; they quickly broil it open-faced. So that's a major difference, but there's still something else that I can't identify," Anne said.

I made a mental note that the next time I came to this café, I would definitely order a tuna melt!

Alex was talking about how good the waffle fries were and passed them around for all to sample. They were crispy and delightfully seasoned. This place was a real hit!

Mary said "Does Alex know the NOINO story?"

"Hmmm, no, I don't think he does."

"What's the NOINO story?" Alex asked.

"Back when I was a teenager, my mother and I went to the supermarket to do the week's grocery shopping. We had a list, but went up and down every isle just in case we forgot to write something down, or if there was something that caught our fancy. We had gone through the entire store and were in the last isle, the bread isle. We needed bread, but weren't sure which kind to get. I saw one label that I had never seen before, and I picked up the loaf of bread. It said 'NOINO'. I showed it to my mother and she said she'd never heard of it, and let's give it a try. So, I put it in the shopping cart, and we proceeded to the check out, talking about that NOINO bread and wondering what it was like."

"We got to the check out line, and started to unload the cart, and I picked up that loaf of NOINO bread, and we looked at it some more and were talking rather excitedly about this new, strange kind of bread, and how we couldn't wait to get home to try it. I noticed that the clerk and the person behind us in line were looking at us rather strangely. But I figured they were amazed by this NOINO bread as well."

"We got home, and carried in all the grocery bags, and started to unload the contents, and I pulled out the loaf of bread, but this time it didn't read NOINO, it read ONION. Get it, NOINO is ONION spelled backward. When we picked up the bread on the shelf, we were looking at an upside down label, and when we picked it up at the checkout, we also were looking at an upside down label. I said to my mother 'No wonder the clerk and the lady behind us were looking at us strangely, they must have thought we were nuts to be talking about NOINO bread, when clearly it was ONION bread!'

"We erupted into hysterical laughter. My legs got weak and I slid to the floor rolling around laughing. My brother ran upstairs from the basement because he couldn't tell if we were screaming or laughing or what. And he looked at us like we were lunatics. Maybe he was right."

It's a good thing the restaurant crowd had cleared out, because we were all quite loud with our laughter now. Ah, it was one of those silly days filled with laughter. How nice.

After lunch, we headed out to see what the shops had to offer. Alex noted that there were dark clouds on the western horizon, so we better be quick about continued shopping.

There was a local Vermont artisan shop that I definitely wanted the girls to see. It was just around the corner in a beautiful old brick building that had been remodeled. We walked in, and again, my sisters just gravitated to the jewelry counters. However, most of this jewelry was pretty highly priced, and they had been spoiled by the prices at Uncle Jim's. They admired many items, but didn't buy.

There was a copper roofed purple martin house which Alex and I admired. We had always wanted to put up a purple martin house, but never found one that we really liked. Alex had said he would build one, but there were so many other things to do, he never got to it. Anne and Mary said they would buy it for us for Christmas. We said no, they said yes. We said no, they said yes. We went back and forth a few more times, and they won. Purchase in hand, actually in Alex's arms, we walked out and those dark clouds were definitely on the increase and very ominous looking.

"I think we better head for home right now," Alex said. "This doesn't look good".

There were other shops we could have seen, and we could have driven around the lovely Middlebury College campus, but we headed right home. And a good thing it was.

The first drops of rain were just starting as I turned into our driveway. I pulled straight into the garage, as it was now pouring rain. We entered the kitchen through the mudroom off the garage. Mary and Anne were talking about their jewelry purchases again. It tickled me that they were so happy. It had been a good day.

Just then there was a flash of lightening, followed by rolling thunder a few seconds later. It was almost as dark as night outside, so I lit some candles. Alex was pouring wine for the girls. I made a martini for myself, and we headed into the living room.

Alex said we might as well have a fire in the fireplace, as the temperature will be dropping fast now that the front is starting to move through. He went out to the garage and came back with an armful of wood and in no time we had a lovely fire going. Even Itzy was enjoying it, getting as close to the screen as she could.

Through the French doors we could see frequent vivid bolts of lightening over the mountains and lake and the thunder was following much more quickly now. It was cozy sitting there in front of the fire in big comfortable chairs hearing the rain pelt the windows, watching the storm outside. We sat there in silence for a few seconds and then Alex said "Did you know this house is haunted?"

Anne and Mary looked at him in shock.

I said "But they're friendly, and we haven't had much contact from them lately."

Anne asked "What kind of contact have you had with them? And do you know who 'they' are?"

Alex explained that we believed they were the spirits of Gene and Hilda, the couple who had built this house and who had lived in it the rest of their lives.

"One day we were outside working in the yard and we saw this car coming slowly down our driveway. A man got out, approached us, and introduced himself as Richard, nephew to Hilda. He said he was very familiar with the house, and had done work on it in the past, and would be available if we needed any help. He handed us his card, and left."

"The house did need considerable work. We thought it might make sense to bring in someone who was familiar with the house, so we called Richard. He helped with various aspects of the renovation."

"During the time he was working here, Connie and I would have conversations with him about his aunt and uncle, as we were curious about them. He brought us some pictures of them. He said they loved to entertain and would have card parties quite often. They kept two horses in the barn, Satin and Silk, and rode the horses down the dirt road almost every day in good weather. Both Gene and Hilda delighted in landscaping the property. They planted many varieties of perennials and some unusual trees and shrubs."

"That explained the poncirus trifoliata," I said.

The girls gave me a quizzical look

"The poncirus trifoliata! It's a hardy orange that is out in the border around the stone foundation. It should not be growing in this hardiness zone, but it is. It's protected from the north wind by the stone foundation, and that combined with the heat radiation coming off the stone has kept that shrub flourishing for decades."

"What does it look like?" Mary asked.

"Oh, it's about 6 feet tall and wide, and has huge thorns. In the spring it has white flowers that produce little fuzzy oranges that start out green and then turn a golden-orange kind of color in the fall. It's beautiful, actually," I responded.

Alex continued, "There was a small cemetery down the road, and one day I asked Richard if his aunt and uncle were buried there. He gave me a strange look, and then said, no, the family had scattered their ashes on this property, Meghalaya. He said that Gene and Hilda loved this spot so much, that the family felt it fitting that their ashes be scattered here. Connie and I were happy that their ashes were strewn about the land that they so loved."

Just then there was a brilliant light display outside with lightening filling the entire Western horizon. The house shook from the thunder that followed.

Alex got up to get a beer, and when he came back he said the temperature had already dropped over 20 degrees from what it had been when we arrived home.

I continued with the Gene and Hilda story. "One evening later that first summer in the house, Alex was bringing in his tools. He had set up sawhorses outside, as he was doing carpentry work. I had dinner going inside. It was almost dark. Suddenly, Alex came running in, and he stuck out his arm, and said "Look at the hair on my arm, it's standing straight up."

I said "What's going on?"

He said, I was gathering my tools when I could feel electricity in the air and then I distinctly heard a female voice say "Why don't you..." and then I heard a male voice interrupt and say "Shhhhhh..."

"Gene and Hilda?"

"I think so; it must be." Alex said.

Both girls reached for their wine, and took a sip. I could by the flickering fire light that their eyes were open wide.

Alex said that he still had to go back outside to pick up his tools. By now it was very dark. He could still feel the electricity in the air. He bent over to pick up his toolbox and he touched fur! He couldn't see anything, but he heard that Louie Armstrong kind of meow and knew it was Black. It would make sense that Black would be right there as he had been Gene and Hilda's cat for twenty years.

"I finished picking up my things and came inside. By now the moon was coming up. As I looked out the back door, I could see two things which looked like wisps of smoke floating down the path and they disappeared as I watched."

"What I'd like to know is what Hilda wanted to say when she was interrupted. 'Why don't you...' what?" I said. "We'll never know."

"Once when Alex was away for several days working at a job down in Newport, I heard what I believe was Hilda," I said. "I was sound asleep in my bedroom, and I awoke because I could hear Itzy running around like crazy in the living room below making a racket. Then I heard a female voice say 'Stop it!' And Itzy stopped. I can remember thinking to myself, 'Thanks, Hilda'. It didn't bother me in the least; I was glad she was around watching over things."

I continued, "And then I had one episode where I was awakened in the middle of the night with the feeling that someone just sat down on the edge of the bed. I mean I could actually feel the bed move just as if someone sat down. I said "Go away and don't do that again." I could feel the bed move again as if someone got up, and it never did happen again. I don't know if that was Gene, Hilda or someone else"

"We feel their presence at times, and sometimes if we're missing an item, it will almost magically appear, and I attribute that to them," Alex said. "The do appear to be benevolent. I think they like what we have done to the house and grounds. They definitely are not evil spirits, so you don't have to worry!"

The worst of the thunder and lightening seemed to be over, but now the wind was howling!

Anne said "I think I'd like another glass of wine." Mary said "Me, too!" We all got up and walked to the kitchen. I started putting some lights on as we walked.

"Hey, how about we watch 'Close Encounters of the Third Kind'?" I asked. Even though it was pitch black outside, it was only 6 p.m.

Everyone agreed that it sounded like a plan. We positioned ourselves in the den, and I put the DVD on. We had a large flat screen TV with this amazing surround sound type speaker system.

As we watched, either Mary or Anne would say "I don't remember this part." Of course, it was three decades ago that they last saw it.

I especially liked the special effects with the UFO's in the clouds. It seemed that they beautifully and realistically depicted Ezekiel, Chapter 1, Verse 4: "And I looked, and, behold, a whirlwind came out of the north, a great cloud, and a fire infolding itself, and a brightness was about it, and out of the midst thereof as the color of amber, out of the midst of the fire." Some versions of the bible substituted the word "amber" with "glowing metal".

I paused the movie halfway through as I knew I was getting hungry and I figured I wasn't the only one. I popped some popcorn, and put out some extra sharp cheddar cheese and sesame crackers and olives.

We watched the second half of the movie. The part toward the end when the spaceships come to the landing site by Devil's Tower was my favorite. The visual effects were magnificent, and the sound communication between the ship and the humans was spectacular.

After the movie ended, Anne said "That was better than I remembered it."

"Yes, I really enjoyed that," Mary added.

The wind was still howling and rain was still hitting the windows. Anne and Mary said they were going to call it a night.

Mary said, "If I feel someone sitting on the bed tonight, I hope it's only Itzy."

Chapter 17 –Snow Scenes

I woke the next morning and everything was unusually quiet. No more wind; no more rain. It also seemed the bedroom was extremely bright. I got up and looked out the window and everything was white. Snow clung to the tree branches and even coated the northwest side of the tree trunks. I looked out windows on the other side toward the lake, and the Adirondacks were coated in white as well. Lake Champlain was a deep steely color blue. What a beautiful sight.

I put on my robe and slippers and went downstairs. That amazing pure white light was pouring through every window. Itzy was sitting by one of the French doors, looking longingly outside. She was always fascinated by the first snow.

I put the coffee on. Seconds later Alex appeared in the doorway with a handful of logs.

"I think a morning like this calls for a fire, don't you?" he asked.

"Absolutely. Isn't it beautiful?"

"Sure is."

Alex set up fires in the den/dining room fireplace as well as the living room. No sooner had the fires caught, when I could hear both Mary and Anne coming down the stairs. They walked into the kitchen with this amazed look in their eyes.

"It's a winter wonderland," Anne said.

"It's been so long since I saw snow," Mary said. "Who would believe it was almost 80 yesterday afternoon and this morning we have snow!"

"Very unusual, but beautiful," Alex said.

I put some bacon on the grill, as this seemed to be a bacon and eggs kind of morning.

Mary said that Itzy had slept with her again last night, and she was happy for the company.

The girls poured some coffee for themselves, and then

proceeded to walk around the first floor of the house to look at the views out of every window. Alex was watching the weather on the TV by the time they circled back to the kitchen.

"It's going to stay cold enough today that there won't be much melting of the few inches that fell, but tomorrow it's going to warm up again," he said.

"Good, at least we'll have a day to enjoy looking at this snow," Anne said.

They sat down at the kitchen table, as breakfast was almost ready. Anne said "I was reading that book 'Disclosure' by Steven Greer that you gave me to read, and there was an interview with some monsignor which was startling.

"That was Monsignor Corrado Balducci, if memory serves me correctly," Alex said.

"Yes, that sounds right. The monsignor was saying that, in his opinion, the human race is the lowest of the low. You can't get any worse than we are. Isn't that surprising?"

"But it's very true, isn't it?" Alex said.

We all gave him a look and pondered that statement.

Anne said, "and then the monsignor continued by saying perhaps extraterrestrials will intervene and help us."

"And earlier this year there was another announcement by the Vatican about extraterrestrials," Alex said. "We printed out some news articles on it."

Alex got up and went into the living room and, because of his amazing organizational skills, was able to immediately put his hands on the appropriate file. He walked back into the den and started to read:

"The Vatican's chief astronomer, Reverend Jose Gabriel Funes, confessed in an interview that he saw no conflict between the religious doctrine he serves, and the scientific knowledge he pursues – including the possibility of 'extraterrestrial brothers'. He also stated that it remains entirely possible that humanity represents the 'lost sheep' of the universe, and that there is an entire community of highly-evolved extraterrestrials that remained in 'full friendship with their creator'."

Alex turned to the next article and read:

"Asked about the difficult theological question, Father Funes said 'If other intelligent beings exist, it's not certain that they need redemption. They could have remained in full friendship with their creator without committing original sin.' "

Turning to another article, he continued:

"...in an interview published Tuesday in the Vatican newspaper L'Osservatore Roman, the Reverend Jose Gabriel Funes says rejecting the notion of extraterrestrial life outright would mean 'putting limits on God's creative freedom'."

"Oh, and here's a couple more comments from Monsignor Balducci which I stuck in this file. 'We are at the bottom of the ladder for our ability to see good but do evil.' And, 'we earthlings are nothing...The Lord certainly did not limit his glory to this small earth. On other planets other beings exist who did not sin and fall as we did.'"

"Very interesting," Mary said. She looked at me and asked, "So how does Jesus fit into the scheme of things in your opinion?"

"Well, I believe he does have extraterrestrial DNA in him, and a double dose of it, as Alex would say, as his mother was a result of extraterrestrial intervention as was he. I do believe he sincerely believed his message of love your neighbor. And I also believe that an equally important message of his was the power of faith, which I interpret as the power of our mind."

"The power of our mind?" Mary asked.

"Yes, my favorite quote of Jesus is about the fig tree where he said the tree will no longer bear fruit and immediately the tree withered and his disciples were amazed. And he said to them '...if you have faith and do not doubt, you will not only do what was done to the fig tree, but even if you say to this mountain, 'be taken up and cast into the sea,' it will happen.' You might recall that Jesus also said 'your faith has made you well', and 'it shall be done to you according to your faith'. And then there's the ever popular 'if you have faith the size of a mustard seed, you will say to this mountain, 'Move from here to there,' and it will move; and nothing will be impossible for you.'"

I continued, "These are powerful words from Jesus. You could interpret the phrase 'your faith has made you well' as faith in the ability of Jesus. However, the fig tree and mustard seeds parables are definitely saying to us that if we believe we can do something and have no doubt that we can do it, it will be done. The power of our mind is amazing. It can alter us physically and it can alter our life experience."

Anne said, "I know I can think my self well, or think myself sick. I've done that many times."

"Absolutely," I said. "And that's just the tip of the iceberg. But for us humans it is so difficult to master control over one's mind. Thoughts just constantly pop into our heads, going from one subject to the other. How many of us make an effort to control all those bizarre thoughts that come and go like a flash through our minds?"

"I am certain that the beings inside the UFO that mother and I saw back in the 1960's were picking up on our thoughts, reading our minds, knowing that we were watching and curious, and that's why they zoomed in our direction from a dead stop." I said.

"You and mommy saw a UFO?" Mary asked.

"Yes, didn't you know?"

"No, I didn't. Did you, Anne?"

"No, I think I would have remembered that." Anne responded.

I told them the story and they were amazed. They asked if I thought we had been abducted. I told them I honestly didn't think so, but I do remember being afraid to look out the windows at night after this episode.

Then Mary said, "I saw several UFO's from my balcony on Blueberry Hill."

"It was in the late 1970's and it was a beautiful

summer evening, and I was on the balcony looking out toward Long Island Sound and out of the blue there appeared three objects with multicolored lights. They zoomed and zigzagged and did maneuvers no airplane could do. They were so fast. It was amazing and only lasted less than a minute when they disappeared. But there is no denying I saw something that was not of this world."

"Gee, I feel left out; I've never seen a UFO", Anne said.

Alex said, "Me neither. At least I don't think I have."

"What does that mean?" Anne asked.

"Earlier this year we were watching a show on television on the History Channel or maybe the Travel Channel and it concerned UFO sightings. They mentioned a sighting at a campground in Old Saybrook, Connecticut, during the summer of 1965. They said there were several teenage boys who were attending the outing who claim they saw a spaceship land, and beings emerge from the ship."

"I'll tell you, when I heard that, my hair stood on end. When I was a teenager, we had a church camp for two weeks down at a campground in Old Saybrook. It was the summer of 1965. The funny thing is that I don't remember any details of that outing. And it was immediately after that trip that I stopped believing in God. Prior to that I had gone to church, and even taught religious classes. But something happened, and I don't know what it was, that turned me off religion during that two week period. And that is pretty weird considering it was a church camp."

"And Alex has a very good memory. He has told me stories of his childhood and youth in amazing detail. So it is unusual that he can't remember anything about that outing."

"And it was right about this same time that I became interested in UFO's. I read everything I could find on the subject. I've been interested in extraterrestrial life ever since."

"Weird," Anne said.

"Very weird," Mary echoed.

"So going back to Jesus," Mary said, "do you think he knew he was extraterrestrial?"

"Yes, I do. He didn't begin his public ministry until he was 30, and we can only speculate on what happened during those hidden years, but I do believe he was in communication with extraterrestrials and was being taught and prepared for his ministry by them. The question I do have is: did he truly expect to die on the cross? His words on the cross, 'My god, my god, why hast thou forsaken me?' make me wonder. And if he did expect to die on the cross, did he know he would be resurrected?"

"Or did he really die and was he actually resurrected?" Alex asked.

"In any case, I do believe Jesus' intentions were good as his message was admirable, but the intended result was not what happened. The Roman Catholic Church was formed, they picked what scripture they wanted to include in the bible, they created dogma, put a huge bureaucracy together, made themselves the intermediary between god and man, gave themselves the power to forgive sins, judged others and killed many in the name of religion. Somehow I don't think that is what Jesus had intended."

"And you have to consider that there is not just one group of extraterrestrials out there, presumably looking out for our good. There are probably extraterrestrials from many different galaxies, solar systems, planets, stars or whatever, and they each might have different agendas. Who's to say that the ones that were involved with Jesus had our best interests in mind? Maybe they duped him, and the resulting current chaos on this planet is just what they wanted," Alex said.

"That's a possibility," I said.

We all got quiet, each mulling this over.

"Well, ladies and gentleman, we'd better finish up our breakfast and get ready to head on out for the day's adventure," I said. "We were going to go into Burlington today, but we'll wait to do that until tomorrow when it's supposed to be warmer. There are two huge antique centers on Route 7 that I thought we could check out today. What do you say?"

There was agreement all around that this sounded like a plan, and we soon headed out the door, eager to look at yet more antiques!

The snow-covered landscape was spectacular. I slowly drove down our dirt road and we all took in the scenery. Everything was white and sparkling in the sun. It seemed to be a surrealistic wonderland as it was so beautiful, so perfect. Mary had her camera with her and I had to stop several times as she hopped out to take a picture.

We spent the next several hours rummaging through antiques. Since we had a substantial breakfast, we didn't even stop for lunch. My sisters appeared to enjoy the search for antique treasures as much as Alex and I. Today everyone found something special to bring home with them.

I picked up a couple of pizzas on the way back to the house. We were all exhausted by our day of antiquing and hours and hours of standing on our feet and walking and bending over looking at display tables and cabinets. I'm glad everyone thought pizza was a good idea, because I couldn't bear the thought of making dinner.

These pizzas were incredible; we were very fortunate to have such a wonderful pizza place relatively close to home. What I really liked was that they weren't baked; once we got home, I'd put them in the oven and bake them. We got one with mushrooms, eggplant and spinach, and the other with shrimp, broccoli and pesto sauce.

It was getting dark as we pulled into the courtyard and all of the solar lights were already on. It was a little winter wonderland with the snow and the white lights. Mary said she was going to grab her camera and try to take some pictures outside of the house with the lights on. She wasn't sure what setting to use, and Alex said he'd show her.

We brought all of our purchases inside and put them on the bench in the mudroom. I put the oven on, and poured drinks for everyone. Anne said she had a marvelous day. She had such fun going through those shops and finding all those little treasures.

Mary came back with her camera and Alex showed her what setting would work at night, and together they headed for the front door. I was looking down the hallway toward the door as they opened it, and I could see Itzy make a run for it. Mary yelled "Itzy" but it was too late. Anne and I ran to the front door and we all watched as Itzy pranced around in the snow. I don't know if 'prance' is the right word. What she was doing was a cross between a jump and a leap. I guess you could call that a prance.

There she was, a solid white cat, out in the snow under the white lights of the crabapple tree. It was an amazing sight. Mary started taking pictures and Alex ran to get the video camera. He came back in no time and started taking video of the action.

Itzy would stop and look at us every now and then; and go right back into her prancing. The snow would fly up into the air from her back feet pushing off on every leap. I said "Itzy, you're so beautiful!" And it seemed that she knew it and she was putting on a show for us.

The thought came to mind that she might just take off into the woods, but my ace in the hole was she hadn't had her dinner yet.

She had stopped her prancing and was sitting under the tree, and I said "Okay, Itzy, time for dinner!" and she ran like crazy toward the open front door, down the hall and into the kitchen. I immediately opened a can of cat food for her and told her what a good girl she was.

Mary and Alex were still outside taking pictures. Anne was sipping her wine. She said "Weren't you worried that she was going to run off?"

"The thought did come to mind, but I wasn't really worried about it. She does this every year when we have the first snow. She doesn't really like the cold, but there is something about all that white out there that calls to her. She's got it out of her system for this season now."

Just then Mary and Alex came back into the house. Mary said she got some really good pictures and was showing them to us on her digital camera. Alex plugged the video camera into the TV and we had a few minutes of Itzy in the snow show. I was so glad he taped that.

While Alex was starting a fire in the den fireplace, Mary said, "I didn't notice that pile of stones up on the hill with the spotlight on it. How pretty that is in the snow!"

"Hey, that's not just a pile of stones," Alex said, "it's a cairn!"

"What's a cairn?"

"A pile of stones!" "Actually, I believe the word 'cairn' originated in Scotland. These stone piles were sometimes used as markers, even as markers of graves. I recall there were two trains of thought regarding why they were used to mark graves. One was to dissuade grave robbers."

"And the other?" Anne asked.

"To keep the dead from rising."

"Is someone buried under that cairn?" Mary asked.

"No, when I built it I thought of it as a monument to Gene and Hilda. I built it using stones from their property, and it overlooked their house and grounds."

"You never mentioned that to me before," I said. "What a lovely thought."

The buzzer went off telling me the oven was hot enough to put the pizzas in, so in they went.

Anne went to retrieve the packages containing today's purchases off the bench in the mud room. We sat down around the kitchen table, and she placed the appropriate bags and or boxes in front of each of us. It was almost like Christmas. We each displayed what we bought.

Mary showed us her new thimble which she was going to add to her collection. It was sterling silver with an intricate vine and leaf design and the tag said it was Victorian.

Then she opened the box containing her other purchase, an opal necklace. The box itself was beautiful. It looked very old, and had worn brown leather on the outside and green velvet on the inside. The necklace had a gold clasp, including a safety clasp, and small round gold beads in between oval shaped opals which had a tremendous amount of fire in them. The flashes of color in each stone were amazing. The opals were all the same size and went entirely around the necklace. Mary's birthday was in October, and opal was her birthstone. She had tried on the necklace in the store and I judged it to be around 17 inches long, which I thought was a perfect length.

"Want to put it on again?" I asked.

"Okay."

I got up and put it around her neck and made sure the safety clasp was latched. It looked beautiful in the firelight. I got up and brought back a hand mirror so she could see it for herself.

"If I didn't buy this today, I'd be thinking about it for the rest of my life. I absolutely love it. It was well worth the price."

Anne went next. She removed the sterling silver ring box from the bag. It had beautiful scroll work on it, and the letter "A" engraved on the top. The interior was lined with blue velvet. She then took out a little cardboard box from the bag and opened it up. Inside was a beautiful gold ring with an oval shaped spessartite garnet that was set with 13 prongs. The tag said that this garnet was mined in Virginia and the setting was 14kt gold. I didn't know that spessartite had been mined in Virginia and I made a mental note that after dinner I was going to look it up in one of my reference books.

Garnet was Anne's January birthstone. She wasn't aware that this incredibly vivid orange variety of garnet existed. The ring fit her perfectly. I especially liked the 13 prongs, as they were slightly asymmetrical. This was obviously a handcrafted ring, and a beauty.

I had only one purchase. I took the item out of the box. It was a brown and white transferware narrow pitcher, about 10 inches tall and 4 inches wide. The design pattern was 'Crusoe' and the potter was Gildea & Walker. This was the only pattern that I had searched for, but never found. The pattern dated back to the mid 1880's. The scene showed Robinson Crusoe on the beach and a palm tree on the right side with a monkey climbing up. It was in perfect condition. I was incredibly happy with this find. Alex knew that I had been searching for this pattern for years, so he knew how delighted I was. My sisters probably thought I was crazy.

Alex went last. He opened his bag, reached in, and pulled out red, clip-on suspenders. He had been looking for these for a while, too. Not necessarily red, but clip-on suspenders. He was always complaining that his pants were falling down, and these would be put to good use.

Then he pulled out his other purchase, an old copper oil lamp. It looked like a genie would appear if you rubbed it; that was its shape. It looked very, very old. The workmanship was beautiful, and it was also functional!

The pizza was ready to come out of the oven. I carefully put my Crusoe pitcher on the mantle in the dining room.

As we devoured the pizza, we commented on what a lovely day it was. It began with the snowy surprise, then very productive antique shopping, followed by Itzy in the snow, and now this wonderful pizza!

"I can't believe that in a couple of days you'll be going back to Hilton Head," I said.

"We've had so much fun with you both," Anne said. "I have to admit that I had no idea that antiques could be so much fun."

"Are you calling us antiques?" Alex asked.

"Very funny; you know what I meant." Anne replied.

"You really have been wonderful hosts," Mary added. "And now I've got so much to think about; so much to research and read on creation, UFO's and the bible!"

"Really," Anne said, "we're going back home with a whole new perspective on the human race. It is amazing, isn't it?"

"Before I forget," I said "I'm going to grab a book on gemstones as I want to check out spessartites in Virginia."

I went over to the bookcase behind Alex and found just the book I wanted. I have to admit that quite often Alex's organizational skills came in handy. He had the bookcases organized by subject matter, and then alphabetical by author.

"Yes, here it is, it says starting in the mid 1800's spessartite crystals were mined in the Rutherford Mines, Amelia County, Virginia. That gives you some provenance to add to your ring."

We continued to sit around the fire, sipping herbal tea, eating cookies and talking.

Anne said "You both have amassed a great amount of evidence pointing to the possible involvement of extraterrestrials in human creation. What are you going to do with that information?"

"What do you mean 'do with it'?" I asked.

"Is it your intent to just keep this to yourselves? Don't you think it should be shared with others?"

"We have briefly discussed that." Alex said. "We've been so caught up in the day to day research, we haven't considered exactly what the next step would be."

"I imagine most people would think we're nuts." I said. "But then again, I don't give a hoot about what most people think."

"And all we would be doing would be to reference our sources, mainly the bible, and ask others to read, research, think and draw their own conclusions." Alex said.

"How about starting a blog? I really don't know anything about blogs, but I think it might be a good way to share this information." Mary suggested.

We all turned to look at Mary. "What a wonderful

idea!" I said.

"That way, others can leave their comments and we could share ideas." Alex said.

"I'm sure there will be some comments that I'd rather not see, but I'm really excited about this." I said.

We talked way into the night about the blog, and even viewed some blogs on the internet to see how they were set up.

I know I went to bed that night with visions of blogs dancing in my head.

Chapter 18 – Of Heaven and Earth

Because of our late hours the night before, we all got up a little later than usual the next morning. We sat around the kitchen table, sipping coffee and eating bagels. The plan for the day was to go to Burlington. I mentioned that we could have a late lunch in town as well.

Mary said "No, we've discussed this and Anne and I would like to make dinner tonight. If you just stop at the grocery store on the way home after our Burlington visit, we'll run in and get what we need. Then you just sit back and relax and we'll cook."

"No, you are my guests. I don't want you cooking for me."

"Mind your elders, baby sister, we are going to cook!" Anne said.

"Okay, I'm outranked and outnumbered. You win."

"Just curious," Alex said, "what are you going to make?"

"Wouldn't you rather be surprised?" Mary asked.

"Not really. If it's something I don't like, I can pickup some really good appetizers."

"It's seafood lasagna," Anne said. "It is delicious and so easy to make. It's a white sauce, not red."

"Well, it sounds like I don't have to worry about appetizers," Alex responded.

We continued to just sit and drink coffee and started talking more about the blog idea. We had seen some blogs that were very nicely formatted in our search last night. I liked the idea of inserting links to our source materials, as well as the comments feature. I needed to do research on blog hosting sites after the girls went back home.

We finally mustered enough ambition to get dressed and head on out for the day's adventures. It was warmer out today, perfect weather to walk up and down Church Street in Burlington.

On the way up Route 7, I made a detour and headed over to Shelburne and Charlotte for a scenic drive along the lake. Although they had viewed the lake from the air when they were flying in, I wanted them to see it up close. We were driving by a rocky beach area and Mary asked if we could stop for a few minutes as she wanted to take some pictures. The rocks on the beach were black, grey and white smooth ovals. Some of them had a solid black or grey color with white lines going through them.

Mary finished taking her pictures of the lake and the Adirondacks. Then she said she wanted to take a group picture. She took a picture of Anne, Alex and me. Then Alex took a picture of us three girls.

We drove back out to Route 7 and continued into Burlington. This time I took a right at the fork just before town and headed up into the Hill section. The houses were absolutely gorgeous up there. They weren't huge estates on large pieces of land, but were older homes on moderate size lots. Each one was unique and charming and all were extremely well-cared for. What was great was that it was an easy walk downtown or to the lake from here. I wouldn't trade my "Meghalaya" for any of these houses, but if you wanted to live in-town, this was the place to be.

We passed by Champlain College and the University of Vermont campuses. Then I headed down the hill toward town. Now they had a panoramic view of the town, the harbor, the lake and the Adirondacks. Mary asked me to pull over to get a picture. I have to admit that it looked like a picture postcard. The sky was blue with a few fluffy clouds, and there was still some snow on the mountains in the background.

When she was through with her picture taking, I proceeded down into town and parked in one of the lots close to Church Street. We started up the street and the plan was to check out the shops on one side, and then come back down the other. I had a fondness for jewelry, and there were several spectacular jewelry stores, and some specialty shops that also had a nice selection of jewelry. Alex, of course, was interested in antiques and books. And Mary and Anne just wanted to see everything.

For the most part we skipped the large national brand stores. We went into every Vermont artisan type shop and there were quite a few of those. The girls especially liked the Champlain Chocolates place. They had to get a bag full of goodies to give them the strength to walk up and down the street and in and out of all those shops.

It took us several hours to make the rounds, and I have to admit that chocolate did give us a jolt of energy when we were dragging. But no one bought a thing, other than those chocolates. I think we were 'shopped out' by the prior two days experiences.

We got in the car and headed south on Route 7. I stopped at Hannaford and we all got out. Mary and Anne headed to the fish counter and picked up fresh shrimp, sea scallops and flounder. They also picked up spinach, garlic, scallions, ricotta cheese, mozzarella cheese, white sauce mix and no bake lasagna noodles.

Thanksgiving was the next day, but I was prepared for that. I had purchased a Kosher turkey the day before Mary and Anne arrived. I thought Kosher turkeys were the best; they were soaked in brine and they were so moist and flavorful. You didn't really have to do a thing with them except stick them in the oven.

I had the ingredients for the rice stuffing and the corn bread stuffing, turnips, sweet potatoes, mashed potatoes, green bean casserole, and cranberry orange relish. I also had the ingredients for a pecan/pumpkin pie.

So I picked up more cat food, and milk and coffee and that was all I needed.

In no time at all, we were headed toward home.

Mary and Anne wasted no time in getting to work

assembling their lasagna. Of course, they had to have a little wine to provide them with culinary inspiration.

Alex and I sat and sipped our drinks while watching my sisters working on the lasagna.

"I have another ghost story to share with you," I said.

That got everyone's attention. All eyes were on me.

"I knew Grandma had died when all 3 of my hard wired smoke detectors went off in the middle of the night. The smoke detectors were at the bottom of the basement stairs, the back hall on the first floor, and at the top of the stairs on the second floor. It was around 4 a.m. and I woke with a start, as one of those blaring smoke detectors was right outside my bedroom door. I jumped up and ran into the hall and flicked on the light. No smoke, no flames. I ran down the stairs and checked out the other two levels and no smoke, no flames anywhere. Having confirmed there was no fire, the thought came to me that Grandma must have passed away. We all knew she was severely ill and she could go at any time, and I believed she was telling me her time had come."

"After several minutes, one by one, the smoke detectors stopped. The call came a few hours later that Gram had passed away just before 4 a.m."

"Several months later, I was moving into the house in Farmington. Alex and I had moved some of the smaller items and plants into the house over the weekend. As we were leaving the house Sunday night, we had left one of the Persian rugs rolled up under the chandelier. There were no lights left on in the house, and Alex used a flashlight so that we could safely see our way out of the house and out to the car."

"The next day was Grandma's birthday. I remember thinking of her that morning as I got dressed to go to work. At lunch time I took a ride over to the house to drop a few more things off. I unlocked the front door, walked in and stopped dead. The chandelier was on, the rug was unrolled and placed directly under the chandelier and the mantel clock, Grandma's mantel clock, was ticking away. I had placed the clock on the mantel the day before, but I did not wind it up, and it was not ticking when I left the house the previous day."

"I remember thinking 'Today is Grandma's birthday and she wanted me to know she is close by, that's why she did this.' I sat down on the only chair in the house and spent the rest of my lunch hour just sitting there, thinking about this."

Alex said "I've heard that spirits can work with electrical impulses to use to contact people, so the fire detector story makes perfect sense."

Anne added "Wouldn't you love to have seen that carpet unroll and position itself? There's no doubt in my mind Grandma did that."

The lasagna was assembled and put in the oven. Anne and Mary helped themselves to another glass of wine. Alex went into the living room and lit the fireplace. We followed him in there and sat down around the fire.

"And that wasn't the end of it." They all looked at me with anticipation.

"The following year, on Grandma's birthday, I was in Seattle on business. I was sound asleep in my hotel room, when the smoke detector started doing that little noise that it makes when the battery is going low. As soon as I heard it, I knew it was Grandma doing it. I figured I'd try to ignore it. But I couldn't ignore it; and I couldn't go back to sleep because of it. After about 20 minutes or so of that feeble little beeping noise, I called the desk and told them the battery was running low on the smoke detector and it was making noise. They said they would send someone right up. About five minutes later, I hear a knock on the door. As soon as I heard that knock, the beeping stopped. The maintenance man comes in with his tool box and a ladder. I tell him that the smoke detector was beeping, but it just stopped. He looks at me like I'm nuts. He says he's going to check it anyway. He positions the ladder, climbs it, removes the cover from the smoke detector and checks the battery. He says its fine; there's nothing wrong. He replaces the cover, climbs down the ladder and leaves with toolbox and ladder in hand."

"I'm mentally having a conversation with Grandma saying 'So you had to wake me up out of a sound sleep, and embarrass me in front of the maintenance man, just to remind me that it's your birthday and you're still close to me? Couldn't you have done it some other way? That was the last contact I had with her."

Mary asked "How do you relate ghosts with extraterrestrials? And I know you did believe in reincarnation; do you still believe in reincarnation?"

"I believe that intelligent life exists not only on Earth."

"And there isn't much intelligent life existing on this planet today anyway," Alex interjected.

"I believed in life after death before. I believed in ghosts and reincarnation before. And now that I'm convinced there is intelligent life on other plants, solar systems and galaxies, that doesn't change my mind."

"So although you believe that human beings on the planet Earth were created by extraterrestrials, you still believe in a Divine Being of some sort?"

"Yes, and this is where Alex and I differ. Alex doesn't believe in God. I believe that we have spirits that are eternal. And I believe that we are searching for perfection of the spirit through reincarnation. Maybe I should say some of us are searching for perfection of the spirit. I'm not convinced that all spirits inhabiting human bodies on Earth today are searching for perfection. Who those spirits are and what they are looking to accomplish, I'm uncertain."

"God has been fabricated by religion," Alex retorted.

"But even before organized religion, man worshipped gods," Anne said.

"And maybe those gods really existed," Alex responded. "Maybe they were extraterrestrial entities that were worshipped as gods because they had abilities and knowledge unknown to the beings on the Earth in those days. It is the all knowing, all powerful God of today's religions that doesn't exist. There is no God, and there is no heaven or hell."

Anne said "Remember that Cardinal from Rome said '…we are the lowest of the low…' and the other Vatican priest saying that perhaps we are 'the lost sheep of the universe'. Maybe that is the basis for reincarnation; to perfect ourselves to the point that we can get off this planet and go to a better place. And as we continue to perfect ourselves, to improve, we continue to move up and up to a better place, to a higher level."

"Exactly!" I shouted.

"But that doesn't mean that God exists. I can pretty much buy into what Anne just described, that we keep coming back to improve and, hopefully, get off this planet. But I cannot buy into God," Alex exclaimed.

"But then," Mary said, "there's some 'thing' out there rewarding us as acknowledgement of our spiritual growth by allowing us to reincarnate in a better position. Wouldn't that 'thing' be God or something similar?"

"I think that we have a spark of that 'divine essence' in each of us," I said. "And I think we determine who we come back as and when we come back, not some divinity. Hopefully, we choose a life that will present us with challenges that will help us to grow, if we react to those challenges properly. And if we choose wisely and act properly, we keep moving up and up and up until we reach the ultimate level, the highest level."

"And, perhaps it follows, that if that divine spark is within each of us, then all others at the highest level are collectively all 'god' and not just one entity," Mary said.

"Yes! I can accept that!" Alex shouted.

"Me too!" I exclaimed.

"I think we just experienced an epiphany here," Anne said.

"So that highest level could be considered heaven," Mary responded.

"If you had to give it a name, then I guess 'heaven' would work," Alex said.

"I think Jesus said 'In my father's house are many mansions. If it were not so, I would have told you.' Maybe he was alluding to the various levels to which we can ascend," I said.

"You know, I think I made some notes on the Hindu religion that relate to this. Just let me grab my notebook." Alex went over to the tables piled high with books and reached for his notebook.

In no time at all he was reading, "Most Hindus believe that the spirit or soul — the true 'self' of every person, called the Atman — is eternal. According to the monistic /pantheistic theologies of Hinduism, such as the Advaita school, this *Atman* is ultimately indistinct from Brahman, the supreme spirit. Hence, these schools are called non-dualist. The goal of life, according to the Advaita school, is to realize that one's Atman is identical to Brahman, the supreme soul. Whoever becomes fully aware of the Atman as the innermost core of one's own self realizes an identity with Brahman and thereby reaches *moksha* (liberation or freedom)."

And listen to this, "The Hindu scriptures refer to celestial entities called Devas, 'the shining ones', which may be translated into English as 'gods' or 'heavenly beings'. The *devas* are an integral part of Hindu culture and are depicted in art, architecture and through icons, and mythological stories about them are related in the scriptures, particularly in Indian epic poetry and the Puranas."

"Celestial entities or heavenly beings called the shining ones. Kind of sounds like something out of Exodus," I said.

"But you can't just wake up one morning and realize that your Atman is identical to Brahman," Mary said. "You have to work up to it, cause and effect and all that stuff, until, through your own efforts, you reach the highest level. Right, isn't that what we decided?"

"Right," Alex said. "But I don't think that the 'innermost core of one's own self' would realize that until it had reached that level.

"You said you didn't believe in God, heaven or hell," I said to Alex. "We have just now provided a definition of 'God' which is acceptable to you, and we have also provided a definition of 'heaven' which is acceptable to you. I have to admit it was a collaborative effort to reach these definitions. But I have to put the question out there, not just to you, Alex, but to all of us; do we believe in hell? Is there a place that is lower than this earthly existence? If 'heaven' is the highest level, then is there a corresponding 'lowest level'?"

"Maybe the lowest of low is Earth. Isn't that what the monsignor said? This is hell on Earth. Maybe we can't go any lower than this." Alex muttered.

"That could well be. But, Connie, you said earlier that you didn't think all spirits on Earth today were searching for perfection. Maybe those spirits are here to try to entice other spirits to follow them to lower and lower levels until they reach the lowest level…hell." Anne said.

Just then the over timer went off.

"And, Anne, you've had the last word on that subject!" Alex shouted.

We all got up and walked into the kitchen. Mary took the lasagna out of the oven. It looked wonderful and smelled delicious.

As the lasagna was cooling, I set the dining room table. The thought came to mind about a book that I had read decades ago about a man in England who had lost his brother during the Second World War. An Indian mystic visited the living brother and taught him the art of astral travel. While in his astral form, he could see other astral entities, both living and dead. He saw the spirit of his dead brother in a pub, with other friends who were now deceased, having a grand old time. The man met a teacher on the astral plane who instructed him about the existence of various levels of advancement. If I recalled correctly, the highest astral level was heaven. But was there a lower level than this planet Earth?

As we sat down to dinner, I mentioned this book and

asked if anyone recalled it. I believe the book was originally published in England in the 1950's. It was told in the first person and appeared to be a true story. I recalled that this book was my mother's and I happened to pick it up and read it and was very impressed with it. I thought I had bought a duplicate and given it to one of my sisters to read. Of course, no one remembered it. And I couldn't remember the title. Alex said that after dinner I should look at the reincarnation section of the bookcase to see if any of the titles rang a bell with me.

The lasagna was incredible. The blend of seafood, cheeses, herbs and spices combined with the white sauce and noodles was delicious. And it really took very little time to assemble.

"Tomorrow will be a busy day, what with baking and cooking for Thanksgiving." Mary said.

"Yes, but I'll have a lot of help out there in that kitchen. It shouldn't be too bad. The first thing I'll do is get the pumpkin pecan pie made and into the oven. Once that's baked, I'll pop in the turkey. The rest of the preparation should be a breeze."

"Food, food, food…is that all you girls think about?" Alex asked.

"No, we think about heaven, hell and the meaning of life at times, too," Anne exclaimed.

Mary raised her glass and said "To heaven, hell and the meaning of life!" We all raised our glasses and toasted.

After dinner I started to clear the table and Mary said, "No, we're cleaning up tonight. Why don't you go look for that book you were talking about." I didn't even bother putting up a fight about this; I knew I wouldn't win.

I went into the den and started to look through the books in the reincarnation section. Dear Alex had all the New Age type books together, and there was a separate section for reincarnation. I started to look through the titles and in no time I found it: 'A Soul's Journey' by Peter Richelieu.

"I found it!" I exclaimed. Everyone came over to take

a look, and they all thought it looked vaguely familiar. I was looking forward to rereading it, starting tonight.

Chapter 19 – Bad Bat Karma

Thanksgiving morning I awoke early, as I knew I had a lot of things to do. To my surprise, Mary and Anne were already downstairs and coffee had been made.

"How come you're up so early?" I asked.

"We knew you needed help preparing Thanksgiving dinner, so we wanted to be up bright and early," Anne responded.

"I told Anne to wake me up on her way downstairs," Mary said.

"That is so sweet of you, thank you!"

"I've been thinking about our conversation yesterday about heaven, hell and god," Alex said. "We all are in agreement that heaven is the highest level of achievement or evolution of the spirit. And all those who have achieved this highest level are collectively gods. And we briefly touched on the converse, the lowest of the low or hell. I believe there are intrinsically good people and bad people on Earth. And then there are those on the fence, those who could go either way, and are constantly in play.

"On this planet, wealth and power are looked at as something to strive for. Greed and lack of concern for your fellow man help you attain wealth and power. It's every man and woman for themselves. Step on everyone you can to get ahead. Dog eat dog. Look out for number one.

"If Jesus was an emissary of extraterrestrials that were more highly evolved and who wanted to help man rise up above this hell on Earth, doesn't it make sense that there are also extraterrestrials who are interested in seeing us fail? Certainly not all extraterrestrials have our best interests in mind. I could name presidents and popes who I think would be candidates as emissaries of a dark force of extraterrestrials who would like to topple any balance of good and evil on this planet."

"I did read enough of 'A Soul's Journey' last night to confirm that there was no mention of a level lower than our human existence on this planet." I said.

"But does that mean that a lower level doesn't exist?" Alex asked. "If there are benevolent extraterrestrials looking out for us, maybe there are malevolent extraterrestrials who would love to see us annihilated. Just think a minute about the gods in the bible. The Old Testament god was an eye for an eye and a tooth for a tooth type of god. Look what he did to poor Moses just because he tapped the rock twice. That god was ready to annihilate the human race over and over again."

Alex continued, "But the god in the New Testament is a turn the other cheek kind of god, the complete opposite from the Old Testament god. I don't think that the Old and the New Testament gods are the same god. The god of the Old Testament was always testing humans, picking sides and destroying those who were not in his favor. To my way of thinking, that is one malevolent extraterrestrial.

"And you know what's funny? It's right there in black and white in the bible 'Let *us* make man in *our* image, after *our* likeness...' and not just once, several times. And the poor human is so stupid that he didn't pick up on it. The extraterrestrials that created us are probably thinking that we earthlings are getting what we deserve because we blindly followed organized religion and the belief that there is but one god. And it's this belief that our religion and our one god is the only true religion and the only true god that creates all the unrest in the world. We have killed and continue to kill each other in the name of religion. It's ludicrous!"

"You know what I think?" Mary asked. We all turned to look at her in expectation.

"I think the devil symbolizes the human's lower nature. And religion has exploited the concept of the devil, making it seem as if it were a battle between good and evil, god and the devil. But in reality, the devil is the lowest form of human and it is here on Earth. This is hell on Earth."

"And I believe that through karma we can work our way up from hell here on Earth to the highest level, heaven. Once it dawns on us that there are laws of cause and effect in the universe, our existence will begin to change for the better. We get back what we give out. Karma will always win out," I said. "And, not to change the subject, but I've got to get that pie made and in the oven!"

I got up and turned the oven on, and assembled the ingredients for the pie. Mary, Anne and Alex were sitting there, sipping their coffee in silence and watching me.

"Talking about karma, do you still have that story you wrote about the bat karma?" Anne asked.

"Sure do."

"What bat karma story?" Mary asked.

"It's a true story about my experiences with bats. Didn't I send it to you?" I asked.

"I don't think so."

"You would definitely remember it if you had read it," Anne said. "Come to think of it, I think I was up in Connecticut visiting you one summer when you gave it to me to read."

"I know where it is. Want me to get it?" Alex asked.

"That would be great. I'll read it out loud while we watch Connie work," Anne said.

Alex returned with my notebook in hand, and Anne began to read:

"BAD BAT KARMA:

I'm going to tell you a little story. Several years ago when my daughter was still in high school and my daughter, mother and I all lived together in a little house in New Milford, CT, we had a winged visitor one night.

It was a warm summer evening and my mother, daughter (Jennifer) and I were watching TV in the family room. Around 9 p.m. or so my mother announced she was going up to bed, and off she went. All remained quiet and calm for about an hour and then we heard these footsteps pounding down the stairs toward the family room. My mother never walks that fast; what could be wrong? Then as she approached the family room we could hear this labored breathing. Jennifer and I looked at each other with alarm. Then she appeared around the corner and was barely able to speak. Finally she got out the words "There's a bat in my room and I was laying on him!"

"A bat? And you were laying on him?"

Yes, she answered. She said she had propped her pillows up in order to read before going to sleep, and when her eyes started to get heavy she took some of the pillows off, and there sandwiched between the pillows was this bat.

"Is he dead?" we asked.

"No" she replied, "Just a little stunned, but he's coming around!"

She figured that when she had opened the window in the bathroom to close the storm window because it was getting cold, the attic fan must have sucked in the bat. She never saw it and it ended up lying on her pillow and she didn't notice it when she picked up another pillow and put it on top.

So now what were we going to do? Well, I did the sensible thing and sent my daughter upstairs with a big plastic garbage bag. My mother accompanied her, not me, as I was terrified of bats. So my mother folded the pillow over on the bat as it was just coming back to its senses, and stuffed it in the plastic bag that Jennifer was holding wide open. They sealed it and carried it outside and the poor little thing suffocated to death.

I felt awful about it at that time. Not the fact that I had sent my teenage daughter and elderly mother upstairs to tackle a bat which could conceivably have been rabid, who knows? I felt awful about that poor little bat suffocating in that plastic bag; that must be an awful way to go. I have thought about this episode quite frequently in the years since.

Just recently in our house in Salem, CT, I was sitting on the sofa in the family room with my mother around dusk one evening and thought I saw some movement near the lamp on the table against the opposite wall. It couldn't be. It must be my imagination. I looked away and looked back and sure enough there was definitely something moving toward the base of the lamp. It was a bat!

I was literally speechless. All I could do was make these little shrieky noises (I kind of sounded like a bat myself). My mother kept saying "What's wrong? What's wrong?" but I couldn't even get the words out.

Finally, I managed to tell her there was a bat on the lamp. What to do....what to do? Call an exterminator! That's it, I'll call an exterminator. I reached for the phone book and started flipping through the Yellow Pages. But wait, I didn't want the bat dead. That little bat didn't want to be in my house any more than I wanted him there. Bats serve a purpose; they eat tons of insects. It would throw the whole ecological system out of whack if there were no bats. I couldn't let him die!

So, the only thing left for me to do was to carry the lamp outside, hopefully with the bat still clinging to it, and pray that he flies away. So we opened the sliding door wide open, and I walked over to the lamp. He was still moving slightly. I pulled the end of the table away from the wall so I could unplug the lamp. So far, so good. The lamp itself had a lot of scrolled wrought iron and I took a firm hold of it, picked it up and held it out in front of me as far as my little arms could go. I walked very quickly out through the door and onto the deck and put the lamp down. But one of my fingers was caught in the scrollwork! And the bat was definitely revived by the evening air. He was starting to really move! I gave my finger a good yank and managed to extricate it, pulling some of the skin off with it. My mother and I stood at the far side of the deck and watched.

Mr. Bat slid off the lamp onto the deck and just sat there. He really was kind of cute. He had a beautiful minky shade of fur and he was tiny. He seemed to be shaking or shivering or something. Oh no, don't tell me he's sick! Will I have to nurse a sick bat? Maybe he was just as scared as I was and that was all. So we watched. He started to stretch his wings a little, and then, up, up and away. And that was it! We applauded his departure and we felt pleased that it had turned out well.

Later that night I was reflecting on my earlier bat experience in New Milford and it occurred to me that I had repaid my bad bat karma. I had always felt bad about that little bat suffocating, and now I had repaid that life with this new bat's life. The score was settled. We were all even. I should have no more bat experiences.....hopefully.

OVER A DECADE LATER...

So I had a "bat" night last night. At around 3 a.m. some sort of noise woke me up. I'm laying in bed trying to figure out what the noise is and where it's coming from. It's a combination of a whooshing and a flutter. It's definitely not a mouse in the attic. It's not coming from one location, it's kind of everywhere. Then it stops. Of course now I'm fully awake. I decide to go downstairs to see if Coalbee is at the back door (she didn't come in before I went to bed). I put my glasses on and head out the bedroom door and turn to go down the stairs and "vrooommmm" flying toward me and slightly above me is a bat!!!!! Well, of course I start screaming and I run downstairs. I'm thinking maybe it was just a really big moth, maybe it wasn't a bat. It's still upstairs somewhere.

I go to the back door and there is Coalbee . I let her in and she's hungry, so I get the cat food and start to put it out for her and I see her standing in the middle of the family room looking up......there's the bat (definitely a bat) flying desperately around the room, trying to find a way out. Well, the screaming starts all over again and I run to the downstairs bathroom and slam the door shut, making sure he didn't follow *me in there! After a few seconds I slowly open the door and peek out and there he is zooming down the hall towards me! More screaming. More door slamming. This little scenario repeats itself a few times, and then, finally, he's not around. I put the little leopard print hand towel over my head (having heard about bats getting tangled up in human hair) and run to the sliding door to the deck and open it. I figure if he's zooming around the family room, maybe he'll head on out. Coalbee takes one look at me with the towel on my head and she heads out the door. Can't take it.*

Then I go to the basement and get a broom, to kind of push him in the right direction should he try to swoop down on me. I come back up and open the front door. I'm standing in the front hall and he swoops down (and I scream) and he sees me and turns to go back up the stairs. (I'd turn, too, if I saw me standing there with a towel on my head, broom in hand, screaming) He comes back down a few more times but always turns around. Finally, after about 15 minutes of standing there, broom in hand and leopard towel on head, I pull out a dining room chair to sit and wait. I can't go to bed, obviously. Poor Mother is up there sleeping unaware there is a bat zooming over her head (maybe even sitting on her pillow). What to do, what to do. Well, thankfully, as I'm sitting there watching, he zooms straight down the stairs and right out the door. I jump up and slam it shut and then run to the back door to make sure he doesn't decide to come in the back door. Coalbee is no where in sight. I went to bed, but couldn't sleep. I guess he slipped in somehow when we were going in or out, or letting Coalbee in or out. Don't know.

A FEW DAYS LATER...

Some sort of sound woke me from a sound sleep. Wasn't sure what it was or where it was coming from. Could have been from outside, as all my bedroom windows were open. I lay there very still, listening. I could faintly hear something, but couldn't figure out what it was or where it was coming from. After a few minutes I knew, I could hear the flutter of wings. It was a bat. My stomach did a kind of flip-flop and I felt nauseous. The bat from the night before was not just an isolated incidence. I had a problem.

I knew I had to get up and open the front door. My heart was pounding. I put my glasses on, ran to the bathroom and threw a towel over my head. I slowly turned the corner to go down the stairs. Half way down, I saw the bat fly by the bottom of the stairs into the living room. I screamed, but that was the only time I screamed. I knew what I had to do. I reached the bottom of the stairs and pulled an umbrella out of the stand by the front door. Then I flung the door wide open, pulled out a dining room chair and sat there, towel on head and umbrella in hand. He swooped by several times and flew up and down the stairs several times, and finally, after what seemed like a very long time, he flew out the front door. I slammed the door shut, put the dining room chair back where it belonged, and went back upstairs to bed.

I still had the towel on my head and the umbrella in my hand. I knew that most likely this wasn't one misguided bat, most likely there were more somewhere in the house, probably in the attic. The guest bedroom light was on. I left it on so that at night my mother could see where she was going in case she got up to go to the bathroom. I lay in bed with several pillows under my head in pretty much a sitting position. There was a bureau on the opposite wall and a mirror over the bureau. Looking at the mirror I could see into the upstairs hall and guest bedroom. I laid there, awake and staring into that mirror, pretty much the rest of the night. I kept the towel on my head and the umbrella in my hand all night. I just watched and listened. But no movement, no sounds.

The next morning, exhausted, I decided I had to call an exterminator. I went through the Yellow Pages, and most of the exterminators appeared to be more into ants, termites and such. Then I spotted 'Animal Evictions' who dealt with skunks, raccoons, squirrels, and yes, bats! My kind of guy! It was only 7:45 a.m., but I called. At first the answering machine kicked in, but then a real live human being came on the phone. I explained my situation, and he seemed very nice and knowledgeable. The only problem was, he could not come over to check it out until the following morning. I had to go through one more night of this. He was telling me how bats can get through tiny openings only 3/8ths of an inch wide. I told him I would see him the next morning.

So I decided that I had to look for all possible ways the bat could be getting into the house. Obviously, the fireplace opening was one. And the opening to the attic at the top of the stairs was another. There seemed to be a space at the side of the attic opening that was large enough for a bat to squeeze through. I went to the hardware store and bought duct tape. I came back and took large plastic garbage bags and the duct tape and sealed off the fireplace opening and the attic opening. That made me feel a little better.

Later that night, as I was getting out of the shower, I noticed the exhaust fan in the bathroom ceiling. There were openings on the side of that fan which were definitely large enough for a bat to get through. Grabbed the duct tape and sealed off those openings in my bathroom and in my mother's bathroom as well. We decided that we would keep our bedroom doors closed at night. And we went to bed. I had a towel folded up next to me in bed, should I need to cover my head during the night. Again, I laid there and listened most of the night. Nothing. Maybe all that duct tape worked.

The next morning, right on time, a red truck with 'Animal Evictions' printed on the side pulled into my driveway. I was hoping my little kitty 'Coalbee' wasn't looking. She might think she was being evicted! I opened the front door and a very nice looking man was standing there. His name was Brian. We talked for a bit and then Brian headed upstairs to the attic opening. He carefully removed the duct tape and plastic garbage bag, and proceeded up into the attic. I could *hear him moving around. He was up there for what seemed like a very long time. Finally, I could see him descend. He replaced the duct tape and plastic around the opening. As he came down the stairs I said "Well, I see you replaced the duct tape and plastic, so I guess that means there are bats up there." He said there were. He could not see them; he said they most likely were hidden in the insulation. But their droppings were up there, so they were there. I was somewhat relieved. I had envisioned him telling me there were hundreds of them up there hanging upside down. I'm going to have to stop looking at the 'Star' at the supermarket check-out counter where I see all those horrid stories.*

Brian and I take a walk around the outside of the house and he is showing me all the tiny openings that a bat could possibly get through. They need to be sealed up. He suggests I put a cap on the chimney. And then he would leave the bats a one way out exit, that would close and not allow them back in. So when they left at night, they wouldn't be able to get back in. Sounded good to me. Only problem is, just as the birds were doing, the bats, too, were having their young. If he did this now, the baby bats wouldn't be able to fly out at night, and they would die in the attic. I definitely didn't want that to happen. Brian said by mid-August the baby bats would be flying out at night with the parents. I agreed to wait over a month for Brian to return and seal up the house.

A COUPLE OF WEEKS AFTER THAT...

Well, since I got the verdict from the 'Animal Evictions' guy that I was certifiably batty (in the attic, that is), my mother and I have been keeping our bedroom doors closed at night, since there appeared to be no way those bats could get from the attic into our bedrooms, unless they figured out how to turn a doorknob. Well, we were wrong.

Last night was warm and humid and I had my ceiling fan on. The bedroom door is closed. I hear little scratchy-type noises soon after I turn out the light. I figure it's coming from the attic and those mother bats are probably showing their little baby bats how to fly and other bat-related functions. That's okay. They are in the attic and I am in my bedroom with the door closed, safe and sound. Each time I doze off, the noises wake me up again. I keep telling myself it's okay, they are not in my room.

At 3:15 I wake with a start. Those noises sound like they are in my room. I lie very still and listen..... Sure enough, I hear the flutter of wings. I couldn't possibly hear the flutter of wings unless those wings were in my room. My digital alarm clock is very bright and I lay there with the sheet pulled way up. There is definitely a bat flying around in my room. My heart is pounding and I'm sweating. I've got to get out of bed and open my bedroom door. I kind of slide off the bed and crawl to the door and open it. The light is on in the guest room, illuminating the hall. I crawl back to bed and pull the sheet way up. I hear the flutter of wings above me. I watch. I swear I saw a baby bat (tiny little thing) fly out the door into the hall. I watch. He flies back in. I watch. He flies back out. A second or two later mother bat flies out behind him. I jump up and slam the door shut and put a towel at the bottom of the door, just in case they decide they want to crawl back in.

I'm laying there wondering how the heck did they get in my room? Were they in the room when I went to bed? Or did they get in some other way during the night? I'm assuming that was mother and child. Where was Dad? Was he coming to find them? And what were mother and child doing flying around the rest of the house? They were waiting for me to get up and open the door. Well, I couldn't. I was so upset to think that they were in my bedroom and I didn't know how they got there, I just couldn't bring myself to put a towel on my head, sit-crawl down the stairs, open the front door, pull up a chair and wait for them to fly out. I just couldn't. Of course, then I worried about them not able to get out. And the next morning they would be somewhere in the house....but where.

At around 4 a.m. I heard my mother's bedroom door open....she was heading across the hall to the bathroom. I'm thinking "Hurry, run. Get into the bathroom and close the door behind you." I hear the bathroom door close. No screaming, so she didn't encounter a bat. I hear the toilet flush and I hear the bathroom door open. Same thing. Hurry. Get into you bedroom. I hear her bedroom door open and close. No screaming. Good.

Shortly after my mother gets back into her room, I hear a thud. Not sure where it's coming from. Could it be Coalbee? I call her name, but don't hear anything. And I'm sure not going to open the door and walk around to see what it is.

At 4:17 a.m. I hear the first chirp of a bird. Thank God, morning is coming. I'm lying in bed, wide awake, waiting and listening. Not another chirp until 4:39, and then the birds start their morning chatter in earnest. It's comforting.

At 6:00 a.m. I get up and take a shower. I come out and slowly open my bedroom door. My mother is standing in her bathroom. She doesn't have her hearing aides on yet. I make a flying motion with my arms and point up. She says "Bats?" and I nod. She said "You heard bats?" And I shake my head and point to my eyes. She says "You SAW bats?" And I nod yes. She says "Where?" And I point to my room. She says "Oh my God....I'm going to put my hearing aides on." She does and I tell her the whole story. We're both baffled about how they got in my room. She says she is going to take a shower, and I head on downstairs to make the coffee.

I have some laundry with me and head into the downstairs bathroom to put the laundry in the washer. There is movement coming from the toilet bowl. No. It can't be. Yes, it is. The mother bat is in the toilet bowl, head above water, looking at me and swimming for her life. I start sobbing. I can't take this. I run upstairs and tell me mother. She runs down with me. I am just sobbing and sobbing. Not screaming.

Sobbing. I'm sobbing because I have to experience this, and I'm sobbing for the poor little bat who must have been doing the breast stroke for a couple of hours....(must have been that thud I heard)....desperately trying to stay alive. I'm sobbing because I know I'm going to have to get her out of there. Those little bat eyes are looking at me.

I get a big bowl and a slotted spoon. My mother opens the deck door, ready for me to carry the bat out. I go into the bathroom and I run out. I can't do it. I can't get that close to a bat. But I have to. There is no one else to do it and it has to be done. My mother suggests a long handled pot with a lid to it. Scoop him up in that and put the lid on. Sounds like a good idea. I'm still sobbing....non-stop. I have the pot in one hand and the slotted spoon in the other. My mother has the lid. We go into the bathroom. She's still swimming. I put the toilet seat up, and put the pot into the water, trying to get it under her. I'm directing her in with the slotted spoon. I get her in!!!! She's really moving around. My mother puts the lid on the pot and I carry her to the deck. I turn the pot on its side and remove the lid. Out comes water and the bat. We run inside and close the sliding door. We watch. She is sitting in a puddle of water. Alive. I hope I didn't hurt her when I scooped her out. A few minutes pass. She is kind of shaking herself off. She is looking around. Probably glad to be alive and wondering where to go now. She moves over to the edge of the deck and looks around. She sits there for a few minutes, looking. Then she kind of slides off the deck and flies up and away to the tall pine trees at the edge of the woods. And that's that.

But what happened to the baby? My mother thought maybe the baby was the first into the toilet and mother followed her. But baby couldn't swim and went down. Too terrible to really contemplate. Don't want to think about it. Know I won't be sleeping much tonight.

The End."

By now the pie had been in the oven for several minutes, and I was sitting down sipping coffee.

Mary asked "And that was all true?"

"Every word of it."

Chapter 20 – Food for Thought

"I really thought that I had paid off my bad bat karma when I carried the lamp out to the deck with the little bat clinging to it. But there must have been some karma that carried over from another life that I had to deal with."

"Do you have bats here?" Anne asked.

"Just outside. They swoop across the lawn on summer nights gobbling up the flying insects. We've never had one in the house though."

I got up to take the turkey out of the refrigerator and put it in the roasting pan. All I needed to do was sprinkle it with a little poultry seasoning, and that was it. No stuffing. I'd prepare that separately outside the bird.

"Is there something I can do?" Mary asked.

"You can chop some celery, onions and red pepper if you'd like. I need them for the stuffing. I've got them out on the counter by the sink."

"How about me?" Anne asked.

"You can peel and chop the turnips."

"Do you have a hammer?"

"A hammer?" Alex asked.

"Yes, my mother always used a hammer to hit the back side of the knife. Turnips are hard, you know."

"I'll get the hammer," Alex responded.

I got out the big wooden cutting board for Anne and placed the bag of turnips in front of her. In a minute Alex returned with a hammer.

The oven timer went off, signaling the pie was done. I took the pie out and put the turkey in.

Anne started pounding away with the hammer on the knife. Alex stopped her and said "Let me do that. Once I get them cut in big chunks, then you can peel them and dice them, okay?"

"Okay! Thanks! I think I'll have a little more coffee."

We all worked together dicing, slicing and cooking for a little better than an hour. Everything was ready for final cooking or reheating in a couple of hours when the turkey was roasted.

A little while later, after we got cleaned up and dressed, we reassembled in the living room. Alex had a fire burning in the fireplace. It was a crystal clear beautiful day outside. He had some Willie Nelson playing. It was my favorite Willie CD, the one with 'Hello Walls' and 'Crazy' on it. The aroma of the turkey was starting to waft through the house, as was the smell of cooking turnips. There's probably not that many people who love the smell of cooking turnips, but I did. I know my sisters did, too. We were a turnip crazy family. Always had been. Actually, my little toy fox terrier that I had as a girl, Tinkerbell, loved to eat raw turnips. She'd jump up and down like mad until she got a piece. Go figure.

"So, do you agree with me that most likely there were various extraterrestrials depicted as gods in the bible?" Alex asked?

"Yes, you are most likely correct. Remember I had noted that even the name of god changed from 'God' in Genesis Chapter 1, to 'Lord God' in Genesis Chapter 2, and just 'Lord' thereafter? And there were two separate creation stories contained in each of the first two chapters? I think there were different sets of extraterrestrials involved."

"Wait, you say there are two separate creation stories in Genesis?" Mary asked.

"Yes, Chapter 1 tells the story of God creating man and woman 'in our image' and 'our likeness'. And then in Chapter 2, the Lord God created a man, Adam, and woman, Eve, and put them in the Garden of Eden with the Tree of Knowledge and the Tree of Life. Then in Chapter 3, the snake comes along. Actually, the snake could be another type of extraterrestrial, along with the God of Chapter 1 and the Lord God of Chapter 2." I said

"Maybe the humans created in Chapter 1 were still in

existence when the second set was created in the Garden of Eden." Alex said.

"Could well be. I always wondered where Cain and Seth found their wives."

"But if we were created in their image and likeness, then those extraterrestrials must have looked pretty much like us, right?" Anne said.

"Yup, I would say so. Supposedly there are different types of extraterrestrials," Alex said. "There's the humanoid/Nordic, which are our creators I would assume, various types of grays and the reptilians. Maybe it was a reptilian that was the snake in the Garden of Eden."

"But who do you suppose actually authored Genesis 1 and 2?" Anne asked.

"Good question!" Alex said. "I believe it was our creators themselves. When Moses went up into the cloud on top of Mount Sinai, god supposedly wrote the Ten Commandments down himself on the clay tablets and gave them to Moses. Since no one could possibly have witnessed the creation of man, it had to be recorded by our creator and then given to Adam. Remember, St. Luke said that Adam was the son of god? I believe Adam was taught to write by god, and he picked up recording after the creation story was concluded. And the story was passed along to succeeding generations to document their history."

"I agree with Alex. The creation story had to be recorded by our creators. But what really baffles me is that organized religion has left the plural references to our creators in Genesis. For example, the Roman Catholic Church was very particular in what gospels and epistles were included in their bible. Anything questionable was left out. Why did they leave that 'in our image' in there? I'm glad they did, but I just don't understand why they did."

"How long before we eat?" Alex asked.

"Oh, about an hour or so. The turkey should be coming out within a half hour and then everything else can be heated."

"Okay, then I'm taking drink orders, ladies!"

"Do you have the makings for a Manhattan?" Anne asked.

I was surprised because I never saw Anne drink anything but wine.

"Yes, I do. Would you like one?"

"I think that would be very nice," Anne said.

Mary said "I'll join you!"

"Martini for me, please," I said.

Alex returned in a few minutes with our drinks on one of my silver serving trays along with my monogrammed cocktail napkins. Such a nice presentation! He even had a little bowl of macadamia nuts for us.

"I'm going to set the dining room table. I'll be back in a few minutes," he said.

"He is a dear, isn't he?" Mary said.

"When he wants to be," I responded.

I got up and put another log on the fire. I really hated the thought of my sisters leaving tomorrow. I had enjoyed their company so much. I know Alex did too. And it meant that I had to buckle down again, research blogs and decide on one, set my blog up and begin to fill it with all we had discovered over the last few months.

Anne had gotten up and went over to the table with the books piled on it and picked up the bible and came back and sat down. She started reading Genesis Chapter 1.

"What about the humans that were created in Chapter 1 of Genesis. What's with that?" Anne asked.

Just then Alex walked back into the room and said "I believe they were beings that were somehow created by extraterrestrials, but didn't have extraterrestrial DNA as did Adam. Adam was the son of god, those other creatures weren't. Because Adam and Eve ate fruit from the tree of knowledge, they knew right from wrong. Remember it says in Genesis, Chapter 2, "Behold, the man has become like one of us, knowing good and evil…"

"I just had a chilling thought." All eyes turned to me.

"Remember we just mentioned that perhaps the beings that were created in Chapter 1 were still in existence when Adam and Eve were created in Chapter 2?" I said. "Maybe those beings who were created in Chapter 1, who do not have the DNA of our creator, and who do not know the difference between good and evil, maybe they are still on our planet today."

Silence.

"And these beings have interbred with the progeny of Adam and Eve, diluting it further and further from what it was originally, creating a population on this earth that is no longer able to discern the difference between good and evil. Also a possibility is that there are still beings on earth today who are pure first creation offspring. They have not been tempered at all by an infusion of extraterrestrial DNA. Perhaps they are pure evil. When you hear of vile crimes and you can't imagine what kind of person could do something like that, maybe it's these first creation beings who don't know any better."

"Wow…" Mary said.

More silence.

"And that's why this is hell on earth. Those who do have some of the DNA of our creators really have to work hard, lifetime after lifetime, to become better and more spiritual. And all the while they are surrounded by beings who have no clue," Anne said.

"I would guess that they don't have souls or any spiritual essence. They are like clay figures…like that little Venus of Willendorf…except that they live and breath, but are really just hollow shells. And when they die, that's it. They just die," Alex said.

"So instead of destroying those first beings who were flawed, they just conducted a second experiment with creation, this time actually using their own DNA. Adam and Eve were physically put in the Garden of Eden so they could be watched, and also be kept separate from those 'mistakes' made earlier. Then when they ate the apple, they were booted out of the garden, free to associate with the earlier soul-less creatures," I said.

"Another thought just popped into my head," I continued. "It says in the bible that the beings created in Chapter 1 were made 'in our image'. It doesn't say that about Adam and Eve in Chapter 2. Maybe the two sets looked completely different from each other."

"Right," Alex said, "the first creatures were little grey people with big eyes."

That got a big laugh from all of us.

Just then the oven timer went off signaling the turkey was ready to come out.

"No one move!" I commanded. "I just have to take the turkey out and warm up everything else. I'll be right back."

I went into the kitchen and juggled all the side dishes around so they were either in the oven or on the stove heating. I covered the turkey with some aluminum foil and left it to rest.

I walked into the living room to hear Alex talking about 'god's chosen people'.

"What were you saying?" I asked Alex.

"I was talking about how important the genealogy listing of the line of Adam is. The New Testament's creator's DNA was in that line. That is why they were the 'chosen' people. That is why they were not to marry outsiders. What do you think?"

"Very possible," I responded. "Isn't it amazing how much we've stumbled upon today? I've got my work cut out for me, putting this all down in writing in a blog. I don't even know where to start."

"Start at the beginning, just like it happened. Begin with that foggy morning when you opened the bible and began to read Genesis and just take it from there," Alex said.

"I'm just going to post my blog every day. I'm not going to wait until I get the whole thing down in writing. I'm just going to write for an hour or two every day and post that day's entry, and then continue the next day."

"Sounds like a plan to me. Hey, are we going to have wine with dinner?" Alex asked.

"Of course! We have Grgich Hills Chardonnay and Cabernet."

"Grgich Hills! I love their wine!" Anne said.

"It's my favorite," I said.

"Okay, let's move into the kitchen. Alex, could you open the wine? I'll carve the turkey."

In no time we were seated in the dining room enjoying a fabulous meal, if I do say so myself.

We took a walk down the road after dinner. It was late afternoon and the sun was low in the sky. It would be getting dark soon, but we needed the exercise and we needed the air. When we approached the driveway of the elderly couple, Herbert and June, who had brought Itzy to me, we saw them out with their dachshund, Heidi. They waived and came over to us. I introduced Anne and Mary to them.

They invited us to have a little Old Krupnik with them.

"Old what?" Alex asked.

"Old Krupnik. It's a Polish honey liqueur," Herbert said. "You'll love it!"

Well of course, we couldn't pass that up. As we walked toward the house we could see the sun was just about to set behind the Adirondacks. The blues, purples, golds, pinks and peach colors of the clouds were spectacular. We decided to have the drink in their solarium in order to take in that remarkable view. I really liked their solarium. You could enter it from French doors on either side of the fireplace in the living room, similar to the arrangement in my house, only my doors went out on the patio. June had some beautiful African violets and spectacular poinsettias out there.

The Old Krupnik was like nothing I'd ever tasted before. And I'm not sure I'd want to taste it again. It definitely had a honey and herb kind of flavor that most likely was an acquired taste.

The sun had set and we thanked Herbert and June for their hospitality and headed back up the road toward home. I could see through the woods that the solar lights had come on, which was a good thing as it was getting dark fast.

We had some coffee and pumpkin pecan pie, and played Monopoly well into the night. It had been a good day.

Chapter 21 - In Black and White

It was fortunate that Anne and Mary didn't have an early morning flight. None of us were early risers the next morning. Maybe it was that tryptophan in the turkey that had wiped us out. Maybe it was the Old Krupnik. Maybe both.

After breakfast Mary and Anne said their goodbyes to Alex, and off we went to the airport. On the way the girls were talking about this being a mind altering trip. Their basic religious beliefs had been challenged and they now had their own research to do. And besides that, they had a lot of fun, too!

After a teary little goodbye at the airport, I headed home. I was thinking about all the work that was ahead of me. The majority of the research had been done; now it had to be put down in writing. And there was no point in dawdling.

As soon as I got home I got on the internet and started checking out blog hosting services. In no time I found that there were free services and services that charged a fee. I expected, or at least hoped, that my blog would have high traffic volume. I felt I needed a service that was professional and reliable. I zeroed in on one that looked very professional and which appeared to be very easy to use (which was very important for me). It also had a chat widget option which I liked.

I had Alex take a look at the website for this service and he thought it looked good as well, so I dove in and signed up.

Later that day I designed my blog. I have to say it was fun! Now all I had to do is write. I figured I might as well jump into this. There was no point in procrastinating, which I was so good at. So start I did. I started with the story of seeing that UFO back when I was a teenager. I continued with a brief history of my religious background. I provided a brief description of Alex and me. I then described opening the bible to Genesis that foggy morning and reading the words "in our image".

Alex came over to see how I was doing and I asked him to read what I had written thus far. I got up to make myself a martini and he sat down and began to read. I thought to myself that at least I didn't have to cook for the next few days as we had lots of leftovers.

I walked into the living room. Gazing out across the lake, I saw clouds coming in from the west. It looked like it was going to be a rainy night. Good thing the girls got out before this front came in.

I walked back to the den and stood looking over Alex's shoulder. I saw he had made a couple of notes on the pad. A couple minutes later he turned to me and said he thought it looked great. He did catch one typo and one grammatical error.

I sat down, made the changes, and said to him "Okay, this is it. I'm going to post this." And with a stroke of the key, it was posted. It was kind of scary, really. What kind of response would I get? Would I get any response at all? But at least I did it. I set up my blog and I posted my first entry. I was feeling pretty proud of myself!

We went into the kitchen and pulled out all of the leftovers and had a lovely dinner in no time. There was still quite a bit of turkey left, and I had plans to use the carcass for soup in a couple of days.

I guess that tryptophan kicked in again, as I slept very soundly that night. When I awoke the next morning and went downstairs Alex was waiting for me.

"You had 83 visitors to your blog overnight," he said.

"You're kidding!"

"No, I'm not. 83 and one left a comment."

"What did they say?"

"It was a she, her name is Kate, and she said she found this topic very interesting and wanted to know if you would be posting frequently."

"You know I had absolutely no idea how many people I would reach. 83 the first night is great! Don't you think?"

"I certainly do. It's amazing, really."

I poured myself a cup of coffee, sat down and basked in the glory of my initial success. Now I was psyched. I was ready to blog my little heart out.

And continue I did later that morning. I described the other reference to plural gods in Genesis, the "man has become like one of *us*" after Adam and Eve ate from the Tree of Knowledge, and the section about the "sons of god saw that the daughters of men were fair". I explained how we came to the natural conclusion (natural for us, at least) that we were created by extraterrestrials and how we went to the bookstore and found books that supported this theory.

At this point, I wanted to link in those sources. It didn't take long before I figured out how to do this and I was quite pleased with myself. I included brief comments on some of the highlights of those books. Actually, my comments on the Matthew Hurley book, 'The Alien Chronicles' were not brief. I described some of the art work contained in that book, and even went on to say that I actually obtained a copy of 'The Baptism of Christ' on the internet, framed it and enjoy looking at it hanging on my living room wall. Okay, enough for another day!

Of course, I asked Alex to proof read it. He was quite impressed with my technical ability to link in those source books. The text was perfect, so I posted it. I was on a roll.

I responded to the woman, Kate, who had left the comment overnight. I told her that I hoped to continue to post daily until I had documented everything that I felt needed to be documented. And I hoped that she would continue to read.

I looked out the window and saw that it had started to snow. It was not windy out and the flakes seemed to softly meander toward the ground. I saw Itzy was sitting by one of the French doors, looking out. I hoped she remembered that she already did her snow thing for this year.

It seemed as good a time as any to remove the turkey meat from the carcass and start cooking soup! In no time at all, the turkey bones were simmering in a big pot of water on the stove. That would take a few hours worth of cooking.

Alex asked if I was finished with the computer, and I said I was. He sat down and started to search something.

I had the urge to bake, but what? How about some whole wheat bread to go with that soup? I had a tried and true King Arthur flour whole wheat bread recipe and the bread would be ready in time to have with the soup tonight. My father used to bake bread and he always used King Arthur flour. Little did I know all those years ago that King Arthur was up here in Norwich, Vermont. At least a couple of times a year I'd drive over to their store to stock up and see what was new.

Just as I was ready to start making the bread, Alex comes over and says "You probably don't want to do any more research on the subject of extraterrestrial creation, but I found a book on the internet that I think you're going to want to read".

"You're absolutely correct. I don't want to do any more research on the subject. I've done enough. I've drawn my conclusions. I'm finished with that part. Now all I want to concentrate on doing is to put my conclusions and supporting documentation on my blog to share with others. That's it. End of discussion."

"What about if this book supports what you've already found and perhaps even explains some of it?"

I gave him this look, like 'go away', but he wasn't budging.

"Anyway, I've already ordered it," he said.

Now I gave him an exasperated look. "Okay, what is it?"

"The title is 'The Yahweh Encounters: Bible Astronauts, Ark Radiations and Temple Electronics' by Ann Madden Jones.

I responded by raising my left eyebrow and staring.

"Really, I think you should read this. I think it explains the technology behind the voice booming from the spaceship in the clouds saying '...this is my beloved son in whom I am well pleased...' plus all the other technology referred to in the bible."

I had to admit it did sound interesting. "Okay, I'm glad you ordered it, I guess."

"And I ordered one other book."

Now I was really getting exasperated with him.

"It's 'The World's Greatest Deception: The Bible UFO Connection' by Patrick Cooke. I believe the author discusses the incredible human body and the power of the mind. I know how much you believe one of the important messages of Jesus was the power of the mind. Come on, doesn't this sound like a book you'd like to read? And now that you have sworn off any further research on the subject, what do you read before you go to bed at night?"

"Okay, this book does sound interesting as well. And for your information, I'm reading 'Jane Eyre'. Again. It must be the fourth time I've read it. And I'm reading it out loud. It is written so beautifully, the words flow so wonderful together, that it should be read out loud. Itzy lays there and listens to me read. You must think I've gone off the deep end, right?"

"No...I've read it several times myself. I can't say that I've ever read it out loud to a cat, though. You're making soup and bread?"

"Yes, the snow seemed to inspire me to cook and bake!"

I looked out the window and saw that everything was completely covered with snow and it looked like a couple of inches had fallen. The flakes were no longer meandering to the ground, they were falling with determination now.

"I think I'll get a fire going in the living room fireplace," Alex said and walked off toward the garage to get some wood.

I continued to work on the bread and thought how odd

it was that usually we had fires in the living room fireplace, but not in the den fireplace which was visible from the work area in the kitchen. I figured it must be that if I was in the kitchen, I was usually cooking or cleaning. And if I moved over to the den area, I was either on the computer or watching television. But in the living room, the burning fire was the focal point. You'd sit there and stare and get lost in it.

Alex walked back through the kitchen with a load of wood in his arms. I had the mixing and kneading part of the bread done and it needed to sit and hopefully rise for an hour.

"Do you want a drink?" I called out to Alex. "I'm making a martini for myself."

"Okay, thanks. I'll have scotch on the rocks with a twist of lemon."

Scotch, actually that sounded good. It was more a scotch kind of day than a martini day. I grabbed the bottle of Dewar's out of the cabinet, poured out two drinks, added ice and lemon twists and walked into the living room just as Alex was lighting the fire. That man could set a great fire. Must be his Eagle Scout training.

"Wow, I haven't seen you drink scotch in a long time," he said to me as I handed him his drink.

"And it is such a healthy drink," I chuckled.

"It is?"

"That's what my mother said when we were sipping scotch at around 10 o'clock one crisp morning at the Dewar's Distillery in Scotland. We drove past the fields of barley. And we saw the clear stream of water running close to the distillery. This was the barley and the water they used to make the scotch. My mother figured that this had to be good for you."

"I've got some Scottish blood in me. I've always wanted to go there," Alex said.

"It is absolutely beautiful. I'd love to go again. We flew by helicopter from the east coast over to the west coast. We saw flocks of black faced sheep running across the hills, and lochs and abandoned castles, heather, heath and salmon farming. And then we landed on one of the islands off the western coast and had lunch at a manor house. It was fantastic. And of course, we drank a bit of scotch and ate smoked salmon just about every day."

We stared into the fire for a bit and sipped scotch. Daylight was quickly slipping away, but the fire and the lights from that beautiful Christmas tree that spread out across the ceiling were cheerful.

"So, do you have any guess as to how many visitors you'll have to your blog overnight?" Alex asked.

"If I have just as many as I did last night, I'll be very happy."

"I bet you'll have over 100 at least," Alex said.

"I wonder how long it will take me to get everything written. Of course, with you ordering more books, who knows if I'll ever be through with this."

Alex got up and put on the patio lights so we could watch the snow fall. The wind had picked up and little drifts were forming next to the stone wall. We sipped scotch, watched the fire, talked and later had a wonderful supper of homemade turkey vegetable barley soup and whole wheat bread.

And then I went to bed and read out loud from 'Jane Eyre' to Itzy. It had been a good day.

Chapter 22 – So Much More to Learn

It was still snowing the next morning. It looked like we had over a foot on the ground. I put on my robe and went downstairs. Alex was asleep on the couch and the television was on. I fed Itzy and then got the coffee going. The local weather person was saying that the snow would be tapering off mid morning.

Alex opened his eyes and said "Good morning. Did you look at your blog yet?"

"No, not yet."

"Mind if I do?"

"Go right ahead."

I got two clean coffee mugs out of the dishwasher and started to pour the coffee when I heard him say, "You had 124 visitors overnight and six of them left comments. Kate was one of the comments."

I walked over to the computer, handed Alex the cup of coffee, and peered over his shoulder. I was speechless.

"Well I guess you'd like to sit down and look at the comments," Alex said and got up.

I sat down and read Kate's first. She said she'd be checking my blog daily. She also said she had the Joe Lewels book that I had linked and she found it very interesting.

And to my surprise, the other five comments were all positive, and all of them were from women.

"You know what you should do?" Alex asked.

"What?"

"Call your sisters and tell them you have the blog up and running and let them know how it's going. I'm sure they'd like to read it as well."

"Excellent idea. I'll call them a little later this morning."

"And what's today's blog about?"

"Well, I have to pick up with rereading Genesis and

realizing there were two separate creation stories. Adam and Eve were the second creation. And the word 'God' was changed to 'Lord God' in Chapter 2 and was changed again in Chapter 3 to just 'Lord'. And then I'll go on to Chapter 4 and the tower of Babel story and the quote '... let *us* go down, and there confound their language...'."

"Are you going to mention that we believe the first beings created in Chapter 1 did not have our creator's DNA, whereas the second group did? Are you going to mention that we believe it is possible that the first group were still alive when the second group was made? Are you going to say that we believe it is possible that some of the first group are still walking the earth today?"

"No. I'm going to put this down in the exact order that we discovered it. We didn't reach that decision until much later. Actually, we didn't reach that first group/second group decision until a few days ago when we were discussing this with my sisters. I don't want to hit my audience with all this at once."

"You're right. Take it step by step and build on it; makes sense."

"It looks like the snow has just about stopped. What do you think; we've got about 15 inches or so?"

"Looks like it. I guess I'd better get the snow blower out in a little while. I hope those books I ordered are delivered today."

"You just ordered them yesterday, didn't you?"

"I specified overnight delivery."

I sighed and shook my head. I had no idea what the big rush was to get these books, but there was no point in talking further about it.

After I showered and got dressed, I called my sisters. They already knew that we had over a foot of snow overnight. However, they did not know that I had already started my blog and they were delighted to hear it. I gave them the web address and told them about the number of visitors I had during the first two days. They said they would read it daily as well. We chatted a bit more about mundane things like turkey soup and the homemade bread my father used to make and then we said our goodbyes.

It was time to sit down and blog.

As I had outlined to Alex earlier, I wrote about what I found when I reread Genesis. I explained that there were two separate creation stories and Adam and Eve were the result of the second creation, not the first. I recounted the tower of Babel story in Chapter 4 and the phrase '… let *us* go down, and there confound their language…' And I mentioned the usage of the word 'God' in Chapter 1, 'Lord God' in Chapter 2, and just plain 'Lord' in Chapter 3 and speculated on whether this meant these were three separate entities.

I felt like writing more, so I continued with a discussion on ziggurats that had been built in Mesopotamia and how they were believed to be dwelling places for the gods. Priests were the only ones allowed within the ziggurats in order to attend to their needs. I explained how these ziggurats first appeared during a sudden scientific and philosophical golden age and speculated that the 'gods' who were being attended to by the priests, were actually extraterrestrials who were teaching human beings and helping them to create these extremely advanced civilizations.   I also brought in reference to Joseph Campbell and his 'Masks of God' book. I even put up a link to the book. Okay, that was enough!

I looked out the front window and saw that Alex had plowed the driveway and was clearing the snow from the front path when the UPS truck approached. I saw him go over and talk with the driver for a little bit. The driver handed him a box and left.

A few minutes later he walked in and put the box down on the kitchen counter. He said "Okay, more reading material for you!"

Great, just what I needed.   "Thanks," I said rather unenthusiastically.

"I've finished writing today's blog. Want to read it before I post it?"

"Sure. Is there any more coffee left?"

"No, but I'll make some."

The coffee was ready just about the same time he finished reading.

"Connie, it's great. I'm glad you included the part about the ziggurats as they're linked with that tower of Babel story. And you even put a link for that Joseph Campbell book. Really good. Let her rip!"

I handed him his cup of coffee and posted my entry.

Alex had opened the box containing the books and asked, "Okay, which one are you going to read first?"

I sipped my coffee and looked at the front and back covers of both. The back cover of the "Yahweh Encounters" was intriguing as it alluded to both the tabernacle of Exodus and Solomon's temple as being part of the communications system between earthlings and a spaceship. Reading further, I had to admit that it appeared that this book contained information that I had not read elsewhere.

"'The Yahweh Encounters' it is," I said. "It looks very interesting."

"Good! I'm going to finish clearing the snow and then I'm going to bring more wood from the woodshed into the garage."

I sat down in the living room with 'The Yahweh Encounters' and looked at the Table of Contents. I saw a chapter entitled 'Jesus Christ: Not of this Earth', and thumbed over to that chapter.

One of the premises of this chapter was that although through genetic interbreeding various barren women in the bible had been impregnated, Mary's pregnancy was different. But the author speculated that perhaps Jesus represented the first actual intermingling of the seed of Yahweh with a human. Hey, I thought to myself, what about Sarah? The "Lord did unto Sarah what he had spoken." It didn't sound to me like he sent an emissary for that one.

The author suggested that Jesus must have been fathered by a very important entity. She also quoted from 'The Lost Books of the Bible' that the angel, when speaking to Joachim, predicted that Mary would, in her virginity, conceive and give birth to the Son of God 'in an unparalleled way'.

I had noted that same phrase as well when I read this portion of the 'The Lost Books of the Bible' a few months earlier.

I walked over to the 'book table' and found 'The Lost Books of the Bible' and found the page where the angel was speaking with Anna and, predicting what would happen in the future, using the phrase 'an unparalleled instance'. I had taken this to mean the double dose of extraterrestrial DNA. I had not considered the origin of the DNA of the fathers of the children of all those barren women in the bible. It was extraterrestrial DNA and I just left it at that. But of course, there could be different levels of hierarchy of ET and different groups, both benevolent and malevolent. I don't know why I didn't think of that before. If I was correct in thinking that the god of the Old Testament was not the same as the god of the New Testament, then of course the ET DNA used in impregnations in the Old and New Testaments would come from different alien groups.

I also found very interesting the author's discussion of both the tabernacle and Solomon's temple. Solomon's temple was the new and improved home of the Ark of the Covenant, and the author believed the Ark was the central piece of the communication system with the extraterrestrials.

I picked up the bible and looked through Exodus for reference to communication and the Ark, and found Chapter 25:22 "And there I will meet with thee, and I will *commune* with thee from above the mercy seat, from between the two cherubim which are upon the ark of the testimony..."

And also, just as the glory of the Lord appeared above the tabernacle, it also appeared at Solomon's temple as described in 2 Chronicles 7:3: "And when all the children of

Israel saw how the fire came down, and the glory of the Lord upon the house, they bowed with their faces to the ground upon the pavement, and worshiped..."

I decided I should read Kings and Chronicles in their entirety, as verses from those chapters were being referred to with regard to Solomon's temple. But first I needed a cup of tea. I walked into the kitchen and found Alex at the computer.

"Want to know what the activity is on your blog?" he asked.

"No, I'd rather wait until tomorrow morning and be surprised."

"Okay."

Now he got me wondering what kind of activity there was. He didn't say anything more. I tried to put it out of my mind as I waited for my tea to brew.

"I have to admit that I'm enjoying 'The Yahweh Encounters' very much. Thank you for ordering it."

"My pleasure."

I carried my tea into the living room and sat down at the book table. That's what we called it now, 'the book table'. It was piled high with books. Religious books, UFO books, art books, reference books. There were piles and piles of them. I picked up the bible and opened to Kings and started to read.

In 2 Kings, 22, King Josiah initiated a project to renovate the temple. I read: "... and Hilkiah the high priest said unto Shaphan the scribe, I have found the book of the law in the house of the Lord...and Shaphan the scribe came to the king....saying, Hilkiah the priest delivered me a book, and Shaphan read from it before the king."

What is this all about, I wondered. The Book of the Law of the Lord that had been given to Moses were the tablets that were in the Ark of the Covenant, no? It sounded like they found this book lying around in the temple, like in a corner under some rubble or something. Was it translated onto paper? Were the original tablets still in the Ark? Or was this book separate and distinct from the tablets inscribed with the Ten

Commandments, the tablets that had been inscribed by the hand of god?

I continued to read "And it came to pass, when the king heard the words of the book of the law, he rent his clothes. He gave these orders... Go ye enquire of the Lord for me, and for all of Judah, concerning the words of this book that is found. For great is the wrath of the Lord that is kindled against us, because our fathers have not hearkened unto the words of this book, to do according unto all that is written concerning us."

They went to the prophetess Huldah and she said to them, "Thus saith the Lord God of Israel, Tell the man that sent you to me, Thus saith the Lord: Behold I will bring evil upon this place and upon the inhabitants thereof, even all the words of the book which the king of Judah hath read. Because they have forsaken me and burned incense to other gods, that they might provoke me to anger with all of the works of their hands, therefore my wrath shall be kindled against this place, and shall not be quenched. But to the king of Judah which sent you to enquire of the Lord, thus shall he say to him, thus saith the Lord God of Israel, as touching the words which thou hast heard; Because thine heart was tender and thou hast humbled thyself before the Lord, when thou heardest what I spake against this place and against the inhabitants thereof, that they should become a desolation and a curse, and hast rent thy clothes and wept before me, I also have heard thee, saith the Lord. Behold therefore, I will gather thee unto thy fathers, and thou shalt be gathered into thy grave in peace, and thine eyes shall not see all the evil which I will bring upon this place. And they brought the king word again."

What curses were written in the book? I thought Moses was given the Ten Commandments, I didn't remember anything about curses. Moses broke the first pair of tablets when he came down the mountain and saw the people worshipping the golden calf, but was given a second set presumably written by Yahweh himself.

I got up and found Alex still on the computer. "Could you do a search for me?" I asked.

"Fire away."

"Search 'Ten Commandments - Law of Moses' and see what you get."

"Why, what are you trying to find out?"

"Were the Ten Commandments separate from a book of the law of the lord that Moses had?"

Less than a minute later Alex said, "Okay, I think I found what you want. And the answer is, yes, they are two separate things: stone tablets inscribed by god with the Ten Commandments and a book of law written by Moses as instructed by god. Listen to these quotes."

"Deuteronomy 4:13-14, 'And he declared unto you his covenant, which he commanded you to perform, even ten commandments; and he wrote them upon two tables of stone. And the Lord commanded me at that time to teach you statutes and judgments, that ye might do them in the land whither ye go over to possess it.'"

"Deuteronomy 31:24-26, 'And it came to pass, when Moses had made an end of writing the words of this law in a book, until they were finished, that Moses commanded the Levites, which bare the ark of the covenant of the Lord, saying, Take this book of the law, and put it in the side of the ark of the covenant of the Lord your God, that it may be there for a witness against thee.' "

"And here's another that came up which mentions a curse:

"Daniel 9:11, 'Yea, all Israel have transgressed thy law, even by departing, that they might not obey thy voice; therefore the curse is poured upon us, and the oath that is written in the law of Moses the servant of God, because we have sinned against him.' "

"That's exactly what I needed. It's amazing how much we don't know. I don't think the search will ever end."

"And if it did, what would you do with all your free time?"

"Honestly, I don't even remember what I did with my days before we stumbled upon this whole thing. But that's it for today. I think I'll do a little housework for a change! The dust bunnies are taking over the place."

Chapter 23 – Kindred Spirits

I woke exhausted the next morning. I barely slept at all. It troubled me that there were curses contained in the book of the law that god instructed Moses to write. What were these curses? Did this book still exist?

I walked downstairs and smelled the aroma of coffee. Alex had just poured cups for both of us.

"I heard you coming down the stairs. How are you?"

I told him about my sleepless night and the thoughts going through my head about the Old Testament god's curses.

"I guess there's more research to be done," he said.

"I don't want to do any more research! I thought I was through with all that. I was just going to put what I had found on my blog and be done with it!"

"Speaking about blogs, why don't you go take a look at yours?"

I took a sip of my coffee, gave him a look, and walked over to the computer. I couldn't believe what I saw. I had 312 visitors since yesterday's post and 24 left comments. It was incredible to me that 312 people looked at my blog within a 24 hour period. Yet, if you consider that this blog is on the worldwide web, 'worldwide' being the operative word, 312 is nothing.

Kate left another comment. She asked if I thought it was possible that the beings created in Genesis Chapter 1 were still in existence when Adam and Eve were created in the second attempt.

"Did you read what Kate wrote?" I asked Alex.

"No, I didn't; what did she write?"

"She asked if I thought the beings created in Genesis Chapter 1 were still in existence when Adam and Eve were created."

"Wow, very astute! It took us several months to even think about that as a possibility."

"I'll respond by saying I do think it is a possibility and will discuss further in a future posting."

I looked at the other comments. One said I was an agent of the devil and another pretty much said I was nuts. The remainder, however, were encouraging. And what was interesting was that all of the positive comments were from women. Fourteen of those women said that they, too, had seen a UFO when they were younger. And several of the women commented that they hardly ever used the internet, but for some reason they felt compelled to search 'UFO/creation/Genesis' or some combination thereof and found my blog.

Alex came over and read the comments. When he finished he said "It's almost as if some force were bringing you all together."

"Don't get carried away now," I said. Although I have to admit the same thought crossed my mind.

"Really, don't you think it's kind of weird that it was completely out of character for several of these women to get on the internet and search this topic for some reason that is inexplicable even to them?"

"Weird…"

"Okay, I can see I'm getting no where with you. So you left off with the tower of Babel and the ziggurat hypothesis. What's next?"

"I'm going to discuss the extraterrestrial impregnation of Anne, Mary, Elizabeth, Rachel, the mothers of Samuel and Samson, and of course, Sarah. I'll also add my theory about the double dose of DNA in Jesus."

"Boy, I can't wait to see what tomorrow's comments will bring."

After breakfast I sat down at the computer and started my post with "The Lord visited Sarah…and the Lord did to Sarah as he had spoken…" Ah yes, the comments should be interesting regarding this post, I thought.

About an hour later Alex asked "Are you finished?"

"Yes, just now."

"Want to go for a ride? I have to look at a property down in Shoreham. It's directly on the lake and they're looking to put in a terrace, wall and steps."

"It's December, isn't this a little unusual to be doing estimates in December?"

"Actually, I'd be happy to do estimates all winter and get my spring and summer jobs all lined up. Usually people don't think about landscape projects in winter, but these people were different. So, do you want to go for a ride?"

"I'd love to get out of this house for a while. Sure."

I grabbed my coat and Alex gathered his paraphernalia and we headed out the door. The sun was out and the snow was dazzling. We got in the Outback and headed down the drive. The last time I was out of the house was when I brought my sisters to the airport. It's not healthy to be housebound, glued to the computer and reading all the time, I thought.

Shoreham was mainly an agricultural community. It had several wonderful niche farms. One of my favorites was Champlain Orchards high on a hill overlooking the lake. They had fruits, vegetables and meats. And their pies were to die for.

"Do you think we could stop at the Champlain Orchards farm store on the way back? I could pick up a couple of pies and some cider and some of their wonderful sauerkraut."

"Sauerkraut!"

"I know you don't like it, but I do. I'm kind of craving it. It's been months since I had it last. Even you like those little potato dumplings that I make with sauerkraut."

"Okay, we'll stop."

About a half hour later we arrived in Shoreham and Alex turned onto a dead end road that was on the lake shore. I didn't even know this road existed. The icy blue lake and snow covered mountains in the background made this look like a picture postcard. A bend in the road took us to a federal style house on the lake side at the end of the road. It was brick with black shutters and although it was probably a couple hundred years old, looked to be in good condition.

There was another good sized brick building off to the side. It looked like part of it was a garage, part was maybe used for storage, and there was a second floor with a large window facing the lake.

We parked and walked up the steps to the front door. Before we could ring the bell, the door opened and a man who I could only describe as looking like 'an old hippy' said, "Hi, I'm Joshua, you must be Alex." They shook hands and then Alex introduced me.

I expected to see a country gentleman, corduroy jacket and tassel loafer type guy living here. Joshua had overalls on that were paint splattered and torn, and his work boots looked like they had seen a lot of work. His longish hair was reddish blond with streaks of grey, and so was his beard. I had a feeling he and Alex would get along famously.

The foyer was spacious, which was surprising for a federal style home. There was a round table centered in the space with a large urn filled with various types of evergreens, dried grasses and bittersweet. There was a through hall that ended at a glass door at the back of the house. The view out the door was the lake and the mountains. It was spectacular. On the far right side of the foyer the stairs went up to a landing with a large Palladian window and a window seat. Between that window and the back door and the front door with the fanlight and side lights, the interior was flooded with beautiful natural light.

I was standing there in awe, when a woman started to descend the stairs towards us. She had long brown hair with a few streaks of gray pulled back into one long pigtail. She wore no makeup, and didn't need to as she had a beautiful face and complexion. She was wearing a denim jumper with a black turtleneck and black tights. She seemed to float down the stairs.

Joshua introduced her, "This is Jane and this is her house."

We shook hands and she seemed to be familiar to me, like she was an old friend I hadn't seen in a long, long time. She looked at me and said "Haven't we met before?"

"Funny, I was thinking the same thing, but I don't think it was in this lifetime."

She looked at me like she understood, and nodded.

"Your house is beautiful," Alex said.

"Thank you. It's always been in my family. When my mother died last year, I inherited it."

The dining room was to the left of the foyer and on the sideboard against the far wall was a large tureen. It looked to me like it was Staffordshire, the Indus pattern.

I realized that everyone was looking at me staring into the dining room straining to see that tureen.

"Oh, I apologize. My eye caught that tureen on the sideboard and it looked to me like it might be the Indus pattern."

"You're familiar with that pattern?" Jane asked rather excitedly.

"Yes, I have several pieces myself."

"You collect transferware?"

"Sure do, especially the aesthetic period."

"I can't believe it. I knew there was some special connection between us when we met. Follow me."

Alex and Joshua were standing there looking rather dumbfounded by this whole thing. We all followed Jane into the dining room. Yes, that was the largest Indus tureen I had ever seen, and it even had the matching ladle. I was standing there admiring it when Jane said, "Look over here."

At the far end of the room were two corner cupboards, all filled with transferware, mostly brown and white.

I'm sure I gasped when I saw it. I walked over to the nearest cupboard and saw that it was filled with Indus plates, bowls, cups, saucers and all sorts of serving dishes. The other cupboard was filled with many pieces of different aesthetic designs of various shapes and sizes. I was familiar with most of the patterns.

"I am amazed. I have never met anyone who collected aesthetic period transferware or was even interested in it. What a collection you have!"

"The Indus pieces were my great, great grandmother's. I always admired it and started to collect other patterns. I'm especially fond of the asymmetrical collage patterns."

"Me too!"

"Okay, I hate to interrupt," Alex said, "but I just wanted to mention that I have written a book on asymmetrical collage transferware patterns."

Jane was looking at him like she didn't believe him, and I said "Really, he did. He's got pictures of the various patterns and it's indexed by both potter and pattern name. He even has pictures of the potter marks and dates of the patterns."

"Oh, I'd love to see that!"

"Well, why don't you two come over to our house and you can see my collection of transferware and look at the book as well?"

"Great, we'd love to!" Jane responded.

"Alex, how long will it take for you to get computer images and sketches completed of the work that needs to be done here?"

"Well, it's kind of hard to say as I haven't seen the area yet, but probably a couple of days."

"So that would be Wednesday. How does Wednesday around 2 in the afternoon sound?"

"Perfect." Jane said. "Joshua, does that work for you?"

"Sounds good."

"I'll write down the directions."

"I've got a notepad in the kitchen, why don't you follow me?"

Joshua said "Hey Alex, why the girls are bonding here, why don't we go outside and take a look at the property?"

"Oh, I'm here as his assistant," I said. "I'm supposed to help with measuring."

"I'll help with measuring. You ladies look like you have a lot of talking to do."

Alex and Joshua walked out the back door and I followed Jane to the kitchen, which was to the rear of the dining room.

The kitchen was charming. It was large and had a rectangular table in the middle with six chairs around it. It had worn black and white linoleum squares on the floor. And the sink was large, deep and made of copper!

"A copper sink! Isn't that lovely!" I exclaimed.

"Thanks. The kitchen was the only room in this house that I felt really needed to be remodeled. I really did like the worn look of the floor. But the cabinets and countertops were in bad shape. I had them replaced and at the same time had the sink put in. I went with copper because it's antimicrobial thus reducing the surface germs and bacteria."

"And it's beautiful as well," I said.

"Would you like some coffee? I made a pot just before you arrived."

"Okay, thank you. I take it black."

"Sit down at the table. Here's the pen and paper for the directions."

After I finished writing the directions, we sipped coffee and talked about transferware for a while. Then Jane said, "Come on, let me show you the living room."

We walked across the back hall and into the rear of the living room. I glimpsed Alex and Joshua out back laughing about something and seeming to be very comfortable with each other.

The living room had the largest Persian rug that I had ever seen. The room must have been 30 feet long and 15 feet wide and the rug filled a good deal of the floor space.

"Is this a Sarouk?" I asked.

"Don't tell me you know Persian rugs, too?'

"Alex is the expert. All I know is what I've learned from him over the years. But this looks like a Sarouk to me."

"Yes, it's a Ferahan Sarouk from the late 19th Century. My great, great grandmother had very good taste."

"She certainly did. The colors are incredible. That celadon green mixed with the coppery brown color with just little hints of teal and cream work wonderfully together. I love it! And the walls are painted that same teal color. It's perfect."

I stood there and took a long look around the room. The fireplace was centered on the outside wall. It had a beautiful mantle carved with garlands. It was painted the same cream color that was in the rug. There were two windows at either end of the room and a window on either side of the fireplace. They were adorned with drapes that appeared to be silk and were of a similar teal shade as the walls. They had piping that was a blend of teal and copper, and the tiebacks were held with huge copper colored tassels. And over the mantle was a painting that was amazing. It appeared to be a painting of clouds with every shade of blue, violet and grey imaginable with a bronze glow in the center.

I walked over to it and stared at it.

Jane said "What do you think?"

"I'm speechless. Was this your great, great grandmother's as well?"

"No, I painted it."

I turned around to look at her just as the men came through the back door.

"You painted this? It looks like the work of a master. And the master is you!"

Alex heard what I said, removed his boots by the back door and walked over to where we were standing.

"It has a mysterious quality about it," he said.

I saw a little twinkle in Jane's eyes. "You think so?" she asked.

"Absolutely."

"Alex, want a cup of coffee?" Joshua asked.

"Okay, thanks. Black."

"Actually, this entire room is amazing. There is so much to take in, the rug being one of them. This is a Ferahan Sarouk, right?"

"I told you this man knows his rugs," I said.

"Correct you are."

Joshua joined us with coffee mugs in hand.

"I didn't know there were any palace sized Sarouks. The pattern and colors are striking," Alex commented as he stared at the rug.

"So, Alex, what are your ideas about the patio out back?" Jane asked.

"The view is the main attraction out there. Nothing could, or even attempt to, compete with it. The stone work should be simple and just fit into the gentle slope of the ground. As I mentioned to Joshua, I think a fan shaped bluestone patio that ran the entire length of the house would work nicely. The curve of that patio would tie in with the window fan over the front door and the curve of the Palladian window at the back landing."

"Oh, I like the way it sounds," Jane said.

"And instead of having a wall or a fence around the edge of the patio with steps at the middle or edge or wherever, I thought the entire edge of the patio could simply be curved wide steps. So you could descend at any point. The steps could act as stadium seating if you had a group of people over. When you are looking out from the house or the patio every inch of the scenery is visible to you. And conversely, when you are down by the water's edge, you are looking up at graceful curving steps and the patio and the house. Nothing is lost from your view from whatever your vantage point."

"Doesn't that sound wonderful?" Joshua asked.

"You know I tried envisioning what I wanted out there," Jane said. "I was thinking rectangular with black wrought iron fencing with stairs in the middle. But would that have been wrong! I love what Alex is suggesting."

"You're coming over on Wednesday," Alex said. "I'll have this sketched out for you by then. I took pictures, so I'll even have computerized images that you can view. I have the measurements, so I'm all set. I'm really glad you like my idea."

"Okay, so we'll see you Wednesday afternoon," I said.

Alex took one last sip of his coffee and said "I'll just put this in the kitchen sink," and started to walk off even though Jane was saying "Oh, don't bother."

"I'm going in that general direction anyway as I have to put my boots back on," he said.

We walked toward the front door and Alex met us there. "Copper sink. It's a beauty!"

Jane chuckled.

We said our goodbyes, and off we went. As we were driving away I asked "Doesn't it seem like we've known them forever?"

"Yes, it's kind of eerie."

"Eerie in a nice way. And what do you think about that cloud painting? I swear it looked like there was a UFO in there. Did you see that bronze glint in the middle?"

"Yup. That was weird, too."

In no time at all we were at Champlain Orchards and I bought two frozen apple pies with the oatmeal crumble topping, several bottles of sauerkraut, a couple bottles of dilly beans, some artesian cheese, apples and cider.

As we continued toward home Alex said "That house is something. The transferware collection is incredible and that Sarouk belongs in a museum. I mean it. The quality and the size are astonishing. It's over a hundred years old and in excellent condition. And the colors are highly unusual for a Sarouk."

"I'm so glad you asked me to come with you."

"I'm glad you were with me, too. And isn't it nice that Jane appreciates it all. The house and all of its contents could have gone to someone who couldn't care less about that stuff and either called in an auction house or had a huge estate sale or something."

"You're right about that. I wonder what Joshua does for a living?"

"He buys, sells and restores antique furniture. His workshop is in the bottom floor of that building which is part garage. And Jane's studio is on the second floor."

"Oh, so you already knew she painted when you came back into the house?"

"Yes, but I had no idea how good she was at it."

When we arrived home, I made a batch of potato dumplings with sauerkraut. Even if I do say so myself, it was delicious. Alex had two helpings.

Chapter 24 - Chatterbox

I woke the next morning refreshed from a wonderful night's sleep. I wonder if that sauerkraut had anything to do with it?

Alex was hard at work on the computer when I got downstairs.

"The coffee is made; help yourself," he said.

"You're working on the presentation for Jane and Joshua?"

"Yep, been working on it for over an hour now. Come over here and take a look."

I poured my coffee and walked over to the computer.

"Wow, it looks great! I don't know how you ever came up with that idea. Look how fantastic it looks with that Palladian window."

"Thanks, I figured I'd better get this computerized rendition going first, and I'll do some sketches later to supplement the presentation."

"I checked your blog earlier," Alex said. "And there's lots of activity."

"What do you mean 'activity'?"

"They're chatting away like crazy."

"Chatting? They're actually chatting?"

"Uh-huh. And what's nice about the way your chat widget works is that you can review the entire history. It's pretty neat. You got them all excited with your extraterrestrial impregnation comments."

"So can I get on there and chat along with them? I've never 'chatted' before."

"Sure, you can. I'll be through with what I'm doing in a half hour or so, then it's all yours."

I walked to the living room and looked out at the lake. It was a grey day and looked like it would start snowing any minute.

I didn't know why I was so surprised that they were chatting on my blog site. After all, that is what I was hoping for when I put that chat widget thing on there.

I just stood there staring out at the lake and sipping coffee, lost in thought, when I heard Alex say "Okay, she's all yours."

I poured myself another cup of coffee and sat down at the computer. Alex had my blog up on the screen. The chatting was still going on. I went back to the history to see who had started it, and, no surprise, it was Kate. She opened with "I don't know if anyone is out there, but I just wanted to say that I do believe that Samuel and Samson and the offspring of Anne, Elizabeth, Rachel and, of course, Mary, were extraordinary beings. And I concur with Connie that it is most likely that they are all the result of extraterrestrial insemination."

She continued, "And I do believe that we are being manipulated and purposely kept in the dark about the true nature of our creation and the existence of extraterrestrial contact by organized religion, government, big business and the media. I believe that the majority of mankind is greedy, complacent and ignorant, more so now than ever. I believe we are spiraling downward to a depth that we will not be able to climb out of and hope for the future of mankind and womankind on this earth will be lost."

"I believe that our only solution is to channel our thoughts towards benevolent extraterrestrial entities and ask them to come to our aid."

Well that's what started it. I continued to read all of the back and forth chat after that opening salvo. Most of those responding to Kate's comments had no argument with her statements regarding the extraterrestrial insemination of the named entities of the bible. And most of them agreed with her that we were being manipulated and purposely kept in the dark. But when it came to requesting extraterrestrial entities to come to our aid, there was much controversy.

The question was raised and discussed by many that we might be asking for trouble, more trouble than we were already in. Who knew who was out there listening, waiting to react? It might not necessarily be a benevolent response. We could be inviting pure evil upon this earth.

Okay, I might as well jump in on this. I entered the chat room, "Hello, all. I knew I'd probably get quite a response to yesterday's posting, but this far exceeds my expectations. Thank you for your interest and your comments. It is evident that we are all researching, thinking and communicating. This is a complex topic. I recently started to wonder if the god of the Old Testament was different than the god in the New Testament. The Old Testament god was vengeful and egocentric and the god of the New Testament was all about love.

"I wholeheartedly agree with Kate's comments about our being manipulated. There are forces out there with their own agendas. I don't know if those forces are of this earth or elsewhere. I don't know if they are truly malevolent or just misguided. But I do know that if we don't react somehow, the human race will never recover. It has crossed my mind countless times that we need an infusion of that same extraterrestrial DNA today to help elevate the human race. We are in a downward spiral.

"Yet, I can understand the hesitancy of those who think we are asking for trouble. That saying 'be careful what you ask for, because you might just get it' could be applicable here. But I'm convinced that it's not going to get better; something needs to be done.

"Today's post is about the reference to the genealogy of Jesus in the Gospel of Luke. My plan is to follow a chronological order in my posts, so you'll get a feeling for the order that I found things and how I reached certain conclusions and when.

"Please continue to communicate. It can only help. Thank you."

I proceed to enter the day's post about "…the son of Adam, the son of God" and the inference that Adam was not just created by extraterrestrials; he had extraterrestrial DNA in him.

I noted that I had 342 visitors overnight and 6 comments. It looked like I was leveling off with daily visitors. And I think the chat room grabbed many people who would otherwise have left comments.

Alex had made a spot for himself on the book table and was sketching various views of Jane's house and patio. He did beautiful drawings. He really didn't need to do them at all because the computer images pretty much showed every detail. But I'm sure he felt his drawings were more personal, which they were. Plus I know he enjoyed doing it.

"Did you read the chat history?"

"I started at the beginning with Kate's and read a little further. That Kate really is right on the ball, isn't she?"

"Well, she certainly is in sync with our way of thinking."

"Did you enter the chat room?"

"Yes. And I also entered today's post about '…the son of Adam, the son of God…' Tomorrow I'm going to start discussing Moses, Mount Sinai and the glory of god."

"I'm going to do a little light dusting and some vacuuming. Jane and Joshua will be here tomorrow."

"Okay, I'll finish up my sketches."

As I worked, I thought about Kate's suggestion that we channel our thoughts to benevolent extraterrestrials and ask them to come to our aid. Did Sarah, or Elizabeth or Mary ask to be mothers of hybrid children? Not to my knowledge. They were chosen. You could say they were manipulated, but manipulated for the good. Or at least I thought it was for the good. What would happen if we did try to channel our thoughts to request help, anything?

I recalled that time years ago when I would fall asleep asking for guidance and knowledge, and then that vortex episode, actually episodes, happened. I believe that someone had heard me, and someone was trying to answer my request. But who?

I finished my dusting and vacuuming and then decided I should really wash all of my transferware. That meant hand washing, not using the dishwasher.

Ah, time flies when you're having fun. Before I knew it, it was evening and it was snowing, a nice gentle snow. Alex had the fire going in the living room and the lights were on the Christmas trees. We were sipping our drinks by the fire and eating popcorn. Itzy was curled up on the hearth. Life was good.

Chapter 25 – Truth is Stranger than Fiction

Only a few inches of new snow had fallen overnight. Just enough to freshen things up a bit outside.

The TV was on, and Alex was asleep on the couch. I got the coffee going and then walked over and turned the computer on.

Itzy was standing by her empty bowl and giving me a piercing look. "Okay, I know you're hungry. I'm getting it right now. Be patient!" I got a can of cat food out of the pantry, put it in a clean dish, and placed it on the floor. I poured some milk in another bowl and put that on the floor. She was happy.

I went over to the computer and looked at my blog. They were still chatting! I had 362 visitors overnight, 14 comments and a whole lot of chatting going on. I saw that Kate was still in there, giving her two cents worth. And it seemed that her major protagonist was a woman named Alice. Alice had provided a quote from the bible with which I was not familiar. It was Ephesians 6:12 and read "For our struggle is not against flesh and blood, but against the rulers, against the authorities, against the powers of this dark world and against the spiritual forces of evil in the heavenly realms." Alice said that she believed pure evil existed not only on this planet, but evil also existed outside of this planet. She felt we would be inviting that evil into our midst if we asked for aid.

The coffee was ready, and I saw that Alex was stirring. I poured one mug for each of us and put his mug on the table next to the couch.

"Thanks. I had some crazy dreams last night. One was about flying dragons zooming down from the clouds and people screaming and running to get away from them."

"It must have been a delayed reaction from the sauerkraut, don't you think?" I said.

"Ah, that must be it!"

"Have you checked your blog, yet?"

"Yes, they are still chatting up a storm. Kate is still in the mix. Her major adversary is Alice who thinks we're inviting the devil into our midst. And she did provide a pretty good quote from Ephesians to support her position. Let me read it from the blog, just a second."

I walked over to the computer and found the quote. Okay, listen to this "For our struggle is not against flesh and blood, but against the rulers, against the authorities, against the powers of this dark world and against the spiritual forces of evil in the heavenly realms."

"That sounds ominous. Who wrote Ephesians?"

"St. Paul."

Alex was sitting up now, and sipping his coffee.

"Remember when we were reading books on the power of positive thinking and the law of attraction?" he asked. "We read that if you thought about something long enough, you would attract it to you, even if it was a thought like 'I don't want to get sick before my vacation,' or something like that. You were still attracting sickness to you because you were thinking about it. Instead you needed to picture yourself in radiant health, and leave the sickness part out."

"Yes, but what does that have to do with the quote from Ephesians?"

"The law of attraction responds to the vibration you are emitting, whether it be positive or negative, by giving you more of it. What I'm trying to say is that if you are asking for and dwelling on aid from benevolent beings, I think you will get it. If you are dwelling on evil out there somewhere, you are attracting it to yourself. Don't dwell on the spiritual forces of evil in the heavenly realms. My suggestion is to dwell only on the positive, and only positive things will come to you."

Okay, I couldn't help it; I felt a song coming on. I stood there looking at him for a couple of seconds, then I put down my coffee mug and started singing 'Accentuate the

Positive' by Harold Arlen and Johnny Mercer. I even did a little dance with it.

Alex chuckled, and said "That's it. You've got it. That's what I mean. How do you know those lyrics?"

"I was in the glee club in high school and that was one of the songs we performed. Those lyrics always stuck with me for some reason."

I sat down and sipped some more coffee and said "So I guess I have to go into that chat room and basically do that song and dance for them, is that it?"

"I think it is the way to go, don't you agree?"

"I do."

"So Jane and Joshua are coming over at 2, right?"

"Right. What should I offer them? Coffee, tea, wine, beer, martinis?"

"Well, it's only 2 o'clock in the afternoon, so I would not offer them martinis."

"Party pooper."

"Coffee, tea, wine or beer would be okay, I think."

"Well, I guess I better go chat and then enter my post on Moses with the shining face, Mount Sinai and the glory of god!"

I refilled our mugs and went over to the computer to chat. I certainly didn't want to make light of this topic, and I didn't want to appear to support any one particular view. I did want to encourage further discussion, however. So I discussed the law of attraction theory, and suggested that we all dwell on a positive result from our request for aid. And then I mentioned Jesus' teachings on faith, including "it shall be done to you according to your faith" and "if you have faith, and do not doubt...it will happen". And then, I couldn't help it, I had to include part of that song, as the word 'faith' was used in there as well. How apropos.

I started to read the comments left overnight and came across one that was extremely interesting. The comment was from Skye who referred to my questioning whether the god of the Old Testament was different from the god of the New Testament. She said that the "'Gospel of Judas', published by the National Geographic Society in 2006, mentions a 'god' named Saklas." In researching further about this Saklas she learned this entity is an imposter god who claims he created the Earth. This is the god of the Old Testament, and not the god of the New Testament. Skye claimed the god of the Old Testament is an Archon and the god of the New is an Aeon. I guess I had more research to do.

I entered the day's post about Moses and his shining face and the glory of the lord on Mount Sinai. At this point the great majority of those reading this blog were already on board with the idea that we were created by extraterrestrials, but I wanted to continue to make a case for my beliefs and I wanted to provide the quotes, by chapter and verse, so individuals could research for themselves and draw their own conclusions.

I got up and poured a little more coffee in my mug and saw that Alex was already outside cleaning the paths and driveway of the new snow. I sat down by one of the front windows and thought about Jane and Joshua. I was so looking forward to having them over. I didn't have any female friends in Vermont. I knew my neighbors, and we did socialize every now and then, but I had no true friend nearby. Alex was my friend, but it wasn't the same as a female friend. And the same held true for Alex. Ron was the closest to a male friend that Alex had, but they were more like co-workers and not really friends.

I cleaned up the kitchen and went upstairs to shower and dress. I put on jeans and a faded yellow turtleneck. I decided to wear my chakra pendant, after all this was a festive occasion! I pulled my graying blond hair back into a ponytail. I kind of liked the way the gray looked in my hair. It looked like platinum streaks, or so I liked to think.

Before we knew it, it was almost 2 o'clock. I could hear a car coming down the driveway and Alex was already by the window.

"I don't believe it, they're driving a 445."

"A what?"

"A Volvo PV445."

I looked out the window and saw a red vehicle with an off-white roof pulling up. It was a very unusual looking station wagon.

"How old would you say that is?" I asked.

"Probably about 50 years old or so."

We saw Jane and Joshua heading toward the house and we opened the front door before they had a chance to knock.

Before anyone could even say hello, Alex said "That's a cool Volvo. You don't see many 445's these days. And that looks to be in great condition."

"You're familiar with that Volvo model?" Joshua asked.

"I used to buy and restore 544's mostly, but I did have a few 445's."

"Want to take a look at it?" Joshua asked.

"Sure, let me grab my coat."

"Jane, why don't you come in out of the cold?" I asked.

"Don't mind if I do, thank you. So good to see you again. You have an incredible spot here; it's beautiful."

"Thanks, we love it. Let me take your coat."

Alex had his jacket on and he and Joshua headed toward the Volvo and we closed the door.

"Is that a chakra pendant?" Jane inquired.

"Yes. Not too many people know what a chakra is, let alone the colors associated with them."

"I'm into meditation and one of my meditations is on the chakra system. I use colored stones to represent each of the chakras. That's an awesome pendant. Where did you get it?"

"I manufacture them."

"You're a jewelry designer?"

"I'm not actively designing now, but this pendant and a few other items are still in production."

"Neat! Oh, and there is your transferware!" Jane was looking toward the dining room corner cupboard.

"Come take a look," I said and walked her into the dining room.

"This is all Burgess & Leigh Hill Pottery Rustic pattern in this cupboard," I said.

"I'm familiar with that pattern, but I have never seen so much in one place before. Wow, it's great."

"I have ten place settings and assorted serving pieces. I started to collect this when I found a considerable amount all together at an antique store on Route 7 in South Burlington."

"And all the plates lining the room above the paneling, what a great display. There are some I don't know. Like that one right there next to the door. What is that?"

"That's the only plate in this room that wasn't made in Staffordshire. It was made in New Jersey by a company named Willet's and the name of the pattern is 'Tropics'."

"I love it. Talk about asymmetrical collage, what a perfect example. I had no idea there was a potter right here in the States producing this."

Jane walked all around the room looking at and commenting on each plate. She got to the niche in the wall where the smaller pieces were displayed and picked up many to look at the potters mark on the bottom. Then her eye spotted the 'Crusoe' pitcher on the mantle.

"You have the 'Crusoe' pitcher I've been looking for. There's the palm tree with the monkey. I love this pattern. I knew this pitcher existed; I saw it on the internet. I even tried to bid on it on eBay, but wasn't successful."

"I've been looking for this pitcher for years myself. I found it just a few days ago at another antique store in South Burlington."

"What a collection you have! And the brown and white pottery is so effective against the dark paneling in this room. It's wonderful."

"Thank you. You have no idea what a pleasure it is to show it to someone who appreciates it."

"Actually, yes I do. I felt the same way when you were looking at my collection a couple of days ago."

"Let's go into the kitchen. Would you like a glass of wine?"

"I'd love it."

"Red or white?"

"Doesn't matter."

"I've got a bottle of white open." I took the Grgich Hills chardonnay out of the refrigerator and reached for a couple of wine glasses.

"Grgich Hills, my favorite!"

"It kind of seems like we're two peas in a pod, doesn't it? Isn't it kind of eerie?" I poured out the wine.

"You know, after you and Alex left on Monday, I said to Joshua that I felt like I always knew you. You seem so familiar to me. It is eerie, but in a nice way."

" 'Eerie in a nice way', that's exactly what I said to Alex."

Just then the front door opened and Joshua and Alex walked in. They were getting along famously, I could tell. Jane kind of gave me a look like that relationship was eerie as well.

I smiled and nodded. We were already into nonverbal communication.

"Wine, gentlemen?"

"I think I'll have a beer," Alex said.

"Beer sounds good to me, too," Joshua said.

"Two beers coming up."

"So, Jane, did you have a chance to look at the transferware?" Alex asked.

"Yes, and I'm jealous. Connie has the 'Crusoe' pitcher I always wanted."

"You two certainly have very similar tastes."

I handed the guys the beer and Alex said he was going to get the book he had written on transferware.

"This setting is exceptional," Joshua said. "A stone house at the end of a dirt road, on the side of a mountain overlooking the lake and mountains. What I especially like about it is that when we started up your drive we couldn't see the house at first. We're driving through the woods and then all of a sudden we're in a clearing with this incredible vista off to the right and your beautiful house and grounds ahead."

Alex walked back into the kitchen and commented "The first time we saw this house we knew it was the one for us."

"We found it by accident while we were out for a drive, called the agent, saw the house the next day and immediately made an offer," I said.

Alex said, "Let's go sit down at the table so you can look at the book."

Jane and Joshua sat on either side of Alex while he showed them how the book was set up, and then reviewed each pattern. I got some of the cheese that we bought at Champlain Orchards, and served it with assorted crackers.

Jane was making notes on patterns she liked so she could watch for them. There were quite a few that she hadn't seen before.

When they were through reviewing the book, Alex said "And now I've got some sketches of what I propose for your patio." He opened the folder and showed them different views that he had drawn of the patio.

"You are an artist!" Jane exclaimed. "The patio concept is wonderful and your ability to illustrate is incredible."

"Why thank you. I didn't really need to draw these, as I also have computerized images that incorporate actual photos of your house. But I get a tremendous amount of satisfaction doing the sketches. I've been doing this for over twenty five years now, and back when I started there was no computer alternative, you had to do your own drawings. Let's go over to the computer and I'll show you those pictures."

I hadn't seen all of the computerized images, so I joined them. It was amazing how you can take an actual photo and build into it whatever you want, and then look at it from various perspectives. Alex had taken photos from the inside of the back door looking out, from various points outside the door and also from the lake looking up. So now Jane and Joshua were looking at the patio and steps as if they really existed from all angles. Alex had even placed some urns containing shrubs, dining furniture and two lounge chairs on the patio.

"I love it!" Jane exclaimed.

"It is perfect; I wouldn't change anything," Joshua said. "Thank you, Alex."

"I'm glad you like it. I've put together a presentation for you containing copies of the sketches and these computerized images, as well as the pricing proposal."

"Anyone want another drink?" I asked.

"I will," Jane said.

"I'll have another beer," Alex said.

"Why not?" Joshua said.

After refreshing the drinks I said, "Okay, let's go into the living room."

Alex had the fire going. It was amazing how long it could burn without the need to poke it or reposition the logs. But it was starting to get a little low, and Alex went over to put another log on.

"Look at that tree!" Jane said staring at the branches fanning their way across the ceiling.

"Alex made it."

"Out of what? How did he do that?"

Joshua was over in the corner touching the trunk of the tree, trying to figure it out for himself.

"PVC pipe, papier mache, and brown paint," Alex said. "It took some time to complete it because you had to apply a layer of papier mache and then let it dry. And put another layer on and let it dry, etc. etc. I was trying to create some sort of semblance of a real tree trunk and branches."

"And the little lights and icicles, red berries, birds and pine cones are perfect," Jane said. "You must hate taking this down at the end of the season."

"She never takes it down," Alex whispered.

"I heard that. Yes I do take it down, but not until sometime in February because I can't bear doing it sooner," I responded.

"She has toyed with the idea of taking the icicles off in February and putting on hearts for Valentines Day, shamrocks for St. Patrick's Day, eggs and chickens for Easter, flags for Flag Day and Independence Day. You get the picture?"

"I could certainly understand if she did do that. And I see you have Persian rugs throughout the house as well." Jane said. "This is a Tabriz, right?"

"Correct," Alex said.

"Come look out these French doors, Jane," Joshua said. "What a view. Is there a patio out there under the snow?"

"Yes, bluestone, just as what I'm proposing for you. I've got a stone sitting wall off to the right side toward the front of the house. The patio wraps around to the rear of the house and that is where we have the grill. But just as at your house, I didn't want anything to hamper the view."

"We spend most evenings, when it's warm enough and weather permits, outside on that patio." I said.

"And look at all these books," Jane said. "It looks like you have some project going on. And what an interesting combination there is: religious, early civilizations, art and UFOs."

Alex and I didn't know what to say. We hadn't contemplated having a conversation on this topic with Jane and Joshua.

"Oh, I'm too nosey. I'm sorry, I didn't mean to pry," Jane said.

"Let's sit down by the fire," I said.

"Are you familiar with the bible?" Alex asked.

"Yes, to some degree. We both are," Jane responded.

"Do you know what Genesis Chapter 1, Verse 26 says?"

"Yes, I do," Jane said. "It begins with 'And God said, 'Let us make man in our image, after our likeness...'.".

We were speechless. This was more than a coincidence. There was definitely something going on here.

"And what do you take those plural pronouns to mean?" Alex asked.

"That we were created by extraterrestrials," Joshua said. Jane was nodding in agreement.

I couldn't help it, I just started to cry. Looking over at Alex, I could tell he was shaken by all this as well.

Jane came over and put her arm on my shoulder and said "Connie, what is it? What's wrong? Did we say something to offend you?"

"No, you gave the perfect response. It is just too incredible. There is a reason that the four of us came together. I'm not sure exactly what it is, but it was meant to be."

"We came to that conclusion about extraterrestrial creation toward the end of this past summer," Alex said. "We researched the bible and books relating to various aspects of ancient civilizations and humankind's creation. You see all of the books we've plowed through since. Connie has started a blog providing the evidence we've discovered, and has received an amazing response."

"Funny, it was towards the end of the summer when we reached that same conclusion," Joshua said. "Both Jane and I have seen UFO's, so we knew intelligent life was out there. And for some bizarre reason we came across that reference to 'in our image' in Genesis and did our own research. But by the looks of those books piled on the table over there, you did a heck of a lot more research than we did."

I was still all teary eyed when Jane said "You know that picture of the clouds over my mantle? Remember Alex said that it had a mysterious quality to it? You know what that mysterious quality is? That bronze glint towards the center of the cloud is a UFO."

Now I was sobbing uncontrollably. I stood up and hugged Jane, and she was crying too. I saw tears streaming down Alex's cheeks. Joshua looked very pale.

It took a while for us to calm down, especially me. It was obvious that some unseen force had brought us together, but why?

Jane said, "I know you are probably familiar with Ezekiel, Chapter 1, verse 4: 'As I looked, behold, a stormy wind came out of the north, and a great cloud, with brightness round about it, and fire flashing forth continually, and in the midst of the fire, as it were gleaming bronze.' That's what I was trying to depict in my painting. I have several others. It's like I'm obsessed with painting clouds with UFO's hidden within; similar to that Richard Dreyfus character in Close Encounters where he is obsessed with sculpting the Devil's Tower."

Now I was laughing and crying. This was too funny.

" 'Close Encounters' is Connie's favorite movie. She can watch it over and over again."

"It's the way they captured the swirling clouds with the spacecraft hidden inside. That's what I love to watch over and over again," I said.

"I've paused the movie at those parts and took photos of those clouds to use as a basis for my paintings," Jane said.

We all broke out into laughter, hysterical, uproarious, uncontrollable laughter. More tears were streaming down our cheeks.

"You know, they say truth is stranger than fiction. Well this just goes to prove that statement," Joshua said.

"And you're wrong, Alex," I said.

"Wrong about what?"

" 'Close Encounters' is not my favorite movie. It's tied for first with 'An Affair to Remember'".

"Gary Grant and Debra Kerr," Jane said. "What a movie. I cry every time I watch it, which is quite often, in between obsessively painting clouds, of course."

We chatted a bit longer and I offered to refresh everyone's drink, but Jane said it was getting late, the sun had almost set, and they should be on their way. I got their coats, and Alex handed Jane the proposal for the patio.

Jane said "Our relationship has taken a dramatic turn today. I don't know why, but there must be a reason. And you have no idea how happy I am."

We hugged them goodbye, they got in their Volvo and drove slowly down the driveway.

Chapter 26 – Six Fingered Giants

After they left, Alex and I just sat in front of the fire and didn't say much. I felt dazed. It was really difficult to comprehend what had just happened. I felt elated and yet uneasy.

After a while, Alex got up and went over to the computer. A short while later he said, "Remember you had asked about the contents of the law of the lord as given to Moses and the curses contained within? I found something on it. It begins in Deuteronomy 29."

I got up and walked over to the computer and started to read. I especially noted verses 20-29:

"The Lord will not spare him, but then the anger of the Lord and his jealousy shall smoke against that man, and all the curses that are written in this book shall lie upon him, and the Lord shall blot out his name from under heaven. And the Lord shall separate him unto evil out of all the tribes of Israel, according to all the curses of the covenant that are written in this book of the law: So that the generation to come of your children that shall rise up after you, and the stranger that shall come from a far land, shall say, when they see the plagues of that land, and the sicknesses which the Lord hath laid upon it; and that the whole land thereof is brimstone, and salt, and burning, that it is not sown, nor beareth, nor any grass groweth therein, like the overthrow of Sodom, and Gomorrah, Admah, and Zeboim, which the Lord overthrew in his anger, and in his wrath. Even all nations shall say, wherefore hath the Lord done thus unto this land? What meaneth the heat of this great anger? Then men shall say, because they have forsaken the covenant of the Lord God of their fathers, which he made with them when he brought them forth out of the land of Egypt, for they went and served other gods, and worshipped them, gods whom they knew not, and whom he had not given unto them. And the anger of the Lord was kindled against this land, to bring upon it all the curses that are written in this book. And the Lord rooted them out of their land in anger, and in wrath, and in great indignation, and cast them into another land, as it is this day. The secret things belong unto the Lord our God, but those things which are revealed belong unto us and to our children for ever, that we may do all the words of this law."

Deuteronomy Chapter 30, verses 17-19 read: "But if thine heart turn away, so that thou wilt not hear, but shalt be drawn away, and worship other gods, and serve them; I denounce unto you this day, that ye shall surely perish, and that ye shall not prolong your days upon the land, whither thou passeth over Jordan to go to possess it. I call heaven and earth to record this day against you, that I have set before you life and death, blessing and cursing; therefore choose life, that both thou and thy seed may live."

"You know, right now it doesn't really seem to matter to me that there are multiple ET gods in the bible, and that there are curses contained in the law of the lord," I said. "That is all in the past. Right now I'm only thinking about the future. I'm not sure what the future holds, but I no longer have an urge to dwell in the past."

"What about your blog? Are you going to continue with that?" Alex asked.

"Yes, definitely, I'm going to continue with it. I feel it is more important now than ever to keep that going and promote continued communication."

After a good night's sleep, I felt more myself. I was looking forward to checking out my blog and entering the day's post about the transfiguration and ascension of Jesus, as I was continuing that 'shining face' theme from the prior day's discussion about Moses.

I lingered over my coffee a little longer than usual. I was just about to fire up the computer when the phone rang. It was Jane.

"Good morning, Connie. How are you today?"

"Better this morning. I have to tell you that I felt dazed after you and Joshua left yesterday."

"I know what you mean. I don't think Joshua and I exchanged two words on the drive back to our house. We were both lost in our own thoughts. But I'm pretty much back to normal this morning, whatever normal is. I meant to ask you for the web address of your blog, I'd like to check it out."

After I gave it to her, she said "Why don't you and Alex come over and we can go up to my studio and you can look at the other cloud paintings I have. I'd like you to choose one for yourself. Also, I've reviewed Alex' proposal and I'm ready to sign, so he can pick up those papers at the same time."

"Sounds great, when is it convenient?"

"How about today? Do you have any plans?"

"Alex, Jane wants to know if we can go over to their place today to look at her paintings. She also is ready to sign your proposal, so you can pick that up as well."

"Sure, sounds good," Alex said.

"Okay. I've just got to check out my blog and enter today's post, that's all I have on my agenda."

"Just come over whenever you're through. We're not going anywhere."

"Okay, then we'll see you a little later."

I got on to the computer and saw that the chat room continued to be extremely busy. Kate was still in the mix. She latched on to my law of attraction comments and went with them. She was quite eloquent. I also noticed that Alice was still firing away. "The road to hell is paved with good intentions..." she wrote. "The law of attraction and positive thinking are fairy tales. You have to understand that you are inviting pure evil into your lives."

I didn't get involved with the chatting going on. I entered my post on the transfiguration and ascension and that was it. I did note that 402 people had viewed the website within the past 24 hours, so it hadn't leveled off as I thought it did.

A short while later we were knocking on Jane's front door.

The door swung open and Jane said, "Hi, guys!" and gave us both big hugs.

"Let me grab my coat and we'll head over to the studio. Joshua is over there already working on some furniture."

She took her jacket off of the coat rack by the front door, and we walked over to the studio, as they called it. As we walked Jane commented "I started to read your blog, Connie. From what I've seen, you're doing a marvelous job of documenting your findings. And that chat room looks very active. I really didn't have a chance to read much of that yet, but it looks like Kate expresses herself extremely well. And that woman, oh what's her name?"

"You mean Alice?"

"Yes, Alice. I don't think she'll be swayed by Kate or anyone. I'm looking forward to reading all the comments."

We reached the studio. There were two garage doors to the right side and an entrance door to the left. Jane opened the entrance door and we walked into an L-shaped space that ran along the left side of the building and along the back toward the right. Joshua was in the back corner working on a beautiful old breakfront with a marble top. We wove our way through furniture that either had been or was about to be restored.

"Hello, I've got tung oil on my hands, so I won't give you hugs."

"You've got some wonderful old pieces here," Alex said.

"Thanks, it certainly keeps me busy."

"Joshua, that photo on the wall behind you, what is that?" I asked.

"Oh, it's a photo I took of a petroglyph in Three Rivers, New Mexico."

"It looks like a hand with six fingers," Alex commented.

"That's what it is, all right. The American Indians tell stories of six fingered giants."

"Six fingered giants?" I exclaimed.

"Yes. Actually there is a quote by Wild Bill Cody in his autobiography to the effect that the Indians, I think it was the Pawnees, told him that these six fingered giants would run along side of a buffalo and grab it with one hand, rip off its leg, and eat it."

"Wow, that's a disturbing image," Alex said.

"And that's why the Indians raise their hand as a greeting when meeting others. They want to show that they have five fingers, and want to make sure that you have five fingers, too!"

"How," Jane said, and raised her hand.

"How," Joshua said and raised his hand.

"How," I said and raised my hand.

We all looked at Alex as he slid his right hand into his pocket.

After a slight pause, I said "So that's why your pinky finger is so long, and that terrible scar..."

Jane and Joshua's eyes got large and they were staring at Alex.

"Just kidding, folks," I said.

Alex pulled out his hand, raised it, and said "How."

Jane and Joshua were laughing, but I noticed that they both were looking intently at Alex' raised hand.

"There were various gods worshipped by ancient civilizations who had six fingers as well. I believe the Incas and Sumerians had six fingered gods. And I think there was one in Russia as well," Joshua responded.

"Goliath had six fingers on each hand and six toes on each foot," Jane said.

"He did?" I asked.

"Yes, actually I think that six fingers thing was common among the Nephilim."

"You learn something everyday," I commented.

"So let's go upstairs to my space," Jane said.

"I'll stay down here and finish what I'm doing and clean up," Joshua said.

We followed Jane to the stairs that were tucked into the far corner and climbed up to her studio. There were two very large windows up there, one overlooking the lake and the other on the north side. There was an easel set up near the north window and framed canvases propped up against the walls. There was a small table with a couple of chairs and a dark red velvet fainting couch as well.

"What a space! What a view! I think I'd be too distracted to paint," I said.

"Hey, when you're obsessed, you're obsessed," Jane said. "I never have a problem painting up here."

"That fainting couch is a pretty piece," Alex said.

"Isn't it? Joshua got it out of an estate in Shelburne and I talked him into bringing it up here for me. Sometimes I just lay on it and stare at the clouds through the window, for inspiration, of course."

Jane walked over to paintings that were stacked against the wall and we followed her. She started to slowly flip through them, commenting briefly on each.

"These are pretty much in chronological order, with the most recent ones on top. I think you'll see a definite improvement in technique in these more recent ones as compared to the earlier attempts. I played with different times of the day, for example this one is a sunrise. And this next one is later than sunset, it is as dark as I could get it and still see the cloud formation with the glint of metal within. And this next one is during a thunderstorm. If you see one you especially like, just let me know. I want you to pick out your favorite."

"They are all amazing. I do like that dark one, the bronze glow has a luminous quality that just draws you in. Wait. Stop. Let me look at this one!" I said.

Jane advised "The sun had just set and the clouds were a wonderful peachy pink color with hints of lavender."

"This painting has the lake and the mountains in it, whereas the others are only of the sky and clouds," I said. The view out the window was identical to that in the painting, only the time of day was different. In Jane's painting the mountains were a dusky purple color and the clouds were beautifully reflected in the shimmering lake.

"This is the one," I said. "I love it."

"I agree," said Alex. You captured the mountains and lake perfectly."

"Thank you. I have to say it was a challenge doing this one. The reflection on the water was tricky, but I think I nailed it. However, you don't see another one of these, as I don't know if I could do it again."

Jane handed the painting to Alex, and we both thanked her profusely.

"You are entirely welcome! Come on, I think it's time for a drink, what do you say?"

We went back downstairs, collected Joshua, and headed back to the house.

"How about martinis?" Jane asked.

"It's a little early in the day for me," Joshua said. "I'll have a beer, what about you, Alex?"

"Beer sounds great," he said.

"You guys are party poopers," Jane said.

"Aren't they, though," I murmured. "Count me in on the martinis."

A few minutes later we were sitting in the living room, sipping our drinks, and munching on celery stuffed with herb cheese.

"From what I've read on your blog, it appears the majority of your readers agree that we've been created by extraterrestrials," Jane said.

"Right. I am very surprised that I've received relatively few negative comments. Oh, I've been called a nut and the devil, but to a very limited extent. And I don't think Alice is too fond of me," I responded.

"Who's Alice?" Joshua asked.

"She's one of the women in the chat room saying that we are inviting the devil into our midst," I said.

"How are you doing that?' Joshua asked.

"The majority of those reading the blog, or at least a majority of those commenting and chatting agree that society today is in a downward spiral and we need to channel our thoughts to ask extraterrestrials to come to our aid. This was in response to my post on the extraterrestrial insemination of Sarah, Rachel, Anne, Mary and others and my comments on how those offspring were extraordinary beings. They were men and women of renown," I responded.

"I'm going to have to read your blog," Joshua said.

"So you ended today with the transfiguration and ascension," Jane said. "What's tomorrow's post?"

"Tomorrow it's going to be a little off track; actually it's going to be a little off track for the next three days. Tomorrow it's going to be about sleep paralysis. The day after that it's going to be about out of body experiences, and the third day it's going to be about the Rh negative blood type," I responded.

"What about Rh negative blood?" Jane asked.

Alex responded, "Only 15% of the world's population has Rh negative blood. The other 85% has Rh positive and the Rh stands for Rhesus like in monkey. Those with Rh positive blood have a factor in their blood that can be traced back to the Rhesus monkey. But the earthly origin for Rh negative blood is unknown. Scientists have no explanation for it."

"An Rh negative pregnant woman's body rejects the positive blooded baby in her womb. But an Rh positive woman's body does not reject an Rh negative fetus. Isn't this interesting? And there's more."

"Quite interesting," Jane said. "What else?"

"Scientists can clone the Rh positive factor, but they can't clone the Rh negative factor," I said.

"There are some sites that suggest that Rh negative

people are related to the ancient astronauts. And it's believed that there is a high percentage of alien abduction of people with Rh negative blood," Alex continued.

"And I have Rh negative blood," I said. Jane gave me a look, and I knew what she was about to say before she said it.

"So do I," she said.

Alex and Joshua were speechless. We all sat there staring at one another when finally Alex said, "50% of the people in this room have Rh negative blood, when statistically only 15% of the entire world's population has it. A little strange, don't you think?"

"Hey, you didn't ask if I have Rh negative blood," Joshua said.

"Do you?" Alex asked.

"No, I don't think so. Just pulling your leg."

"The Basque people of Spain have the highest incidence of Rh negative blood and their origin is unknown," Alex continued. "Some people link Rh negative blood to the fallen angels who mated with human women."

"Have you experienced sleep paralysis episodes and out of body experiences?" Jane asked me.

"Yes, have you?" I asked.

"No, at least not yet," Jane replied.

"I wonder how many readers of my blog are Rh negative?"

"I venture to guess it's out of the statistical ball park. Way out of the park." Alex said.

"I wonder what the future holds for us," Jane said. "We both know this is more than a coincidence; this is not pure serendipity. Someone has a plan for us. A definite plan."

"Oddly, though, I'm not worried. I'm ready for whatever may come."

"And at least we're in this together!" Jane said.

"Have these two bonded, or what?" Joshua commented.

"It's almost as if they were twins, don't you think?"

Alex asked.

"Right, twins."

"Well, I think we'd better take our leave, we've monopolized too much of your time already," I said.

"Don't forget to give Alex the signed proposal," Joshua reminded Jane.

"Thanks, I would have forgotten."

"There're two copies. I'll sign both as well and then we'll each keep one," Alex said.

We all went into the kitchen and Jane handed the documents to Alex for his signature.

"I'm really looking forward to seeing the completed patio," Jane said. "I couldn't be more pleased with your proposal."

"I'm looking forward to construction myself. I couldn't ask for a better location to work, that's for sure." Alex said.

We walked toward the front door and Alex picked up the painting that was propped against the table in the hall.

"And thank you so much for the painting, Jane. I will treasure it," I said.

We said our goodbyes and headed out the door.

Chapter 27 - Be Careful What You Ask For

The next morning I entered my post about sleep paralysis. The following day I entered the out of body experience post. There were several women who said they had experienced one or both of these phenomena, but it was not an overwhelming response.

My post on Rh negative blood the third day, however, received an incredible response. The chat room was going crazy and the comments were piling up. So many women were indicating that they were Rh negative, it was amazing. But not surprising.

I called Jane, "Good morning! Have you seen the blog?"

"Yes, it's just what we expected. As Alex said 'it's way out of the statistical ball park.'"

"Now we know that it's not just the two of us; there are many women out there in this with us. If we only knew what 'this' was. Can you and Joshua come over for lunch? I make a mean tuna salad sandwich."

"Actually, Joshua has to do some appraisals today, but I'll come over. Okay?"

"Sounds great, see you noonish."

"Jane's coming over for lunch," I shouted to Alex.

"What about Joshua?"

"No, he's out doing appraisals today."

After I cleaned up the kitchen, made the tuna salad and got dressed, I sat down to post my blog. Today's post was on 'God, heaven and hell, do they exist?' This topic most likely would have a huge response as well. Before I did that, however, I checked to see if there was some sort of survey widget I could put on my blog. In no time I located it. The survey question I put up was a simple one, 'Are you Rh Negative? Yes or No'.

I entered the chat room. My chat started with, 'I'm not

surprised by your response to my Rh negative post. I think many of us have been brought together for a particular reason. I think our Rh negative blood is part of the equation. I've added a survey to this blog to see what percentage of you are Rh negative. I'd appreciate it if you could please take a moment and indicate 'yes' or 'no' to that question. Thank you.'

Then I started the post with, "I have a friend who didn't believe in God or heaven. We would occasionally discuss our beliefs and I told him that I believed that we have spirits that are eternal. I also believed that some of us are searching for perfection of the spirit. I believed in reincarnation as a way to perfect ourselves to the point that we can leave this planet and go to a higher level. And as we continue to perfect ourselves, we continue to move up and up to yet higher levels. I believed that we have a spark of 'divine essence' in each of us. Hopefully, we choose a life that will present us with challenges that will help us to grow, if we react to those challenges properly. And if we choose wisely and act properly, we keep moving up and up and up until we reach the ultimate level, the highest level. And, perhaps it follows that if that divine spark is within each of us, then those at the highest level are collectively all 'god' and that highest level could be considered 'heaven'."

"My friend really didn't have any argument with this definition of god and heaven. But then he asked me if I believed in hell. I told him I believed that the lowest of the low is Earth. We are experiencing our hell here on Earth, and there was no where to go but up. What do you think?"

A short while later Jane arrived. I brought her right into the living room so she could see where we hung her painting. It was on the back wall, the same wall on which 'The Baptism of Christ' hung, but in the opposite corner.

"How did you get that framed so fast?" Jane asked. "What a beautiful frame, it looks antique."

"Alex did it. We had an old frame out in the barn that he cut down to size, applied a little gilt burnish and voila!"

"Did I hear my name mentioned?" Alex asked as he walked into the room.

"What an amazing job you did framing the picture. That frame makes the painting look like it's hundreds of years old. I love it!" Jane gushed.

"Why thank you very much. It's always nice to put something that's literally been hanging around the place to good use. I think that frame was in the barn when we moved in."

"Let's go into the kitchen and I'll pour us some wine," I said.

"I spoke to Joshua to tell him that I was coming over here for lunch, and he said his two o'clock appointment was not far from here, so he'll be stopping by shortly," Jane mentioned.

"Great!" Alex and I said simultaneously, and laughed.

"I put a survey widget on my blog this morning."

"You're going to see how many Rh negative visitors you have?" Jane asked.

"Right."

"And if it's out of the statistical ball park like Alex thinks it will be, then what?" Jane asked.

"Then we'll know without a shadow of a doubt that you, I and all the Rh negative women reading my blog have all been brought together for a reason. Exactly what that reason is, I don't know."

Just then the door bell rang.

"That must be Joshua, I'll get it," Alex said.

Alex walked Joshua into the kitchen via the living room, as he wanted to show him the framed picture. I went over and gave Joshua a hug as he entered the kitchen.

"Alex did a great job with framing that painting, didn't he?" Joshua asked.

"He certainly did," Jane responded. "It really added a beautiful sense of age to the painting."

"How much time before you have to leave for your

next appointment?" I asked.

"I've got a little over an hour before I have to head back out."

"Good, then we can relax for a bit."

"Want a beer?" Alex asked.

"Don't mind if I do," Joshua answered.

"We were just talking about Connie's blog. She put a survey widget on this morning so she can get a definite percentage of Rh negative readers," Jane commented. "We know by the overnight response there are lots of them out there, but this will give us a much clearer indicator of percentage."

"You know what I find interesting is that the great majority of your readers already believed in UFOs, and they pretty much accept for fact that we were created by celestial beings. Can you imagine if breaking news came on TV announcing that extraterrestrial space craft landed on the White House lawn?" Joshua asked.

"The Secret Service or CIA or FBI or someone would probably blast it to smithereens and then say it was really a weather balloon," Alex muttered.

"Okay, say spacecraft landed at capitol cities around the world, in countries where they wouldn't blast it to smithereens, like Mexico, Brazil, England. It would have to be covered as world news. It couldn't be hidden or considered a joke. What would happen?"

"The world as we know it would immediately change," I said.

"Right, religious organizations, governments, industry, science, communications and our capitalistic way of life would dramatically change. These are the entities that have been able to successfully subvert the truth, and their control would come to an end in an instant."

"And the fate of Earth would depend on whether the inhabitants of these spaceships were the malevolent manipulating extraterrestrials or the benevolent ones," I said, and got up to make our sandwiches.

"That's why we are focused on sending positive thoughts towards the benevolent extraterrestrials for their aid," Jane said.

"You had mentioned that you and Joshua had both seen UFO's; were you together? What did you see?" Alex asked Jane.

"Yes, we were together. And it was shortly after we moved into our house down in Shoreham," Jane responded. "It was a warm summer night and we were laying out on a blanket in the back yard. It was great because the property slopes down toward the lake, so your head is elevated slightly and you can take in the lake to some extent, the mountains and the sky very comfortably."

I put the sandwiches on the table, as well as chips and pickles, and sat down.

Joshua picked up on the story, "We were trying to identify as many of the stars and constellations as we could. We'd see an occasional airplane or shooting star that would divert our attention for a second or two, but then we'd go right back to our attempt at identification. Then we noticed a relatively bright star or light that slowly came up from the west over the mountains toward the lake."

"Right," Jane continued, "and at first we thought it was an airplane. We kept watching and listening, but there wasn't any sound. As it got closer all lights went off on it, and it was descending to a lower altitude. It was slowly moving over the lake and we could see that this was no airplane. It was triangular, huge and silent. I was extremely frightened."

"So was I," Joshua said. "I really felt that they knew we were there watching it. It came to a dead stop and we watched it for several minutes, petrified."

"Then, three smaller, much smaller, objects with white, green and blue lights appeared in the sky and approached the large object from the north. They either entered or merged with the large object, as they were no longer visible," Jane said.

"After another minute or two, the large object started to move slowly again towards the east. It passed directly over us. When it was no longer in our range of sight, we got up and ran around to the side of the house and we could still see it. Then the lights came back on and it picked up more speed and disappeared behind the hills. I'd estimate that the entire episode lasted 15 minutes or so."

"Right, 15 minutes tops," Joshua said. "I was uneasy the rest of the night, yet I felt elated by what we had seen."

"Me too," Jane commented. "And I expected there would be a story on a UFO sighting in the next day's news, but there wasn't. Maybe others had seen it, but didn't report it, as we didn't."

"Wow, what an experience," I said. "I can't imagine laying there watching a UFO pass by directly overhead." I then proceeded to tell them my UFO story.

"You felt the same way we did, that they were aware we were watching them," Joshua said.

"Definitely! I mean they made a 90 degree turn to zoom in our direction and check us out. Sometimes I wonder if I really concentrated, and tried to contact them, would they respond? I've thought about it at times when Alex and I are sitting out on the patio watching the sky, but I never had the nerve to do it though."

"Actually, we're doing it now," Jane said.

"What?" I asked.

"We're asking for aid from benevolent celestial beings, aren't we? We are sending out our thoughts in an attempt to contact them. They could just show up some day or night in response to our request. Don't you think?"

"You're right. For some reason I'm thinking about our request in an abstract manner, and not thinking about the physicality of it," I responded. "But you're absolutely correct."

"I think it would be extremely helpful that, as a result of their intervention, our lifespan extended to several hundred years," Alex commented.

We all gave him quizzical looks.

"What I mean is, if we all lived 969 years like Methuselah, then we would be more apt to think about the long term consequence of our actions, because we'd actually suffer the consequence of those actions. Right now the majority of humans don't consider things like the pesticides that we use to keep our lawns green and weed free leaching into our water supply. Most people will not live long enough to see a serious shortage in clean water, or at least they think they won't. However, if they lived 900 years, it would be a different story and they would think twice about polluting the environment as it will directly affect them, not future generations, but them."

"Good point there, Alex," Joshua responded.

We chatted a bit more, finished our lunch and Joshua headed out to his next appointment. Jane left shortly after as she had a few errands to do.

"It's funny," she said, "I hardly ever get out of the house, and I have no desire to leave it. But there are some things that do need to be done on occasion, like grocery shopping. So now that I'm out, I might as well do some errands."

I thought about Jane's comment about our attempts at mental contact with extraterrestrials. That phrase "…be careful what you ask for…" came to mind again.

Chapter 28 – Blood Count

Alex had the computer all fired up for me the next morning. I grabbed a cup of coffee and went to see the results of my survey. And the survey said: 62% of those polled were Rh negative. 62%!

Just then Alex walked in with an armful of firewood.

"Did you see this?" I asked him.

"Yep, 62%. Right out of the statistical ballpark, just like I expected."

I saw that the chat room was still going crazy. This blog had a life of it's own. If I never entered another post, this chat room would probably keep on going. I had set some sort of wheels in motion, and nothing was going to stop it now.

I got up and looked out the window. The wind was whipping and it looked like it could snow any minute. Alex was setting up fires in both fireplaces. I sat down by the living room fireplace and watched Alex as he positioned the wood.

"Is anything wrong?" he asked.

"The only way I can describe it is post partum blues."

"What?"

"I feel like I've given birth to a self sustaining entity with no control over its direction."

"Do you really need to be in control? You've done what you set out to do, and that is to share the information which you have gathered. What you are sharing is resonating within certain individuals. That is a good thing. Right?"

"You're absolutely correct."

"Can you put that in writing? I don't hear that too often," Alex joked.

I got up and poured myself some more coffee and went to work on my blog.

First, I entered the chat room and commented on 62% of those responding having Rh negative blood. This confirmed what I had suspected earlier, that we had been brought together for a reason. We needed to continue to channel our thoughts and ask benevolent extraterrestrials to come to the aid of this planet. We needed to dwell on only positive results.

My post concerned the two creation stories and the beings created in each. Was it possible that instead of destroying the first flawed beings, they were allowed to live and multiply? Then a second experiment in creation was conducted, this time actually using the creator's DNA? Adam and Eve were physically put in the Garden of Eden so they would be watched, and kept separate from those earlier 'mistakes'. When they left the Garden of Eden, did they associate with the earlier beings? Were the beings created in Chapter 1, who did not have the DNA of our creator, who did not know the difference between good and evil, still on our planet today? Did some of them interbreed with the progeny of Adam and Eve? Did they create a population on this Earth that is no longer able to discern the difference between good and evil? Is it possible that some pure first creation offspring still exist on this planet and they are pure evil? Are they hollow shells with no souls?

I anticipated that this post would get considerable response. And I was right. The next morning there was a lot of chatting going on.

Skye, the woman who had previously mentioned The Gospel of Judas, was part of the chatting. She said that if the god of the Old Testament was a malevolent god, and not the god of the New Testament, then the DNA in Adam and Eve was the DNA of that malevolent god.

She continued to say that she believed that it was that malevolent god, who was an Archon, who impregnated Sarah, Rachel and the other women of the Old Testament. However, she believed Elizabeth, Anne and Mary were impregnated by the benevolent god of the New Testament, who was an Aeon. As a result, Jesus was an Aeon.

I recalled reading that section of 'The Yahweh Encounters' which had prompted me to reflect that I had not originally considered the origin of DNA in the biblical extraterrestrial impregnations. Good for you, Skye!

Although I had seen the term 'Archon' and 'Aeon' before, I did not understand the meanings. I did order 'The Gospel of Judas' as I knew it was discussed in there. But I might as well search on the internet and see what I could find out.

Another woman, in support of Skye's comments, quoted the Gospel of John as evidence that the god of the Old Testament is not the god of the New. She quoted John 8, starting with verse 43 in which Jesus was speaking to the Jews:

"Why do you not understand my speech? Even because ye cannot hear my word. Ye are of your father the devil, and the lusts of your father ye will do. He was a murderer from the beginning, and abode not in the truth, because there is no truth in him. When he speaketh a lie, he speaketh of his own, for he is a liar and the father of it."

Wow! Okay, I had to look this up for myself as it was hard to believe that Jesus called Yahweh, at least I assumed it was Yahweh, the devil, a murderer and a liar. I reached for the bible and found the Gospel of John and, sure enough, the quote was correct. Jesus was speaking to a group of Jews and he did say that to them. If this wasn't evidence that the god of the Old Testament was not god 'the father' in the New, I don't know what is.

I went back to the chat room and another woman had written "Of course they were two different entities! The god of the Old Testament said 'The silver is mine, and the gold is mine...' Can you imagine the god of the New Testament, the father of Jesus, saying that? This is taken directly from the Old Testament, Haggai – 2:8, look it up."

Well, since I had the bible in hand, I did look it up, and sure enough that quote was accurate as well.

And this quote about the "silver is mine and the gold is mine" fueled even more chatting.

Finally, there was Alice, still dwelling on the negative, asking "How are we to prevent the malevolent god from responding to our request for aid? Wasn't he the one that was using man as slaves in the gold mines? Who's to say he won't come back and make slaves of us all again! Read 'Slave Species of God' by Michael Tellinger, or go to his website, 'slavespecies.com'".

Yes, I have to admit that this book by Michael Tellinger was extremely interesting. However, Alice seemed to be still missing the point that we were to direct our thoughts to benevolent extraterrestrials and only envision positive results.

As I said before, this blog had a life of its own.

I went over to the computer and did a search on 'archon' and found the following: "...the 'creator god' that stood between spiritual humanity and a transcendent God that could only be reached through gnosis."

And for 'aeon' I found: "Aeons bear a number of similarities to Judaeo-Christian angels, including their roles as servants and emanations of God, and their existence as beings of light."

Hopefully the UPS man would be delivering 'The Gospel of Judas' today which might shed more light on this subject.

I entered the day's post on the tabernacle of the Exodus and Solomon's temple functioning as microwave transceivers to send and receive messages from the orbiting spaceship. These were the communication centerpieces used by the god of the Old Testament. I inserted a link to 'The Yahweh Encounters: Bible Astronauts, Ark Radiations and Temple Electronics' by Ann Madden Jones.

It was just starting to snow when I heard Alex yell "The UPS guy is here."

I heard him open the front door, talk briefly, and return to the kitchen with the package in hand.

"It's nice to see you haven't stopped researching," he said as he opened the box for me.

"You know that old saying, 'You learn something new every day'. Well it's true."

I sat down by the fire in the living room and started to read 'The Gospel of Judas'. Just a few pages into the gospel, Judas is saying to Jesus that he knew where Jesus had come from, the realm of Barbelo.

In researching Barbelo, I found that it is the name the Gnostics gave to the feminine aspect of the great invisible spirit, the eternal aeon among the invisible ones. I also found that 'aeon' is synonymous with 'realm'.

Reading further in the gospel, I noted that Judas, too, had entered a cloud and there was a voice that came from the cloud, but the remaining text was missing. Sounded very much like the transfiguration story. I'd love to know what the voice from the cloud said.

Chapter 29 – A Very Real Possibility

The phone rang and I heard Alex answer it. He chatted for a while and then called to me, "Jane's on the phone."

"Hi, Connie, how're you doing?"

"Good, I just got 'The Gospel of Judas' and what I've read so far is quite interesting."

"I was reading your blog and see that the chat room is busier than ever. An idea occurred to me. I think it might be helpful to prepare your readers for what might happen to them."

"What do you mean?"

"You've mentioned that we need to channel our thoughts and ask for aid, but you've never suggested in what form the response might be. I think it would be beneficial to suggest what form that aid might take."

"Which would be what?"

"That certain of us will be impregnated by benevolent extraterrestrials, just as Anne, Elizabeth and Mary were."

I'm not sure, but I think I let out a gasp, because Jane continued, "Don't be shocked. You know you have considered this as well. It's just actually hearing it said out loud by someone that is shocking, right?"

"I guess. Yes, of course, I had considered this. But actually hearing you say it did knock the wind out of me. So you are suggesting I enter a post on this possibility?"

"Yes. It would at least allow your readers to decide whether they want to withdraw from this project now."

"You're absolutely right. It's funny; a couple of weeks ago all I wanted to do was share the information I had gathered. Now the reality of it has hit home, thanks to you."

"I hesitated to bring this up to you."

"I'm so glad you did. Do you mind if I mention you in my post?"

"That's fine with me. Say whatever you think needs to be said."

"I will.   And if I misstate something or leave something out, make sure to enter a comment of your own."

"Okay, sounds good. Have a good night, Connie."

"Thanks. You too."

I hung up the phone and was just staring into space when Alex asked, "What was that about?"

I told him about Jane's suggestions; he didn't respond immediately. After several seconds, he said "It is the right thing to do. Let those women know exactly what they might be in for. But what about you, Connie? Are you up for this?"

"I was led here by a being who thinks I can handle it. I can't back out. Remember that vortex dream I told you about? Remember I said the next time I was given the opportunity, I wouldn't back out? Well this is it. I have to go with it. This is going to drastically change both our lives. Are you up to it, Alex?"

"Absolutely. I didn't do all that research and write out and cross reference 400 index cards for nothing," he chuckled.

I spent the rest of the day drafting what I would write. The next morning I posted the following:

"Not too long ago I met a woman named Jane. It immediately became apparent that we had similar tastes and interests. A friendship developed and we learned more about each other. We discovered that over the past summer we both happened to pick up the bible and read Genesis 1:26. This verse prompted both of us to research the possibility of extraterrestrial creation of humans. Separately, we both came to the same conclusion, that mankind was, in fact, created by extraterrestrials.

"We learned that both our blood types were Rh negative.

"While I continued to research, Jane started painting pictures of clouds concealing the bronzy glow of a spaceship hidden within.

"Jane and I were somehow brought together, just as many of us reading this blog have been brought together, for a reason.

"Some of us are channeling our thoughts to benevolent celestial beings asking for help for our planet. It's easy to imagine that the response will come in some vague intangible form, like a spiritual energy shift. We'll wake up some morning and the world will be a better place. It will be full of love, peace, compassion, sharing and caring. But it is possible that we might receive a very physical response to our request instead. Just as women in the bible were impregnated by extraterrestrial intervention, so might we. I believe this is a real possibility as we are asking for aid from physical beings, not mystical entities.

"Those of you who are reading this that are not prepared to face that eventuality should cease all efforts now. And those of you, who are willing to accept the consequences of our efforts, don't waiver in your attempt. Best wishes to all of you."

Over the next three months, my blog remained extremely active. Some women did decide to leave the project, but not many. To my surprise, Alice did not drop out. A bond developed among those women remaining which prompted open dialogue and a close, supportive community.

Chapter 30 – No Moon at All

I was awakened by the smell of coffee. I looked over at the clock and it said 7:30. Normally I was up at around 6 a.m. What happened?

I put on my robe and slippers, went downstairs and found Itzy eating her breakfast and Alex pouring coffee.

"Well, sleepy head, happy first day of spring!" Alex said.

"Right, happy first day of spring to you as well. I was sleeping like a log until the smell of coffee woke me up."

"Ah, so you finally woke up and smelled the coffee? Good for you."

"The moon was so bright last night that it must have disturbed my sleep."

Alex gave me a long look and said "There was no moon last night."

"Oh, yes there was. It was like daylight outside at some point during the night. The bedroom was bright with the light coming in the window."

"I'm telling you, there was no moon last night."

I walked over to the wall calendar and looked at the moon cycle at the bottom. Sure enough, there was no moon last night.

"Maybe I was dreaming. But it seemed so real."

I sat down and sipped the coffee but it didn't taste right. I asked Alex if he had made it the same as he usually did, and he said, "Don't you remember, you set up the pot last night? All I did was turn it on."

I was feeling strange. I wasn't in pain, but somehow I felt different. I couldn't describe it.

Alex had the TV on and was clicking around trying to find the weather. It annoyed me no end when he clicked like that. He did it so fast, how could he even tell what he was clicking by? Why was I so edgy?

Then, as I looked at the screen, something registered in my brain. I don't know exactly what it was, but I said "Stop! Go back!"

He stopped his maddening clicking and slowly started to go back to the channels he had just whizzed by. And there it was, a special report on multiple UFO sightings around the world in the past 24 hours.

I looked at Alex and he looked at me. And just then the phone rang.

I answered and said "Hello, Jane," as I knew without a doubt it was she.

"Have you seen the news?"

"Yes. I'm watching it now."

"I thought there was a full moon last night...."

"Me too. I think what we've been waiting for has at last happened."

Epilogue:

I could hear the car driving into the courtyard and coming to a stop. The car doors opened and closed and I heard my sisters saying hello to Alex. A couple of minutes later they walked out onto the patio.

"Hope!" Anne shouted.

"And Connie!" Mary said.

"Hi! Hi!" Hope exclaimed.

Hope had a big smile on her face and was clapping her hands. I couldn't believe she remembered them from Easter; that was over four months ago. But it appeared that she did. She extended her arms to them and Mary picked her up. Big hugs and big kisses; then the same thing with Anne.

"Love you," Hope said to both of them. She was saying a few words now at 9 months, and "hi" and "love you" were two phrases she used pretty much daily.

Anne said, "I really think she remembers us. But how can that be? She was just slightly over four months old when we were here in April, and it's not quite five months later now. But she is looking at me like she remembers me. And she's talking!"

I have to say that little baby girl was beautiful. Her hair was platinum blond and curly. Her eyes were as blue as the sky. Her cheeks were pink and her little mouth looked like a rosebud. And I had no doubt that she did remember Anne and Mary. She was an exceptional child in many ways.

She was conceived the night of the spring equinox and born on the winter solstice. I was both surprised and yet not surprised by her arrival. The events of the months preceding her conception all led me to that moment. The research and signs all pointed in that direction. Yet, when the reality of it truly hit me, I was shocked. What I suspected, what I had thought to be a possibility, was true.

Jane and many of the women with whom I

corresponded as a result of my blog also conceived on that same date. And they, too, had given birth to exceptional children. These children were born to women on every continent around the world. We knew these boys and girls would grow up to be men and women of renown. They would be today's heroes. And there is hope.

And there is hope.

The end of the world as we know it.

And a new beginning.

To be continued…